John Mitchel

The Life and Times of Aodh O'Neill, Prince of Ulster

John Mitchel

The Life and Times of Aodh O'Neill, Prince of Ulster

ISBN/EAN: 9783337167790

Printed in Europe, USA, Canada, Australia, Japan

Cover: Foto ©Raphael Reischuk / pixelio.de

More available books at **www.hansebooks.com**

THE
LIFE AND TIMES

OF

AODH O'NEILL,

PRINCE OF ULSTER;

CALLED BY THE ENGLISH,

HUGH, EARL OF TYRONE,

WITH

SOME ACCOUNT OF HIS PREDECESSORS,

CON, SHANE AND TIRLOUGH.

BY JOHN MITCHEL.

"Cu ṁaṁ cṛoınıc ᴅo cloın Néıll."
"Come let us make a chronicle for the O'Neills."

NEW YORK:
P. M. HAVERTY.
P. J. KENEDY,
EXCELSIOR CATHOLIC PUBLISHING HOUSE,
5 BARCLAY STREET.
1879.

TO THE MEMORY

OF

MY DEAR FRIEND,

THOMAS DAVIS,

WITH DEEP REVERENCE

I INSCRIBE

THIS BOOK.

JOHN MITCHEL.

Banbridge, Sept. 22, 1845.

PREFACE.

PERHAPS in no country, but only Ireland, would
a plain narrative of wars and revolutions that are
past and gone two centuries and a half ago, run
any risk of being construed as an attempt to
foster enmity between the descendants of two
races that fought so long since for mastery in the
land.

Yet the writer of this short record of the life
of the greatest Irish chieftain, is warned that
such construction may, and by some assuredly
will, be put upon the following story and the
writer's manner of telling it. But as to the narrative itself, undoubtedly the only question ought
to be—is it *true?* And if so—is the truth to be
told, or hidden?—Is it not at all times, in all
places, above all things, desirable to hear the
truth instead of a lie? And for the way in
which it is told—the writer does indeed acknowledge a strong sympathy with the primitive
Irish race, proud and vehement, tender and

poetical; with their deep religion and boundless wealth of sweetest song, and high old names, and the golden glories of Tradition; retiring slowly, and not without a noble struggle, before what is called "Civilization," and the instinctive and un-relenting insolence of English dominion; mostly victors in the field, but always overcome by policy; plucking down the robber standard of England in many a stricken battle—but on the whole, by iron destiny, and that combination of force and fraud and treachery, which has ever characterized the onward march of English power—borne back, disunited, and finally almost swept from the earth, to make way for the greedy adventurers of all Great Britain. And if the word "Saxon" or "Englishman" is sometimes used with bitterness, it is because the writer, carrying himself two hundred and fifty years backward, and viewing events, not as from the Council-chamber of Dublin Castle, but from the Irish forests and the Irish hearths, is sometimes tempted to use the language that fitted the time, and might have lain in the mouth of a clansman of Tyr-eoghain.

But the struggle is over, and can never, upon that quarrel, be renewed. Those Milesian Irish, as a distinct nation, (why not admit it?) were beaten—were finally subdued; as the Fir-bolgs were before them; as the ancient Kymry were in Britain, and afterwards *their* conquerors the Saxons. A new immigration was made, early in the sixteenth century, like that of the Tuatha-de-Danaan and Milesians of remoter times. Once more new blood was infused into old Ireland; the very undertakers that planted Ulster grew racy of the soil; and their children's children became, thank God! not only Irish, but *united* Irish—became "Eighty-two" Volunteers—anti-Union patriots—in every struggle of Irish nationhood against English domination (to which the now impending one shall not be an exception) were found in the foremost ranks, "more Irish than the Irish." The armies of Elizabeth, the planters and undertakers of James, may have been marauding adventurers, or even robbers: let it be granted that they were—so were the Franks who founded Charlemagne's empire; so were the vagabonds and fugitive slaves who flocked into the "asylum" of Romulus—and afterwards, off-scouring of mankind as they were, begat a progeny that bore the Roman Eagle over nations' necks, from Indus to the Pillars of Hercules. Whatever god or demon may have led the first of them to these shores, the Anglo-Irish and Scottish Ulstermen have now far too old a title to be questioned: they were a hardy race, and fought stoutly ... ... the pleasant valleys they dwell in. And are not Derry ... ... Enniskillen *Ireland's,* as well as Benburb and ting the Yellow Ford ?—and have not those men and their fathers, others lived, and loved, and worshipped God, and died there ?—are not their green graves heaped up there—more generations of them than they have genealogical skill to count ?—a deep enough root those planters have struck into the soil of Ulster, and it would now be ill striving to unplant them.

The writer of these pages boasts to be of that blood himself: no Milesian drop flows in his veins; and therefore he may be the more easily believed in disclaiming the base intention to exasperate Celtic Irish against Saxon Irish, or to revive ancient feuds between the several races that now occupy Irish soil, and are known to all the world besides, as Irishmen.

The truth is, that the object of this Life of Hugh O'Neill is simply to present as life-like a sketch as the writer's ability and information enable him to give, of an important era of Irish history, and the deeds of that illustrious chieftain who was the leading spirit of the time; who was the first, for many a century, to conceive, and almost to realize the grand thought of creating a new Irish Nation: and who for so many bloody years, bulwarked his native Ulster against the numerous armies and veteran generals of the greatest English monarch. And, further than this, if any reader shall see a striking similarity in the dealings of England towards Ireland then, and now—towards Ireland Milesian and Strongbownian, and a later Irish nation consisting of Milesians, Strongbownians, Scottish planters, and Cromwellian adventurers ;—and if such reader shall recognize the policy recommended by Bacon, directed by Cecil, and practised by Mountjoy and Carew, in the proceedings of certain later statesmen of England ; and if (which is not impossible) he shall arrive at the conclusion, that the bitterest, deadliest foe of Ireland (however peopled) is the foul fiend of English imperialism; and, further, if he shall draw from this whole story the inevitable moral, that at any time it only needed Irishmen of all bloods to stand together—to be even *nearly* united—in order to exorcise that fiend for ever, and drive him irrevocably into the Red Sea ;—surely it will be no fault of the present writer.

In the days of Hugh O'Neill, the *religious* element had begun to mingle, with terrible effect, in Irish affairs. And as " the business of a religious reformation in Ireland," to use the words of Dr. Leland, " was nothing more than the im-

position of English government on a people not
sufficiently obedient to that government—not sufficiently impressed with fear or reconciled by
kindness,"* it is impossible for an Irishman,
writing of that period, and sympathizing with
the outraged and plundered people, to describe
that most singular transaction with any soft or
conciliatory phrases. Imagine how a native of
Ireland must then have regarded the "Reformed"
church. To him it was simply the church of the
stranger—it was an ally of the enemy :—the spiritual supremacy and the temporal sovereignty of
a foreign king, were to him altogether indistin-
guishable, and alike detestable : the one seemed
but a scheme of plunder for military adventurers,
the other for ecclesiastical. Apart from all considerations of doctrinal truth (with which, as being
wholly irrelevant, the writer of these pages does
not meddle) it was enough for the Irish people to
know that foreign usurpation and foreign religion
were striding over their country, hand in hand,
and planting their footsteps together deep in
blood and tears ;—deposing their chiefs, persecuting their bards, supplanting their ancient
laws, and also prostrating their illustrious and

---

* Hist. of Ireland, vol. II. p. 201. He is speaking of
the religious changes made in the reign of Edward the
Sixth.

hospitable monasteries, dishonouring the relics of their saints, and hunting their venerated clergy like wolves.

But this, also, is all past and over. The very penal laws, last relics of that bloody business, are with the days before the flood. And, though it be true, that the mode of planting this Established Church of Ireland :—*first*, enthroning a whole hierarchy of bishops and archbishops, and *then* importing clergy for the bishops and parishioners for the clergy—was of all recorded apostolic missions the most preposterous—though the rapacity of those missionaries was too exorbitant, and their methods of conversion too sanguinary; yet, *now*, amongst the national institutions, amongst the existing forces, that make up what we call an Irish nation, the church, so far as it is a spiritual teacher, must positively be reckoned. Its altars, for generations, have been served by a devoted body of clergy; its sanctuaries thronged by our countrymen; its prelates, the successors of those very *queen's bishops*, have been amongst the most learned and pious ornaments of the Christian church. Their stories are twined with our history; their dust is Irish earth; and their memories are Ireland's for ever. In the little church of Dromore, hard by the murmuring Lagan, lie buried the bones of Joremy Taylor; would Ireland be richer without that grave? In any gallery of illustrious Irishmen, Ussher and Swift shall not be forgotten; Derry and Cloyne will not soon let the name of Berkely die; and the lonely tower of Clough Oughter is hardly more interesting to an Irishman as the place where Owen Roe breathed his last sigh, than by the imprisonment within its walls of the mild and excellent Bishop of Kilmore. *Sit mea anima cum Bedello!*

When Irishmen consent to let the past become indeed History, not party politics, and begin to learn from it the lessons of mutual respect and tolerance, instead of endless bitterness and enmity; then, at last, this distracted land shall see the dawn of hope and peace, and begin to renew her youth and rear her head amongst the proudest of the nations.

PREFACE

TO THE AMERICAN EDITION.

—

TWENTY-THREE years have gone by since the writer composed this small volume. It was undertaken at the suggestion of Thomas Davis for the series called "Library of Ireland," anp has had quite as much popularity as it deserved.

Since the time of its publication, a very largo mass of historic material, then inaccessible to the writer, has been for the first time brought to light, specially illustrative of the very period of our annals wherein O'Neill and O'Donnell flourished ; so that now, to do justice to the subject, the "Life of Hugh O'Neill" ought to be re-written, and at far greater length than could be attempted in a slight popular sketch like the present. Not having leisure to undertake this agreeable task, which would otherwise please me well, I am obliged to let it go with all its imperfections on its head.

But to many readers it may be desirable and
useful that some slight account should be given
of the actual materials which have now, by the
zealous labours of many eminent scholars, become available for the due understanding of
that deeply interesting era which saw the " Reformation," the great struggle between Irish
clanship and English feudalism, and the beginning of the religious wars in our island. First in
importance is the great work of John O'Donovan—his edition of the *Annals of the Four Mas-*
ters, with copious and learned notes, topograph-
ical, historical, exegetical. It is true that the
portion of those annals relating to the period
embraced in this work was substantially accessi-
ble to me in the Library of the Royal Irish
Academy, in the shape of the "M. S. Life of
O'Donnell," often cited in the following pages.
This Life of Hugh Roe O'Donnell had been
written by one of the venerable Four Masters
themselves, Franciscans of Donegal Abbey, who
indeed were not only Annalists of the Island,
but especially historiographers to the great house
of O'Donnell ; and it had afterwards been in-
corporated almost entirely in the "Annals."
This old M. S. however, was but poor compensa-
tion for the want of that magnificent repertory
of Irish historic lore, which can now be read

(amply annotated) by everybody, in the volumes of Doctor O'Donovan, and without the study of which no writer should undertake a piece of Irish history.

Another indispensable Irish authority for the period in question is the *Historia Catholica* of Don Phillip O'Sullivan (Beare). A copy of the old Latin edition of this book existed in the library of Trinity College, where I could consult it any length; but since then the work of O'Sullivan also (which had become very rare) has been handsomely reproduced in Ireland. These two, besides the History of the Abbe Mac-Geoghegan (in French), which though not contemporary, is an authority for that time, were the only strictly *Irish* sources from whence I could draw.

Of authorities upon the English side, there was abundance. The most useful of these is Camden,—"History of Queen Elizabeth,"—who has narrated at great length from his own point of view, and not with very gross unfairness, the whole of the transactions in Ireland during the life of Hugh O'Neill. Two exceedingly valuable books are Edmund Spencer's "View of the State of Ireland," and Sir John Davies' "Historical Tracts." Each of these books, though composed with the most virulent hatred and in-

solence towards the Irish nation, yet casts a
flood of light upon the social condition of the
people, and the policy of the British Government
about the time of that sad revolution which
transformed chieftain and clansman into land-
lord and tenant.   The most singular English
authority, however, is the *Pacata Hibernia*,
written by Sir George Carew, but ostensibly by
Stafford, his secretary.   This work is valuable
not only for its documents and maps, but also
for the very open and shameless avowal of the
system of treachery, fraud, and assassination
set on foot by the writer himself, and by which
he was enabled to break up the confederacy of
the Munster lords.

The work of Fynes Moryson must not be
omitted, as his narrative covers almost the whole
of O'Neill's wars : but he, though a contemporary writer, residing in Ireland, and witness of
many of the transactions he undertakes to nar-
rate, is extremely untrustworthy, and needs cor-
roboration often, oftener contradiction.   These
books, with occasional reference to Cartes' Life
of Ormond, Captain Lee's " Memorial," and
Bishop Mant's History of the Irish Church,
constituted the rather imperfect stock of authorities on which I was bold enough to venture
upon the narrative of the Life of the last

of the Princes of Tyrone. Those who may hereafter undertake to give a fuller and better account of Hugh O'Neill and his desperate struggle against English "civilization," will have a much more extensive course of reading to go through.

Besides the mighty tomes of O'Donovan's Four Masters, there are numerous family histories lately published, containing innumerable documents and letters, which, though not perhaps worth reading for their own sake, yet often give a vivid glimpse into the interior of some Franco-Hibernian Castle or Scotic chieftain's stronghold, shewing us the inmates as they lived and moved in those wild times. One of the most voluminous of these is "The Life and Letters of Florence MacCarthy Mor"—who was O'Neill's slippery lieutenant in Munster. This is an octavo volume of over 500 pages; written of course by one of the Clan-Caura, and certainly giving all the details concerning that able but treacherous chief, which the world will ever wish to know. Of other family histories may be named: "The Earls of Kildare," History of the O'Briens of Thomond, by O'Donoghue; A "Selection from the Family Archives of the MacGillicuddy of the Reeks, by Maziere Brady," Vicar of Donoghpatrick, &c.

With regard to the changes which took place
in the possession of church property, the suppression of monasteries, and the earliest penal
laws for religion, many good compilations now
exist which are of great value to the student ;
especially "The Irish Reformation ; or the
alleged conversion of the Irish bishops at the
accession of Queen Elisabeth, and the assumed
descent of the present established Hierarchy in
Ireland from the Ancient Irish Church—dis-
proved " by Dr. Maziere Brady.   The author,
though a Protestant Rector, takes part, unex-
pectedly, with the Irish Catholic Church in her
historical dispute with the Anglicans touching
the descent of orders.   His subject necessarily
obliged him to investigate minutely the civil
transactions of the sixteenth century in Ireland,
which accompanied and illustrated the ecclesiastical changes.   It has been heretofore insisted
upon by Anglican writers that the Catholic
bishops in Ireland, as a body, accepted the pretended reformation of Elizabeth ; that the Irish
hierarchy, church and nation, renounced their
allegiance to the Bishop of Rome, and to the
doctrine of the Roman Church ; that the apostolic succession was regularly transmitted to the
Protestant bishops of Ireland, and that the present Roman Catholic hierarchy and church were

established *de novo*, in schismatical manner, by emissaries of the Pope. Consequently, they say, the Protestant archbishops of Armagh and Dublin are the canonical successors of St. Patrick and St. Lawrence ; the other Protestant bishops are also the canonical successors to the ancient Catholic bishops of the sees they pretend to fill, the ecclesiastical property legally belongs to the Protestant establishment, and the Roman Catholic bishops are intruders who have drawn the majority of the Irish people into a schism. Dr. Brady has laboriously and triumphantly refuted all this; and Mr. Froude, the English historian, has given his full indorsement to Dr. Brady's statements. Dr. Brady proves that, at the most, two of the Marian bishops submitted to Elizabeth—Curwen, of Dublin, and O'Fihil, of Leighlin. Curwin's apostacy is a notorious fact, but that of O'Fihil is denied by Dr. Moran, who adduces evidence against it. Curwen was an Englishman, and consecrated by English bishops. Therefore, according to Dr. Brady, but one Irishman, having Irish consecration, deserted the communion of the Pope for that of the Queen and Parker. He goes through all the Irish sees *seriatim*, proving the continuity of succession from their ancient to their modern Catholic incumbents, and

proving, also, the forcible intrusion of Protestants by degrees, and with many breaks, into
the same titular sees. He states the conclusion
derived from his facts and arguments thus : "In
point of fact, the Irish nation, from 1558 to
1867 has continued in communion with Rome,
never having ceased to be, in its clergy, priests,
and people, as thoroughly Roman Catholic as at
the accession of Elizabeth," (p. 199.) The claim
of a succession of orders by a line traceable to
the old Irish hierarchy is also disposed of. The
doctor shows that whatever orders the Irish
Protestant church has are derived from Curwen,
and from him alone, through Loftus, who was
consecrated by him to Armagh, and thence
transferred to Dublin, in lieu of Curwen himself
who was transferred to Oxford. Of course he
does not deny the validity of the orders, but
merely the fact that they descend from an Irish
source.

In examining this canonical controversy the
author also sheds light upon the civil transactions ; and as O'Neill was holding his country
against the English not only as Prince of Ulster,
but as chief champion of the Catholic religion
in Ireland, the ecclesiastical affairs of the period
are altogether relevant, and needful for a due understanding of O'Neill's true cause and position.

With the same view the works of Dr. Moran of Dublin, especially his *Archbishops of Dublin*, as well as the Church Histories of Dr. Lanigan, Father Brenan, O. S. F., and Father A. Cogan of Navan [History of the Diocese of Meath] must all be consulted.

Amongst other needful authorities, or compilations to be consulted, must be mentioned several excellent papers in the *Ulster Archæological Journal*, Shirley's *Original Letters*, State papers, both in London and Dublin, some of which have been published ; and lastly, and especially, the late admirable book of Father Meehan of Dublin, *The Fate and Fortunes of Hugh O'Neill, Earl of Tyrone, and Hugh O'Donnell, Earl of Tyrconnell;* their Flight, Vicissitudes and Death in Exile. Mr. Meehan, indeed, professes to take up the narrative where this present writer has dropped it : yet he has supplied much authentic information with regard to the chief's last campaign, his surrender at Mellifont, his visit to England, his life in his own country afterwards, the conspiracy for his destruction, his escape from the toils of his enemies, his wanderings in Europe, his plans for return and his death in Rome—all of which, for want of space, and also in part for want of authorities, had to be passed over lightly in the unpretending little volume called, "Life of Hugh O'Neill." It may be added that Mr. Meehan has given us, by way of episode, a seperate chapter, from an earlier period of the Prince's life, his courtship and marriage—the romance of the beautiful Mabel Bagnal, sister of his enemy, the Marshal.

It is needless here to speak of the ancient Irish manuscripts and precious materials of our history as enumerated, classified and described in the great work of Eugene O'Curry: for all these documents, except the Annals of the Four Masters, stop short of the time of O'Neill's wars, and this has no pretension to be a general bibliography of Irish History, but only a sketch of the field to be investigated by any one who shall hereafter aspire to write a Life of O'Neill which may be worthy of 'the subject ; as the present volume is not. Nobody can be more sensible of this than the writer ; who undertook it in part to gratify a dear friend, and in part to aid more or less in the awakening of the minds of Irish young men to the dignity and importance of the history of their own native island.

That it has had some share of influence in that direction I am happy to believe.   J. M.

Fordham, N. Y.   St. Patrick's Day, 1868.

LIFE OF HUGH O'NEILL.

CHAPTER I.

CON THE LAME, AND HIS TIMES.

A. D. 1585—1550.

WHEN Con O'Neill, surnamed *Bacca ʏh*, reigned ɲn Ulster, the far greater portion of this island owed no allegiance and paid no obedience to the king or laws of England. More than two hundred years had gone by since the northern Irish, aided by Edward Bruce of Scotland, had destroyed every vestige of foreign dominion in Ulster; and the few Anglo-Norman families that had got footing there, under De Courcy and De Lacy, were long since, by intermarriage, gossipred, and fostering, blended with the Irish tribes used Irish customs, disdained to ride with stirrups, wore *crommeal* and *coolun*, submitted to the Brehon laws, forgot vassalage, and liege-homage, and all feudal tenure, whether by knight service, escuage, or other,—nay, forgot their language and their very names. Like the Ber minghams and De Burgos of Connaught, **who** became Mac Feorais and Mac Williams, Eighter and Oughter, some writers will have it that the haughty Mac Mahons of Monaghan, with **all** their fierce resistance to English laws and English sheriffs, were no more than so many Norman Fitzurses;—true Sons of Bears, and claiming that descent both in their original *langue d'oui* and their adopted Irish. And the Mac Swynes, from beyond Lough Swilly, sent yearly their tribute of cows to O'Donnell, never demurring on the ground that they were a branch of the knightly De Veres of Oxford.*

So attractive and genial was that Irish life of pastoral independence, and "strenuous liberty;" so kindly the Irish affections; so honey-sweet the Celtic accents on the tongue of foster-nurses and Irish maidens:—"which," says Edmund Spenser, "are two most dangerous infections;" for "The speach being Irish, the heart must needes bee Irish."

Laws, indeed, were from time to time enacted by the small English colony of Leinster, in their local parliament, to forbid all such friendly deal-

* Spenser's "View of the State of Ireland," p. 108. But the Irish annalists (probably a better authority) make both these families old Irish. Mac Mahon is said to have been, like the Mac Guires and O'Hanlons, descended from Colla-na-Chrich of the race of Heremon. (See Connellan's "Four Masters," note in p. 3.) For the Mac Swynes or Mac Sweenys, said to be a branch of the north, Hy Niall, see the same book, p. 52; yet Thierry and other writers have adopted Spenser's statement about these two families.—*Norman Con. Conclusion.*

ings with the "Irish enemy," under penalties: statutes which sounded terrible in Kilkenny and Dublin, but were of no force in the Irish country, where the "degenerate" English soon learned to forget the tongue in which those statutes were expressed, and to despise the authority that had presumed to enact them.

Yet there was, in the sixteenth century, no Irish nation. They had no national council, as of old; no supreme monarch or *Ard-Righ*, to concentrate the powers of the island for any common object. Save the tie of a common language, the chieftain of Clan-Conal had no more connexion with the lord of Clan-Carrha, than either had with the English Pale. The Anglo-Norman colony was regarded rather as one of the independent tribes of the island; "an inferior sept,"* often a tributary sept,† which had got settled there; than what it really was, a garrison holding for a foreign king, the insidious enemy of them all: and the Irish in their frequent wars amongst themselves, sometimes had the troops of the Pale, as well as the powerful Scottish colony of Antrim for auxiliaries on one side or the other.

Frequently the English carried the banners of the Pale into some Irish country with which they were then at war; burning and plundering in their march, until a force could be drawn together strong enough to drive them home: and as often were the war-cries of an O'Neill or an O'Connor

* Leland, vol. 2, p. 83.
† State Papers, Temp. Hen. VIII. cited in O'Connell's *Memoir.*

heard at the Boyne and Liffey, to the very gates of Dublin; while the English were shut up everywhere in their castles and walled towns until the black rent was levied and the storm had passed. But, save in the four counties of the Pale and a few maritime cities, there was no attempt at the exercise of either legislative or executive authority on the part of the English government.

The throne of England was filled by King Henry the Eighth, who styled himself King of England, *France*, and *Ireland;*—of France in virtue of the town of Calais, and of Ireland, because of those bands of his adventurous subjects who garrisoned the Pale. But Henry was not satisfied with temporal sovereignty. Like the Roman emperors, he determined to unite in his own person all authority of every kind, and to be acknowledged *Pontifex maximus.* His parliament had, without scruple, bestowed on him the supreme Headship of the Church; never doubting their power to give it: for the legislature of England has always regulated its religion, pronouncing this way or that upon true doctrine, like an œcumenic council, and deciding upon the successorship to the apostles with no more hesitation than on the rival claims to a disputed peerage.

And having established his spiritual supremacy in England, and desiring to encroach further upon the jurisdiction of his rival the pope, King Henry caused an act to be passed in his parliament of the Pale, duly enacting the supremacy of the English king over the church of Ireland—

"forasmuch," say those legislators, "as Ireland was depending and belonging justly and rightfully to the imperial crown of England." And so began the " Reformation" in this island.

Here a difficulty arose, or rather several difficulties; for the claim of England to govern this country had always been held to rest upon that surprising grant of Pope Adrian IV., which conferred Ireland upon Henry the Second as a fief; and to deny the papal authority was to destroy the only title which the crown of England had ever pretended over this island; whereby hangs a controversy, partly political, partly theological, which greatly agitated the pedants of both countries at that period; but is interesting now neither to gods nor men. Yet for the clear un derstanding of some terms which must often occur in the following story, we may refer to the argument for English dominion used by one of its most learned advocates. " Whatsoever become," says Archbishop Ussher,* " of the pope's idle challenges, the crown of England hath otherwise obtained an undoubted right unto the sovereignty of this country; partly by conquest, prosecuted at first upon occasion of a social war, partly by the several *submissions* of the chieftains of the land made afterwards. For whereas it is free for all men, although they have been formerly quit from all subjection, to renounce their own right, yet now, in these our days (saith Giraldus Cambrensis in his History of the Conquest of Ireland) all the princes of

* Religion of the ancient Irish.

B

Ireland did voluntarily submit, and bind them selves with firm bonds of faith and oath unto Henry the Second, king of England."

On which "submissions" we remark, first, that the same Henry the Second did, with firm bonds of faith and oath, submit and perform homage to Louis the Seventh of France; and " with head uncovered and belt ungirt, with sword and spurs removed, he placed his hands, kneeling, between those of the lord, and promised to become *his man* from thenceforward, and to serve him with life and limb and worldly honour, faithfully and loyally ;"*—that King Edward the Third, in like humble guise, did homage at the feet of another French sovereign ;—but that those two English kings were engaged in endless wars with those very suzerains : and never incurred thereby the charge of perfidy or rebellion.† And the second remark is, that such submissions, by an Irish chieftain, either in the twelfth or any other century, were not only a mere form, but had no

* For form of Liege-homage, see Hallam, Mid. Ages, vol. 1, p. 176.
† No doubt it was as peers of France, not as kings of England, they did homage to the French king; but they made war upon him in *both* capacities, and with all the power of all their dominions, insular and continental. Hallam explains the law of the case, and Thierry the *rationale* of it. The former says, " It was always necessary for a vassal to renounce his homage, before he made war on his lord." (Mid. Ages, vol. 1, p. 176, note.) And Thierry informs us that obligations of this kind " were very vague in their tenor, and were mostly taken with a bad grace, and in some sort as a mere matter of form."—Whitaker's edition, p. 161

force or significance even as a form: because those chiefs were not, themselves, feudal lords · they had neither fiefs nor vassals: like the lead ers of the ancient Franks, they were the elected captains of a tribe of freemen ; and could not, by donning the coronet and robes of a foreign noble, change their countrymen into the subjects of an alien prince, nor involve them in that great feudal system, which, like every other form of national polity must grow with a people's growth, and weave itself, in the " Loom of Time" out of the very elements of its being.

But enough of this technical disquisition. As Henry was not free in conscience, to have and to hold under the pope any longer, he caused his Parliament of the Pale, in the year 1542, to declare him "King of Ireland" in his own right, the first English monarch who assumed that title : and in the same year, at his palace of Greenwich, was beheld a notable thing,—the O'Neill of Ulster submitting himself as liege-man to an English king,—renouncing the royal name of O'Neill, " in comparison of which," says Camden, " the very title of Cæsar is contemptible in Ireland,"* —taking upon him the barbarian Anglo-Saxon title of *Jarl*, or Earl, of Tyrone ; and doing homage to Henry as King of Ireland and Head of the Church ; who on his side adorned him with a golden chain, saluted him beloved cousin, "and so returned him richly plated."†

And now we first hear of Matthew O'Neill,

* Camden, 2 Eliz.
† Campion, "Historie of Ireland," p. 161.

Con's son, (or reputed son; for in Ireland he was
believed to be the offspring of a smith of Dundalk,) called by the Irish Fardoragh, but passing
at Greenwich under the outlandish style of Baron
Dungannon, a title which he dearly rued.

Nor are the O'Neills alone in their strange honours. Mac Gilla Phadruig becomes Fitzpatrick,
and Baron of Upper Ossory. The O'Brien of
Thomond, forgetful of the glories of Kincora,
lays down at Henry's feet his dignity of Chief
Dal-Cais, and arises Earl of Thomond; his son,
Baron of Inis-Hy-Quin; his nephew, Baron of
Ibracken, by "letters patent," with broad seal of
England, with official ceremonial of Garter-king,
and the rest; with remainders, expectancies, estates tail and other jargon of English law, portentous in the ears of Filea and Brehon.

The southern chiefs, indeed, had a more sub-
stantial reward for their complaisance than those
empty dignities of earl and baron. The revenues
of all the suppressed abbeys of Thomond with
patronage of church livings, were annexed to
their lordships, and so was upheld the respectabi-
lity of the peerage. For in those years there was
a sweeping "suppression" in progress, of all religious houses in that part of the island which was
under the control of the new Head of the Church;
and many of the local princes, who could well
have defied his power, were content to sacrifice
the ancient monasteries endowed by their ancestors, to the reforming rage of Henry, on condition
of themselves receiving the spoil. The fair possessions of abbeys and priories were therefore
left almost invariably in the hands of their neigh

bouring lords, and seem to have been the stipulated price of their servile allegiance; so that
even George Browne, the king's archbishop of
Dublin, could not by most diligent suit obtain for
his own share the single nunnery of Grace Dieu,
nor even "a very poor house of friars," called
New Abbey, "a house of the obstinates' religion
which lay very commodious for him by Bally-
more." They were both destined for other claimants who had earned them worthily.

In all Ireland were at that time three hundred
and seventy of such establishments, of various
orders, where the religious passed a life of devo-
tional retirement, feeding the poor, entertaining
strangers, and tending the sick, for no earthly
reward, but for love of blessed charity, and the
health of their founders' souls.

There was abundance of plunder in every province for those who would renounce their faith
and betray their country. But Con O'Neill, to
his honour be it said, understood not the power
of his new suzerain, whether regal or spiritual, to
extend so far; nor is it easy to say *how* far he
was willing to admit such power. For this was
the same chief who had formerly cursed his offspring if they should ever speak the Saxon
tongue, sow corn, or build houses in imitation of
the English, and who, to demonstrate his views
of Henry's Headship, had on the first rumour of
" Reformation" led his troops to the south, burned
Atherdee and Navan to the ground, and from
the hill of Tarah warned off the servile nobles of
the Pale and their reforming deputy far from the
frontiers of Ulster.

While Con therefore, held the chieftaincy o'
Tyr-owen, and long after, the monasteries of his
country stood secure. Though formally "giver
and granted" to King Henry along with the religious houses of other provinces, by those who had
no title either to give or to grant, yet the commissioners appointed to reduce them into charge
did not proceed (for excellent reasons) to hold
the usual inquest on their possessions, to inven
tory their chattels and ornaments, or expel their
peaceful inhabitants ; and for seventy years afte
the "suppression" the monks of Donegal, Kilma
crenan, and Rathmullan, of Derry, Dungiven
Coleraine, and Dungannon, under the sheltering
power of O'Neill and O'Donnell " escaped," says
the Abbè Mac Geoghegan, " the sacrilegious fury
of the heretics :" or as the same fact is stated by
the Presbyterian historian,* the abbeys though
long since suppressed, " were not resumed into
the hands of the king, nor their useless inmates
expelled until the reign of James the First."

Yet the northern Irish liked not the new earl,
nor his honours, however unencumbered by foreign
laws and usages. The bards of Ulster had no
songs of praise for the obsequious liegeman of a
foreign prince. O'Donnell refused to send him
his customary tribute for Inis-Owen : Mac Guire
of Fermanagh thought scorn to be the *Uriaght*
of such an O'Neill as this ; and Con Baccagh
soon found that he was no longer the prince of
the North, and must speedily give place to wor-

* Dr. Reid, " History of the Presbyterian Church in
Ireland," vol. I. p. 77.

thier scions of that ancient stock; who happily were not wanting.

For, unmindful of court intrigue, and little versed in the lore of Saxon heraldry, there was, growing up to manhood, amongst the hills of Ulster, another son of Con; one of the proudest and fiercest O'Neills that had appeared there since he of theNineHostages; and his name was Shane. Chasing the wolf and deer with his foster-brethren in the forests of Tyr-owen, and by the shores of the lake of Feval; learning from the lips of bard and seanaghy the ancient glories and achievements of the Hy-Nial, this Shan. had grown to believe, with all his soul, that the Kinel-Eoghain were the hero-race most favoured by heaven; that Tyr-owen was the eye of Erin, and the very pride of the earth: and that of all noble and royal titles of honour and sovereignty, by far the most dread and illustrious was "The O'Neill."

And behold! just as the impetuous youth has reached manhood, and feels within him the strength and fiery spirit to uphold the honour of his race, that proud name is to be extinguished. The golden collar of an O'Neill, the sacred chair of Tullogh-oge, are to be made of no account; lost or forgotten in these unheard-of peerages of the stranger. By the soul of Con More! By the awful grave of Caille Nial! this must not be. Let his father plume himself in his foreign feathers: let the bastard Matthew maintain, as best he may, his "estate tail" and coronet of Dungannon; he, Shane, will be an O'Neill:—The O'Neill; for the clansmen of Tyr-owen, as men are wont to do, soon found out the man who was fit to be their chief.

It were long to tell, how the younger brethren of Shane stood by him for the honour of Tyrowen; how the bards espoused, as ever, the cause of nationhood, and with harp and voice kindled the ancient spirit of Erin; how there was war in Ulster till the Baron of Dungannon fell (by treachery say English chroniclers); how Con the Lame recognized his true son, and repented him of his base homaging and his foreign earldom; and how, at last, the haughty Shane sat upon the chair of Stone, was invested with the white wand of sovereignty, and duly made 'he O'Neill, and Prince of Tyr-owen.

Baron Matthew, as we said, fell: whether by treachery or on battle field, certain it is, in the course of that war he lost both life and coronet :— "a lusty horseman, well-beloved, and a tried souldiour,"[*] but no match for the ardent and resolute Shane. For *that* generation, the blood of the Dundalk smith, was not to prevail; but, in the halls of Dungannon, Matthew left an infant son, one Aodh, or Hugh, who goes a fostering among the English and is "preserved by them from Shane,"[†] (not without a politic design,) and disappears for a season.

* Campion, "Historie of Ireland," p. 189.
† Moryson.

CHAPTER II.

SHANE THE PROUD AND THE REFORMATION.

A. D. 1550—1567.

THE "Reformation" was meanwhile proceeding vigorously in the English colony; and the history of Ireland, from the period at which we have opened its page, is so deeply coloured by that event and its consequences, that frequent reference to its course and progress is essential to clearness of narrative.

On the archiepiscopal chair of St. Laurence O'Toole,* sat one George Browne, an apostate (or reformed) friar; raised to that eminence by the King of England, in the exercise of his pontifical supremacy; and to him, with four other persons, was directed in the thirtieth year of King Henry, a commission "to investigate, inquire, and search out where, within the said land of Ireland, there were any notable images or reliques, at which the simple people of the said Lord the King were wont superstitiously to meet together   *   *   and that they should break in pieces, deform, and bear away the same, so that no fooleries of this kind might thenceforth for

* Properly Lorcan O'Tuathail.

ever be in use in the said land:" a commission which was executed, wherever the English power extended, with all the zeal that religion and rapacity could both inspire.

The *Report* of these commissioners is still extant, one of the most singular statements of account on record; in which they specify the property, "by virtue of the commission of the lord the king aforesaid, into the hands of the lord the king, taken and appraised, and by the before-recited title sold." £326 2s. 11d. is stated to be "the price of divers pieces of gold and silver, in mass and bullion, and also of certain precious stones set in gold and silver, and of silver ornaments and other things upon divers images, pictures, and reliques." Three cathedral churches, St. Patrick's Dublin, Leighlin, and Ferns, with many monasteries, priories, parish churches and chapels, are stated to have been stripped. "The price of divers vases, jewels, and ornaments of gold and silver, and bells, and the utensils and household stuff of superstitious buildings," is set down at £1710 2s. 0d. and "one thousand pounds of wax, manufactured into candles, tapers, images, and pictures," produced £20.*

So far the *material* reform had been effected, but on the death of Henry the Eighth, the doctrinal revolution was to begin in good earnest. Somerset, the Protector, was a Zuinglian: and under the advice of Cranmer, (who was a Zuin-

* Original account in the Record-Office, Custom-House, Dublin, cited in Dr. Mant's "History of the Church of Ireland," p `63.

•lian also, from the moment of King Henry's death,) it was resolved in his councils to make a more strenuous effort for establishing the Reformation in Ireland. In furtherance of that object, Sir Edward Bellingham was sent over, a very singular apostolic missionary, "with 600 horse and 400 foot." An "order of council" was issued, enjoining the use of a new Liturgy. And shortly after one Bale was appointed by the king to the bishopric of Ossory, a bold and uncompromising reformer, who was not content, like the king's bishops in general, to reside in Dublin, under the shelter of the castle, but proceeded at once to Kilkenny, and undertook his charge. A most remarkable " Vocacyon," as he calls it, was this episcopal visit of Dr. Bale to his diocese, and may serve as an instance of the method in which the Church of Ireland was to be reformed.

The new bishop being ignorant of Irish, and most of his clergy, with all their flocks, ignorant of English, his preaching though never so energetic, could have little effect upon such a diocese. Therefore he ordered his servants to invade the churches, to pull down the images and pictures, and to destroy the vestments and ornaments which savoured of popery. The people of Kilkenny bore the preaching very well, so long as they did not understand it; but there was no mistaking such conduct as this. They rose against him, killed five of his servants before his face, and he himself hardly escaped. As he relates the story himself: "I preached the gospel of the knowledge and right invocation of God. I maintained the political order by doctrine and moved

the commons to obey their magistrates. But
when I once sought to destroy the idolatries, and
dissolve the hypocrites yokes, then followed
angers, slanders, conspiracies, and in the end the
slaughter of men."*

Hitherto the religious innovations had been
confined within very narrow limits; and in the
North the alarm of them was not yet heard.
Two clergymen, indeed, named Dowdall and
Goodacre, had been successively appointed the
nominal (or titular) archbishops of Armagh by
Henry the Eighth and Edward the Sixth; but
they scarcely appear to have visited their diocese,
and certainly attempted no reformation there.
The former of these, though not appointed by the
provision of the pope, was a stanch Catholic,
and upon the death of Henry, zealously resisted
any change of doctrine or practice in the church.
Though a king's bishop, he did not shift and veer,
as was expected, with the Court religion of the
day; and for his contumacy in that respect, the
new English pontiff, in October, 1551, issued a
bull, (or, "letters patent," as it was termed,)
gravely depriving Dowdall, and the see of Armagh, of the Primacy of Ireland, and conferring
that dignity upon the Archbishop of Dublin and
his successors;† in acknowledgment of the services of Browne, who better knew the duties of a
court bishop.

But all these arrangements were unheard of or

* "Vocacyon of John Bale to the bishopric of Ossory."
† Waræi, An. 1ª², folio

disregarded in Ulster. The *Coarba* of St. Patrick still sat upon the archiepiscopal throne of Armagh; and the sees of the North, protected by the O'Neills and O'Donnells, and ruled by the primates Cromer and Waucop, long continued free from invasion by the barbarian missionaries of England. In the words of Dr. Leland, " the people, removed beyond the sphere of English law, had not known or not regarded the ordinances lately made with respect to religion, nor considered themselves as interested or concerned in any regulations hereafter to be made."*

Shane O'Neill troubled himself little about the " Reformation" so long as it kept far from his borders. There was work enough for him to do at home. O'Rielly of Cavan dared to question the supremacy of O'Neill, and had to be brought to reason by a fierce inroad and a bloody defeat. The chief of Tyrconnell was a more formidable antagonist. The O'Donnells had long rivalled in power their kindred tribe of Tyr-owen; had reduced some of the tributary chieftains, former *Uriaghts* of the O'Neill, under their own sway; had wrested from the Kinel-owen their ancient territory of Innishowen for which O'Donnell paid tribute to O'Neill, though always with reluctance; and sometimes he set the prince of Ulster at defiance and denied the tribute altogether: which had in former days produced furious wars, and that famous diplomatic correspondence—emphatic protocols, breaking off with significant *apos.*

* Leland, " Hist. of Ireland," vol. 2, p. 194.

pesis.—" Send me my tribute, or else——" "I owe thee no tribute, and if——"

Shane was not the man to suffer the rights of O'Neill to be questioned. With a large army he burst into Tyrconnell, and too recklessly pursued his enemies into the recesses of their mountainous country. In a night attack upon his camp, his troops were entirely dispersed: Shane himself narrowly escaped being surprised in his tent, amongst the galloglasses of his guard: and for that time was obliged to retreat, or even to fly; swimming the rivers, say the chroniclers of Donegal, and traversing the mountains by unknown ways. But he vowed a dire revenge, and fearfully fulfilled that vow another day.

The plunder of O'Neill's camp fell to the victorious O'Donnells: and the scene upon that battle-field might remind us of Chlodowig and his Franks, dividing their spoil upon the plains of Soissons. " A vast plenty of arms, clothing, and horses fell to the share of the victors, the prodigious quantity of which booty may be judged by this, that when they came to divide the spoil by lots, eighty horses, besides O'Neill's own horse, fell to the share of Con the son of Calvagh.*

The O'Donnells did not long boast of their victory, till a fresh army from Tyr-owen crossed the Foyle and carried havoc and ruin to the heart of their country   Calvagh O'Donnell was

* Ware, " Antiq. of Ireland ;" citing the " Annals of Donegal." (Four Masters.)

defeated in battle, his lands were wasted and plundered, and the chieftain and his wife carried off in chains by the triumphant Shane. Calvagh indeed was afterwards set free ; but his wife remained as part of the spoils of war, in the halls of Benburb ; became the concubine of the haughty conqueror, and bore him sons and daughters : in especial one son, whom they christened Hugh, and surnamed *na Gaveloch,* " Of the fetters," or the Fettered—for whom it had been better if he had never been born.

A wild and turbulent career had this Shane, and few days of rest since he took the leading of that warlike sept : quelling Mac Guire of Fermanagh ; bridling the marauding Scots ; on all sides strengthening the friends and crushing the foes of Tyr-owen : crushing them indeed too fiercely ; whereby he treasured up for himself wrath, which was to burst at a future day upon his head.

At last the impetuous energy of this chief prevailed, and carried the sway of O'Neill higher than it had reached under any of his predecessors since the race had given monarchs to Ireland. From Fanad to Dundalk, from Ballyshannon to Dundrum, was no chief able to resist his power. So that, in 1558, when Elizabeth ascended the throne of England, the O'Neill, as reason was, predominated in Ulster.

The English government seems to have determined that either by force or otherwise,* the

* "By all manner of means, as well by force *as otherwise.*"—Instructions to Sussex. *Desid. Cur. Hibernica.* p. 3.

Northern prince must be destroyed. Sir Henry
Sidney (who was administering the government
of the Pale, in the absence of Sussex) marched
northward as far as Dundalk and invited the
chief to a conference. Shane O'Neill was then
at his house of the Fews, between Dundalk and
Armagh ; and he seems to have entertained some
fears that Sidney meant him foul play in this
proposed interview. He therefore declined the
invitation ; but sent a message that if Sir Henry,
of his courtesy, would visit his poor house, and
attend a christening there, and be gossip to his
child, it would please him well. Sir Henry attended him, was treated with all princely hospitality ; and Shane took the trouble to explain
to him, so far as his English ideas would admit
the information, how the Queen of England had
no jurisdiction in Ulster ; how the " surrender"
and re-investment of Con Baccagh were void by
the Irish laws, as he was only chieftain for his
life, " nor could have more by the law of Tanistry ; nor could surrender but by consent of the
laws of his country ;" how he, Shane, being the
lawful son of Con, and also elected by his sept,
and moreover able to defend his rights by the
sword, was now the true prince and chieftain of
Ulster, and that as he meddled not with the
Queen of England's territories, so he would take
care she should not interfere with his.*

* This visit of Sidney was received by the Irish as a
'submission,' and "although the insolence of this overture," says Leland, " was fully conceived, yet it was
deemed expedient to comply with it."

When the Earl of Sussex returned to his government several unsuccessful expeditions were made to the North in order, either by war or diplomacy to reduce this "Arch-Traitor," as the English chroniclers dare to term him; and at length "the queen resolved," says Camden, " to disannul the patent of King Henry the Eighth, wherein he declared Matthew (falsely supposed to be the son of Con) to be the successor of his father, and to bestow upon this Shane, as his undoubted son and heir, the honourable title of Earl of Tyr-owen and Baron of Dungannon."* Yes: they would now shower their tinsel honours upon him; set his foot upon the necks of all his enemies; enrich him with the spoil of numerous abbeys;—let him only consent to kneel at the footstool of a foreign throne, and place his country under the iron heel of English power.

But Shane the Proud despised those paltry coronets. " Letters patent," could not strengthen him in Tyr-owen; and for the abbeys, if he had been reformer enough he could have robbed them for himself. In the language of the English chronicler: " When he saw that he was able to levy of his own followers one thousand horse and four thousand foot, and had already a guard of seven hundred men, he disdained, in barbarous pride, all such honourable titles in comparison of the name of *O'Neill*, and vaunted himself among his own people to be king of Ulster."†

Yet Shane was willing to live at peace with England and the Pale: he appeared in Dublin

---

* Camden, O 72½z.   † Ib

and announced his intention of visiting the court
of London: then hearing from some of his re-
tainers that Sussex meditated seizing him by
treachery, and sending him to England a prisoner, he proudly resolved to attend the Queen.
as became an independent sovereign. He proceeded to London with a gallant train of guards,
bare-headed, with curled hair (as if the statute of
Kilkenny had never been passed) hanging down
their shoulders, armed with battle-axes, and ar-
rayed in their saffron doublets; an astonishment
to the worthy burghers of London and West-
minster. Elizabeth received him graciously and
they conversed upon Irish affairs; but when the
queen inquired by what right he had excluded
young Hugh from Matthew's inheritance, " he
answered fiercely, by very good right,"* and explained to Elizabeth the laws and usages which
prevailed in his country; showed her that Con's
surrender was unavailing; that Matthew was a
bastard, and he the true O'Neill; and that the
authority he exercised over his tributaries of Ul
ster was no more than his fathers had done before
him :—" Which matters forasmuch as the queen
gave credit unto, he was sent home again with
honour."

Yet that treacherous court had resolved on nis
ruin; and Elizabeth while she loaded him with
honours, vowed revenge in secret, and swore
" by God's death" that such a *rascaille* kern
should not long despise her peerages and defy
her power.

* Camden. Q. Eliz.

An alliance, however, was for the present concluded between the Queen of England and the
prince of Tyr-owen. Shane, as a proof of his
good faith was to exterminate the Scots of Dal-
riada, who were declared enemies of England—a
duty which he readily undertook, as the Scots
were also enemies of his own ; or at least had
grown too numerous and powerful to be tolerated
as neighbours by so imperious a chief. Yet these
Scots of the Western Isles, Mac Neills and Mac
Donnells, were his kinsmen and natural allies
were, in fact, an Irish sept, of Irish speech and
usages, and a branch of the great Clan-Colla,
from which had descended the O'Hanlons and
Mac Gwires of Ulster.*   For ages they had possessed the " glynns" or mountainous country of
Antrim, and were the mercenary soldiers of
every chief in the island who required and could
reward their services. Their swords were frequent in our wars ; their names in the songs of
all our bards : and they founded upon Irish soil
the monasteries of Bona Margy and Limbeg, to
make their peace with God : and there, in Irish
earth, their bones lie buried.†

Now, instead of making common cause with
the Scots against their common enemy, Shane,
at the instance of his faithless *ally* of England,
levied a cruel war upon them. On his return
from London he gathered his clansmen of Tyr-

* Four Masters, by Connellan, note in page 3.
† Dr. Reid takes care to distinguish them from his
Scots. He says, (Hist. of the Presbyterian Church, vol.
1, p. 77,) "The Scots here spoken of were piratical
marauders and Roman Catholics from the western isles.

owen, crossed the Bann, and sought the **Mac** Donnells in their strorgholds of the glynns. Here he defeated their in two battles, slew James the son of Conal, their leader, wasted the country, and carried off Sorley Buidhe (the yellow-haired), brother of their chief, in chains to Tyrone.

The English government had in the mean time been steadily pursuing its views of reforming Ireland, to which Shane O'Neill had hitherto paid no attention whatever. Sussex, in the second year of the queen, held a parliament in Dublin which re-enacted the spiritual supremacy of the English monarch, and imposed on all the Catholic clergy (or, as the act expressed it, all who should maintain or defend foreign authority) penalties of deprivation of benefices, for the first offence; for the second, the penalties of *prœmunire;* for the third, penalty of high-treason;— that is to say, that all Catholic clergymen who would not renounce their faith must die.

Another act passed in that parliament, and called the "Act of Uniformity," commanded the use of King Edward's liturgy (yet not the liturgy which had been prescribed before; not his "First Book," but his "Second Book"); under penalty of imprisonment for life in the case of all such clergymen as should *a third time* refuse to use it, or even speak disrespectfully of it. All persons, whether lay or clerical, who should "despise or deprave" the book, or cause any other form to be said or sung (that is to say, all Catholics) were to be visited with like punishments according to the number of their offences in that kind. All persons whatever, "not

having reasonable excuse," were to resort to their
parish churches on all Sundays and holydays,
and to abide there orderly during service, on pain
of the censures of the church and twelve pence
fine:—and the being a Catholic was not to be
admitted as such "reasonable excuse," but was
rather a serious aggravation. Finally, all archbishops and bishops were solemnly enjoined, *in
God's name,* to put this act in strict execution.

Although the government of the Pale had no
power to enforce their laws in the Irish country,
the intention was that those laws should have a
general operation wherever, and so soon as, either
negotiation or the sword might open a way for
them. And as the queen had not for some years
had an archbishop of Armagh it was resolved (in
order to assert a continual claim against the pope)
to supply that metropolitan see with an active reformer. Adam Loftus, a young Englishman who
had made a favourable impression on the queen
at a public act in Cambridge by "the elegance
of his oratory, the comeliness of his person, and
his graceful address," * was raised at the age of
twenty-eight to the nominal dignity of Archbishop of Armagh; "the youngest archbishop,"
says Ware, "that we meet with in this see, except Celsus." And the North, not being yet
ripe for foreign bishops, the queen declares in
the letters patent that as "his archbishopric is a
place of great charge, in *name and title* only to
be esteemed, without any worldly endowment,"
she permits him to hold the deanery of St. Pa-

* **Mant.** "Hist. of the Church of Ireland," p. 268.

trick's in the meantime. It was clear that while Shane O'Neill held such sway in the North, Loftus could be only a bishop, as it were, *in partibus infidelium*. And that his province must be first reduced by the sword before it would peaceably submit to the sway of his crozier.

To make a beginning of that conquest a powerful body of English troops was sent to Derry under Colonel Randolph, ostensibly as auxiliaries against the Scots, but, in truth, to form a settlement there which might be a key to Ulster, and a bit between the teeth of O'Neill. These English, being true reformers, made small account of the sanctity of that ancient seat of piety. They turned the church into an arsenal and fortified themselves upon the hill of Derry.

Now Shane began to perceive that his new allies were his deadliest enemies, and that nothing less was contemplated by them than the subjugation of his people and the ruin of the ancient religion : and he resolved that Randolph and his troops should no longer hold the *Teampol-More*, nor profane the sacred oaks of Colum-kille. He led his forces to the Foyle, yet, for the present, neither besieged the place nor declared hostility : but a party of his men advanced to the hill, and by their insolence, as Cox relates, provoked Randolph to sally out upon them. A skirmish ensued in which Randolph was killed : and Derry became a hazardous post to hold—with the banners of O'Neill floating over O'Cahan's country to the south ; O'Dogherty and Inishowen glooming on the north ; and angry Mac Swynes and O'Donnells hemming it round on all sides. The garrison, however, maintained its ground : till at length—behold a miracle ! a wolf from the neighbouring woods ran to the hill of Derry, huge and hirsute, having in his mouth a burning torch,* rushed straight to the church and flung his brand amongst the powder barrels of the Saxons. Church and fortress, with horrible explosion were shattered to pieces ; hundreds of the soldiery were blown to the elements : and so St. Columkille avenged the desecration of his sacred groves.

Thus relate the Irish annalists : but whether by the miracles of the saint, or otherwise, certainly the fortifications of Derry were dismantled, and the remnant of Randolph's men betook themselves to their ships.

On the south of O'Neill's territory also the English had begun to encroach ; and the venerable cathedral of Armagh was occupied by their troops—unfailing harbingers of the Reformation in Ireland. But now Shane threw off all reserve with these insidious allies. He could not endure this new garrison of Armagh. His blood was up : his standard was unfurled ; and he swore by St. Malachy, and by the crozier of blessed Patrick, that the holy fanes of Drumsailech hill should be no shelter for the reforming bishop and

---

* Or *sparks of fire.*—*O'Sullivan.* There is an obscurity about the cause of the English troops evacuating Derry. The story of the skirmish in which Randolph was killed is given by Camden and Cox ; but O'Sullivan does not mention it at all. And, on the other hand, the miracle of the wolf is an unsatisfactory account of the matter. O'Sullivan, however, does not state it as a fact. but as the popular belief in his day

his troops. He burst upon Armagh like a thun
derbolt, and laid both church and city in ashes.

For this Loftus solemnly cursed him, and in
Dublin pronounced sentence of excommunica-
tion against him;* not with bell, or book, or
candle, (which might savour of superstition,) yet
with sufficient unction and heartiness notwithstanding. But Shane was little affected by his
cursing. With the troops of Tyr-owen he swept
southward like a hail-storm ravaging the settlements of the English and razing the castles of
the Pale. He laid siege to Dundalk where he
met a stout resistance; and Sarsfield, mayor of
Dublin, having marched to its relief with a large
body of citizens, he raised the siege, and retired
northwards, after laying waste half a province.

The whole powers of the English government
were now concentrated against O'Neill. Even
the Earl of Desmond, on whom he had relied for
support, joined with the Deputy in defence of the
Pale. Sidney, with the usual English policy, laboured to raise an Irish party against him in
Ulster, and for that purpose supported O'Donnell
his bitter enemy with troops and arms. The
North was laid desolate by a furious war; and
although O'Neill was generally victorious in the
field, and especially in the battle of the " Red-
coats" (*na Gassogues dearg*), where four hundred of O'Donnell's English auxiliaries were cut
to pieces;† yet his power gradually declined.
Mac Gwire and some Connaught chieftains whom
his pride and ferocity had made his enemies, joined

* Ware.   † Mac Geoghegan.

O'Donnell against him.   His territories were
wasted by incessant attacks : his troops, who rather feared than loved him, fled in large bodies
from his standard : and at last, abandoned by all
his allies, and reduced nearly to extremity, he
resolved to betake himself to his former enemies,
the Scots of Antrim, who were then encamped
in north Clan-hugh-buidhe, under Alaster Oge
Mac Donnell. As a propitiatory offering he sent
home in freedom the Yellow-haired Sorley, whom
he had taken prisoner two years before; and
shortly after Shane himself, with his concubine,
(the wife of O'Donnell), his secretary, and a
poor train of but fifty horsemen, proceeded to the
encampment of Mac Donnell.

Here again he was met by the treachery of the
English. An officer named Piers, an agent of
the deputy, had been negotiating with the Scots;
and on the news of Shane's approach, took care
to remind them of that pitiless raid upon the
glynns, of the slaughter of their chief and all
their ancient enmity to the haughty prince of
Ulster.   O'Neill arrived, and was entertained
with seeming hospitality ; until some dispute, as
previously concerted, arose between the followers
of the two chiefs, which ended in the Mac Donnells falling upon Shane and all his company and
hewing them to pieces. The chieftain's head was
appropriated by Piers, the contriver of this base
slaughter, who sent it, as an acceptable offering
to the lord deputy, " pickled in a pipkin,"* and
received for the price of it, one thousand marks.

That ghastly head was gibbetted high upon a

* Cox.

pole, and long grinned upon the towers of **Dublin** Castle; a new muniment and visible sign
of that inalienable legacy of hatred to the
stranger bequeathed by an O'Neill two hundred
years before;—" Hatred produced by lengthened
recollections of injustice, by the murder of our
fathers, brothers, and kindred; and which will
not be extinguished in our time nor in that of our
sons." The headless trunk of Shane the Proud
was buried where it fell: and they still show his
grave, about three miles from the little village of
Cushendun, upon the coast of Antrim.

English writers have painted this Shane as a
hideous monster of sensual brutality: and strange
tales are current of his wine cellars at Dundrum
castle, on the coast of Down; of his two hundred tuns of Spanish wine and hogsheads of us-
quebaugh stored in the vaults of that fortress;
of his deep carouses and loathsome drunkenness;
and that unheard-of course of earth-bathing,
burying himself to the ears in cold clay, to cool
the raging fever of his blood. But it is the
painting of an enemy. He was no stupid drunk-
ard, who for so many years defied the armies and
defeated the policy of Elizabeth: and his countrymen have only to lament that, by his indomitable pride and cruelty, he armed so many Irish
chiefs against him, and against their native land;
and further to regret that he did not import from
Spain (instead of wines of Malaga) some thousand blades of the Toledo tempering, and Spanish
soldiers, then the best troops in Europe, to **wield
them against the deadly enemies of his race.**

CHAPTER III.

TIRLOUGH LYNNOGH AND THE "BARON OF DUN-GANNON."

A. D. 1567—1584.

AFTER the murder of Shane O'Neill, Queen Elizabeth and her Irish deputy believed that all danger from Ulster was at an end. Sidney held a parliament in that year in which the legislators of the Pale solemnly passed an act for what they called the " attainder" of Shane O'Neill, and the forfeiture of his " estate," meaning all the lands inhabited by his sept. The act then proceeds, after abolishing the very name of O'Neill, and imposing the penalties of high treason upon any who should dare to assume it, to grant to the queen all the other lands of northern and eastern Ulster ; O'Cahan's country, now the county Derry ; the Route, the Glynns, and North Clan-hugh-buidhe (or Claneboy,) now composing the county of Antrim, but then inhabited by the Mac Quillans, Mac Donnells, and O'Neills ; Mac Gennis' country in Down, called Iveagh ; O'Hanlon's and Mac Cann's in Armagh, called Oir-thir (Orier) and Clan Bressail ; and also the whole of the present county of Monaghan, comprising Farney, Uriel, Lochty, and Dartry, inhabited by the Mac Mahons, and Triuch of the Mac Kennas All these territories were gravely confiscated to the queen's use,—upon the map, and after a documentary manner; but her majesty never derived any benefit from those new dominions, being, indeed, kept out of them by the right owners.

The truth is, the northerns never heard of these acts of Elizabeth's Parliament; and never dreamed that the murder of an Irish chieftain by a traitor Scot should give any foreign power authority in Ulster. Tirlough Lynnogh O'Neill, a grandson of Con More was invested with the chieftaincy of Ulster, by the permission, as the English historians say, of the queen's government; which also permitted him to hold (but, they assure us, by "English tenure") a portion of his estate; permitted indeed more than they could have wished, wanting the power to prevent it.

Sir Henry Sidney however proceeded to the North, not on a hostile expedition, but attended only by six hundred men; and there he received from several chieftains what would now be called assurances of friendly relations, or "submissions" in the language of Camden and Cox; and as the latter author with much gravity assures us, "settled Ulster," which, however, will appear not to have been finally settled at that time.

When Shane O'Neill was murdered, the crafty councillors of Elizabeth seem to have fixed their eyes upon young Hugh, son to the ill-fated Baron Matthew, and destined him, according to the usual English policy, as an instrument to weaken and divide the power of Ulster; by degrees to destroy its independence; and so to *reform* it after their fashion,* little knowing the stuff that was in him: for this Hugh was then "a young man little set by."†

Unhappily, we know but little of Hugh O'Neill's early life; except that he lived sometimes in Ireland, but much frequented the English court; in his own country an Irish chief, in London a courtly nobleman; that he was high in favour with Elizabeth, being a youth of goodly presence and winning speech; that he was not very tall in stature, but powerfully made, able to endure much labour, watching, and hunger; that "his industry was great, *his soul large*, and fit for the weightiest businesses;"—that he "had much knowledge in military affairs, and a profound dissembling heart; so as many deemed him born either for the great good or ill of his country."‡

This man was deemed a suitable instrument of English politicians to ruin his country's liberty; and with that view was recognized by the queen as Baron of Dungannon "by his father's right," and was supported as a rival to Tirlough, then the O'Neill; for thus it was expected that the Irish chieftain and the Saxon baron would destroy each other, and that the great house of Tyrone, divided against itself, would fall. Hugh

* For a candid explanation of this scheme see "**Spenser's** View," p. 180.
† Camden, Queen Eliz.
‡ Ib.

O'Neill knew well the purport and meaning of all these honours : he understood what the golden chain of an English noble symbolized, when worn round the neck of a Celtic chieftain : he felt that in those stars and ribbons there lurked danger to his country, ignominy to himself. But he had much to learn amongst the English : he had their mode of warfare to master, their policy to study, in the characters of Burleigh and Walsingham intending, apparently, to try conclusions with them in both those departments at a future day. So with that "profound dissembling heart" of his, he stomached their disgraceful dignities ; nay, bore himself proudly under them, biding his time.

Nearly twenty years passed away, from the death of Shane till 1584, when Perrot came to Ireland as lord deputy ; during which Ulster was comparatively quiet, though as thoroughly *unreformed*, and anti-English as ever. The sacrilegious outrages by which the foreigners and their bishops prosecuted reformation in the south, (and which provoked the Geraldine war there) were still unknown in the O'Neill's country. Abbey lands and monasteries were peaceably possessed by their religious inhabitants ; and three northern bishoprics, those of Clogher, Derry, and Raphoe, seem to have been abandoned altogether to Catholic prelates ; so that as Doctor Leland, lamenting the circumstance, observes, "they were still granted by the pope without control." Not that the pope did not also appoint bishops, as

usual, to the other sees; but for some of those
there were also nominal bishops (without clergy
or flocks), named by letters patent from the
queen.

During this period also the civil policy of the
North remained unchanged; there was not a
sheriff north of Dundalk. No "lord president"
had yet ventured into these regions to govern
with his "course of discretion," as Sir John Davies terms their method of administering justice.
Hugh O'Neill, when in Ireland, seems to have resided quietly at his house of Dungannon, and to
have acquiesced, contrary to all expectation, in
the chieftaincy of old Tirlough, who held his
state principally in Strabane or Benburb. And
so long as the frontiers of the Pale were not advanced northwards, neither chiefs nor people
concerned themselves about the affairs of other
parts of the island: for, alas! there was still no
Irish nation.

Several transactions, however, occurred in
Ulster, during this period, which deserve some
notice. In Queen Elizabeth's reign foreign plantations began to be a favourite project with the
English. Large tracts of North America were
by those all-powerful "letters patent" taken from
the red men and deliberately given and granted
to such of her discontented and adventurous subjects as would undertake to form settlements
there and establish true religion: and Ulster,
which had been so solemnly declared forfeit to the
queen seemed a very suitable theatre for similar
plantations. Accordingly one Thomas Smith, a
secretary to Elizabeth, having a natural son to

provide for, whose illegitimacy was a bar to his
attaining distinction in his own country, desired
to make him the founder of a noble family in Ireland. He moved the queen, therefore, to *grant* this
young adventurer a territory in the Ards, on the
east coast of Down, for the purpose, as Camden
assures us, of civilizing and converting the barbarous inhabitants.   And as it had always been
found that the Irish could not be civilized or
converted, until they had first been largely plundered, every foot soldier who should accompany
Smith, was to take for his own share, one hundred
and twenty acres of land, every horseman two
hundred and forty acres, and all other persons according to their rank, paying Smith, as Lord of
Ards, one penny per acre.   But Brian Mac Art
O'Neill, and his clansmen, to whom all that land
belonged, had not been consulted in these arrangements, and apparently were not desirous of
such civilization as this foreign pirate had to
offer: for when Smith landed, (1571,) and was
proceeding to establish himself in the Ards,
O'Neill and his people fell upon them by surprise,
(by treachery, some historians say, as if the
O'Neills were his natural and sworn allies,) and
killed Smith and many of his troops; the rest fled
to their ships and speedily weighed anchor, carrying their letters patent and their civilization to
some more hospitable shore.

Shortly after, in the year 1573, Walter Devereux, earl of Essex, projected a more extensive
plantation in the same district.   Twelve hundred
troops were to be maintained and fortification
built at the joint expense of the queen and

Essex ; and, this time, each horseman was to have four hundred acres, and each footman two hundred. A few scores of acres, more or less, of the Irish enemies' land seemed to have been reckoned of small account. Essex raised £10,000 (equal to £100,000 of the present money) by mortgaging his English estate to the queen; made vast preparations in men, arms, and stores; and so hopeful was the expedition held, that Lord Rich, Lord Dacre, Sir Henry Knowles, three sons of Lord Norris, and several other Englishmen of distinction, accompanied him to have a share of the glory and the profit. The armament set sail and arrived in the bay of Carrickfergus.

So formidable an invasion seems to have caused for the time a close union amongst the several chieftains of the name of O'Neill. Brien, lord of Clar-hugh-buidhe, whose territories were the immediate objects of this marauding expedition, was speedily joined both by Tirlough Lynnogh, and Hugh of Dungannon, who was then in this country, and seems, notwithstanding his English peerage and high favour with the queen, to have been strongly of opinion that *Ireland was for the Irish.* Several skirmishes occurred between the O'Neills and the troops of Essex. The new colony began to promise more hard fighting than either profit or Protestantism ; and the English noblemen who shared the adventure, one by one, withdrew to England. At last the earl petitioned the queen for liberty to abandon the plantation and return home, which was not however granted him for more than a year : and the only further proceeding we hear of in connexion

with the affair is that, in 1574, "a solemn peace
and concord was made between the earl of Essex
and Felim O'Neill. However, at a feast wherein
the earl entertained that chieftain, and at the end
of their good cheer, O'Neill and his wife were
seized ; their friends who attended were put to
the sword before their faces, and Felim, together
with his wife and brother, was conveyed to Dublin, where they were cut up in quarters."*

Even this expedient, however, did not secure
Essex in his settlement. The Irish of that country would not be civilized notwithstanding all his
exertions, and never could see the justice or ex-
pediency of allotting their lands to English soldiers. The troops were slain or scattered ; the
money was lost ; and at length the earl got permission to return to England.

But the Geraldine war had now broken out in
Munster, and Hugh of Dungannon must be followed to the South.

* Irish M S. Annals, quoted by Leland and Curry.

CHAPTER IV.

THE GERALDINES AND REFORMATION IN THE SOUTH.

1570—1578.

As the wars in Munster were solely on account of religion, it is needful to keep sight of the " Reformation." In the year 1575, a very singular letter was addressed to the Queen of England by Sir Henry Sidney, then lord deputy, in which the writer undertakes an exposition of the state of his province in matters ecclesiastical.* He takes as an example the diocese of Meath, "the best peopled diocese, and best governed country," he calls it, of this realm, of which the queen's bishop at that time was one Brady. Sir Henry says there were in that diocese two hundred and twenty-four parish churches, of which one hundred and five were served by " very simple and sorry curates," and of these curates only eighteen were found able to speak English, "the rest Irish priests, or rather," as he prefers to call them, " Irish rogues." In many places the very walls of the churches were down, " very few chancels covered, windows and doors ruined." And if such be the estate of the church in Meath

* Sir. H. Sidney's *Letters and Memorials.*

diocese Sidney leaves her Majesty to conjecture in what case the rest is. "Yea, so profane and heathenish," he continues, "are some parts of this your country become, as it hath been preached publicly before me, that the sacrament of baptism is not used among them; and truly I believe it." Spenser's account of the state of religion is still more dismal; the clergy, "generally bad"—"the churches even with the ground"—the bishops keeping the benefices in their own hands and "setting up their own servants and horseboys to take up the tithes and fruits of them." In all the world had not been seen "such an overthrown church." "The kingdom in general," says Dr. Mant, "was at this time overwhelmed by the most deplorable immorality and irreligion." Statements these which to those unacquainted with the peculiar phraseology of the writers might convey an impression of hideous national crime. But "religion" and "the church" meant, with them, only the Protestant religion and the queen's clergy. The universal Catholicism of the people was accounted only as so much *irreligion*; for the same Spenser informs us that the popish priests, "lurking secretly in the houses and in corners of the country doe more *hurt and hindrance* to religion with their private persuasions than all the others can do good with their publique instructions." And he much marvels at the zeal of these priests, which he says "it is a great wonder to see;" "how they spare not to come out of Spaine, from Rome and from Remes, by long toyle and daungerous travayling hither, where they know perill of death awayteth them, and reward or richesse." Dr. Leland, while he deplores the gloomy prospect, as he calls it, admits that "where the reformed clergy could neither be regarded nor understood, the priests spoke to their countrymen and kinsmen in their own language, and were heard with attention, favour and affection." And Doctor Mant, after lamenting the general "irreligion" admits, as it were incidentally, that "It is true there existed in the kingdom other intrusive missionaries sent by the bishop of Rome, as opponents of the sovereign, the laws, and the church of the kingdom."

The overthrow of church buildings mentioned by Sidney and Spenser, may be accounted for by their being generally turned into fortresses by the queen's troops ; "for in the churches dedicated to the saints it was most usual with them to reside," says an Irish chronicler.* And as the Irish loved no strong places upon their borders, they made no scruple, when occasion served, of burning and destroying them like the other castles of the English. We have seen how the cathedrals of Derry and Armagh fared in the wars of Shane O'Neill ; and about the same period† the church of Athenry, in Galway, was laid in ashes by the Mac-an-Earlas, sons of the Earl of Clanrickard ; and when men cried out sacrilege and parricide, for their mother lay buried there, one of them fiercely answered, "If his mother were alive in the church he would sooner burn

* MS. translation of Life of O'Donnell in R.I.A. p. 51.
† 1576.

her and it together than any English should fortify there."

On the whole we may collect that little or no progress had yet been made in reducing the Irish people under the Queen of England's jurisdiction, either temporal or spiritual. The peerages created by King Henry had begun to be regarded in their true light as badges of servitude, and despised accordingly. Thomond, like Tyrone, could endure no earldoms within its bounds, and on the death of the first earl of that title, had compelled his successor to nominate a Tanist after the manner of his fathers, and to comport himself in all respects like an Irish prince. Some years later Mac Carthy-More flung to the winds his coronet of Clancarthy,* assumed the title of King of Munster, and " invaded the Lord Roche's country with banners displayed" as an Eugenian chieftain ought.

But the great Anglo-Irish family of Fitzgerald were the most powerful antagonists of English authority in Munster. Gerald, the head of that tribe, (and by his English title, Earl of Desmond,) was then the most potent chieftain of the south ; had a vast following, royal privileges, many fair castles and wide domains ; and through his palatinate of Kerry, and from the Shannon to the Blackwater, from Carrig-a-foyle to his good town of Kilmallock, and eastward to Youghal, the Geraldine administered justice, levied war, and held his state like a sovereign prince as he was. His attachment to the ancient

* Cox. This writer calls the title *Clancar*

religion caused him to be looked to as the champion of the Catholic cause in the south. The earl and his countess had received, with distinction, Leverous, bishop of Kildare, when deprived of his see for refusing the oath of supremacy; and in defiance of the statutes against harbouring priests and friars, gave an asylum to all such as were persecuted under the atrocious penal laws of the Pale.

It was evident to the councillors of Elizabeth that until this chief could be reduced, reformation and English law would make small way in Munster; and, therefore, in the year 1567, while Desmond and his brother John were at the court of England upon a peaceful visit, they were both seized by order of the queen, and committed prisoners to the Tower.

Now it was hoped that some progress could be made. Sidney procured the appointment, successively, of Sir John Perrot and Sir Wm. Drury to the office of "Lord President" of Munster, a functionary whose duty seems to have been to excite feuds amongst the native princes, and so strengthen the influence, and, as far as possible, establish the rule and religion of England upon their ruin. And wherever local dissension or treachery afforded any opportunity of exercising authority, they proceeded to hold a kind of courts, and make the unfortunate Irish amenable to the laws enacted in the Pale Parliament. Sir John Davies explains the functions of these lords president in the case of Fitton then holding that office in Connaught, who governed, he says, " in a course of discretion," partly martial and partly civil; in short, as best he might.

Perrot and Drury, but especially the latter, carried this course of discretion to a terrible length in Munster. The Act of Uniformity and that against harbouring Catholic priests, were strictly enforced wherever these justiciaries could establish their power; and, unhappily, the south was so torn by the wars of native chiefs, that the English officers, though not supported by large military force, were enabled to usurp much authority. Thus, in an expedition made by Drury, in 1578, he bound forty citizens of Kilkenny, in a kind of recognizance, to come to church every Sunday and hear service in English; (for a reformed bishop had at length established himself in St. Canice's;) and during the same circuit " he executed twenty-two criminals at Limerick, and thirty-six at Kilkenny, one of which was a blackamoor, and two others were witches; who were condemned," says Cox, " by the law of nature."* What were the offences of the other culprits, or by what law they were condemned, we are not apprized; but they had probably *three times* asserted the spiritual supremacy of the pope.

In the same year we find a notable instance of the abhorrence in which the reformers held all " superstition," and how they proceeded in abating

---

* Witchcraft and conjurations of evil spirits had so much increased about this time that the queen's government, amongst other acts for reforming Ireland, was obliged shortly after to procure a special law against those crimes, (the 28th Eliz. c. 2.

it. Matthew Sheyn, queen's bishop of Cork and Cloyne, publicly burned at the high cross of Cork the image of St. Dominick belonging to the Dominican friary of that city.*

And now we might sup full of horrors, with the ecclesiastical historians of the period, in detailing the cruel persecutions and painful deaths of the national clergy, wherever the unsparing arm of that ferocious English Reformation could reach them;—how Patrick O'Hely, bishop of Mayo, and Cornelius O'Rourke, a pious priest, were, by order of Drury, placed on the rack, their hands and feet broken with hammers, needles thrust under their nails; how they were at last hanged:—how Dermod O'Hurley, archbishop of Cashel, was arrested by order of Adam Loftus (then Chancellor of the Pale, and Queen's Archbishop of Dublin, Armagh having proved too hot for him, as we saw); how he was loaded with irons until the Holy Thursday of the following year, dragged before the chancellor and treasurer, questioned, tortured, and finally hanged outside the city walls before break of day:—how John Stephens, a priest, having been duly convicted "for that he said mass to Teague Mac Hugh," was hanged and quartered. All this and much more may be found in the martyrologists of the time.† But what is material for us to re-

* Ware. *Bishops of Cork and Cloyne.*
† O'Sullivan. *Hist. Cath.*—O'Daly. *Ralatio persecut. Hibern.—Arthur-a-monasterio,* (quoted in Brenan's Eccl. Hist. of Ireland.) Theatre of Catholic and Protestant Religion, &c.

mark is, the fact that such methods of conversion were then the only known methods ;—that this island had now become one of the battle-grounds on which Europe in those centuries fought out the cruel quarrel of her rival faiths ;—that Philip of Spain was at this very moment striving to crush liberty and Protestantism in the Low Countries, almost as fiercely as another foreign tyrant was warring against liberty and Catholicism in Ireland ;—that, a few years before, in the streets of Paris, was done that deed of horror which makes St. Bartholomew's a day that mankind, while the earth stands, will tremble to name ;—that hideous rumours of intended extermination, —Catholics to be massacred by Protestants, Protestants by Catholics,—affrighted the general ear of Christendom —and, further, that Pope Pius the Fifth had lately, by a solemn bull, deposed the Queen of England from her throne, and absolved her subjects, as far as a bull could, from their allegiance, which, indeed, he had precisely as good a right to do as she to deprive him of his spiritual supremacy.

This confounding of spiritual and temporal authority, upon both sides, led to all those terrible persecutions and "religious wars," as they were called, which devastated Europe for more than a century.

CHAPTER V.

THE GERALDINE WAR.

A. D. 1578 –1584.

AFTER some years' confinement in the tower,
Gerald, Earl of Desmond, and his brother were
sent as state prisoners to Dublin; from whence, in
1574, they had found an opportunity to escape
onhorseback during a hunting party, and by
desperate riding arrived in Munster, whither it
did not seem advisable to follow them. For about
four years after this Desmond seems to have lived
in peace with the English; yet still, as Ware al-
leges, was keeping up negotiations with the pope
and King of Spain, but without much result, until at last James Fitzmaurice, his kinsman, proceeded to Rome, and through the celebrated
ecclesiastics, Saunders and Allen, solicited and
obtained from his Holiness a bull commanding the
chiefs and clergy of Ireland to assist Fitzmaurice
in defence of holy church against the heretic
English, with promise of indulgences and spiritual privileges, such as the Crusaders had earned
by fighting for the blessed sepulchre.

Thus accredited, Fitzmaurice proceeded to
Spain and entreated King Philip, the mortal

enemy of England, to supply men and arms for
the war.   In Spain also he expected to be joined
by Stukely, an English adventurer, who had
shortly before obtained six hundred Italians from
the pope for the invasion of Ireland, and had
proceeded as far as Cadiz on his way.   A strange
career had this Thomas Stukely, and his story is
characteristic of the time.   It was of course from
no patriotic motive that he sought to levy war in
Ireland, where his antagonists were to be his own
countrymen ;—nor yet from religious zeal : for he
was, in truth, an *undertaker*, and was setting
forth under the pope's authority, as Essex had
come under Elizabeth's, to seek his fortune and
make a plantation in Ireland—poor Ireland ! that
hunting-field for all the hungry adventurers of
the earth.   Essex and Smith had bound themselves, as we saw, to establish the queen's religion
in their settlements : Stukely, as deriving under
the pope, was to uphold Catholicity.   Elizabeth
had entitled those adventurers Lords of Ards ;
and his Holiness duly created his missionary
(whether by letters patent or papal rescript does
not appear) Marquis of Leinster, Earl of Wex-
ford and Carlow, Viscount Murrough and Baron
of Ross.   When he and his six hundred arrived
at Cadiz, it happened that Dom Sabastian of
Portugal was collecting all his powers for a descent upon Africa, to reinstate King Mohammed
on the throne of Fez, and also to found for himself a Portuguese empire upon that continent.
Stukely was dazzled by the splendour of this
African *undertaking ;* and when Sebastian prof

ferred him a share in the enterprize he speedily
exchanged his Irish earldom for a principality on
the Mediterranean ;—perhaps was created Duke
of Barbary or Prince of Mauritania—and led
his freebooters to the Moorish war. A true adventurer this—a genuine knight-errant of *that*
age, not vowed to God or ladye-love, but to
Mammon and Moloch. This poor Stukely indeed
never came into the enjoyment of those vast estates and honours of his, whether in Africa or
in Ireland. Neither was the Mauro-Lusitanian
empire ever founded, nor King Mohammed rein-
throned ; for, on the bloody field of Alcaçar-
quivir, swift destruction overtook them all. There
fell three crowned kings, ending quarrel and life
together, and with them died this most singular
Marquis of Leinster and Baron of Ross.

So when Fitzmaurice reached Spain he found
that Stukely had turned his face southward, and
abandoned the cause of Ireland : but for him
those Moorish kingdoms had no attraction. Not
the vales of Atlas, nor the Atlantic island itself
could draw him aside. Northward lay the shores
of Munster, where, perhaps, even now the adherents of the Geraldine were hard pressed by
those accursed English, and from the capes of
Desmond were gazing wistfully over the sea,
pining for the Spanish ships. At last three small
vessels cast anchor in Smerwick bay, carrying
Fitzmaurice and a poor band of eighty Spaniards,
accompanied by Allen and Saunders, and bearing
a consecrated papal banner, in the sure hope that,
if not for love of liberty and old Ireland, yet for
the sake of religion and to save their souls alive,

the Irish tribes would forget their feuds, and
unite against the common foe.

And now it is heart-breaking to read how
poor Fitzmaurice and his Spaniards were received. Desmond's two brothers indeed joined
him at once; but the earl himself, with some
views of crafty policy which one finds difficulty
in understanding, long held aloof, and even at
first pretended to obey the summons of Drury
the English president, and raised his troops to
resist the invaders. Time was wasted, and the
Spaniards were sickened by their cold reception.
In vain the gallant Fitzmaurice traversed Limerick, sent messengers to Connaught and the Scots,
and made a pilgrimage to Holy-Cross in Tippe-
rary, not to perform his vows alone, but to meet
the emissaries of the Leinster chieftains. Before
a blow was struck against the English, Fitzmaurice fell in a quarrel with one of the Burkes of
Castleconnell, and John of Desmond took the
command in his place.

Some obscurity rests upon the events of that
desultory war which followed the first Spanish
landing—English historians asserting that John
of Desmond was signally defeated by Malby at
Monaster-neva, and that Dr. Allen was amongst
the slain*—O'Sullivan and O'Daly† that the Geraldines were victorious, not only there, bu'
shortly after at Atharlam and Gort-na-pissi. On
the whole, there appears to have been nothing
very decisive done upon either side until the fol

* Camden. *Queen Eliz.*
† O'Daly is cited by the Abbè Mac Geoghegar.

lowing year, when the Earl of Desmond seeing his lands laid waste, and himself proclaimed a traitor by the English, at last raised his standard and openly joined in the war. The earl wrote to Pelham, the Lord Deputy, announcing that he was in arms for the Catholic religion ; sent messengers to Fiach Mac Hugh, chief of the O'Byrnes of Wicklow, and Eustace, Lord Baltinglass, that they might lay waste the neighbourhood of Dublin, and keep the forces of the Pale employed ; while Desmond himself marched suddenly against Youghal, which he took by escalade, plundered, and garrisoned.

In the meantime the Earl of Ormond and the English generals, Malby and Pelham, were wasting and plundering the county of Limerick : and indeed on their part the war was entirely carried on by destroying the cattle and growing crops of the country, and reducing Desmond's castles of Carrig-a-foyle, Askeaton, Ballyloghan, and Castlemaine. There was no pitched-battle, " so that in all that warre there perished not many by the sword, but all by the extremity of famine."* The cruellest warfare ever waged by man ; until the whole territories of Desmond lay a smoking desert where neither man nor beast could live. The Catholic clergy who had been the principal cause of the war were pursued with unusual fury ; and eight hundred Spaniards who landed at Smerwick in September 1680 were instantly besieged there by Ormond, and shortly after invested closely both by sea and land, until

* Spenser's *View*

they surrendered at discretion;* and were all in cold blood massacred by order of Lord Grey.

The most powerful opponent of Desmond was his hereditary enemy the Earl of Ormond, who was assisted also by the Lord Roche and other Anglo-Irish lords, and, rather unaccountably, by Hugh O'Neill of Dungannon, who commanded a body of cavalry for the queen. One would prefer to find this Hugh on the other side; but it seems that the nationality of an O'Neill did not yet extend beyond Ulster, at which we can wonder the less when we read that in the southern war the greater portion of the Irish race was on the side of Elizabeth and at feud with the Geraldines. Hugh was content to keep the English at a distance from his own territories, and had not probably at that period conceived the grand design of uniting all Ireland against the stranger. Of his achievements in the South we have no particular record, save that he behaved himself right valiantly, as we can well suppose; and further that he gained the good-will of his ally the Earl of Ormond, for it was one of the gifts of Hugh O'Neill that he irresistibly attracted to himself the hearts of all men, and all women also, whose love he desired to win.

Two other very notable men appear in the ranks of the English, in that Munster war. One is Walter Raleigh, afterwards Sir Walter; then one of the most active of Irish undertakers; destined to be a planter in Virginia, to be an under-

* The Irish historians say they capitulated on sworn articles; but Spenser elaborately controverts this.

taker in El Dorado; to wander wide over earth
and sea, fighting the Spaniard, chasing plate
fleets, navigating the Orinoco:—and alas! destined also to *dree* his weary thirteen years in the
dungeons of London, and write a " History of
the World" there, and at last to lay his gray head
upon the block, and so end the career of the
wildest and most brilliant adventurer of that adventurous age

And the other is Edmund Spenser, a man well
known to Gloriana and all the realm of Faerie.
He came over in the train of Lord Grey of Wil-
ton,* saw the horrible ending of the Geraldine
war, and had his share of the spoils. Kilcolman
castle and its fair domains fell to the poet undertaker; and there, "under the foot of Mole, that
mountainhoar," dwelling contentedly in another
man's house—sitting in quietness under another
man's vine and fig-tree, within view of the smoking ruins of tower and town and the unburied
skeletons of a famished nation, he began inditing
that solemn and tender strain, the intent of which
he has informed us is "to fashion a gentleman
or noble person in vertuous and gentle discipline,"—nay, he drew inspiration from the hideous Golgotha that lay around him; and when his
Merlin tells of the ravage to be made by king
Gormonde,† he has only to describe what the
poet saw with his mere bodily eye in the vales of
Munster:

" He in his furie all shall over-ronne,
And holy church with faithless hands deface.

* 1580.　　　† " Faerie Queene," B. 3, c. 3.

E

That thy sad people, utterly fordonne,
Shall to the utmost mountains fly apace;
Was never so great waste in any place,
Nor so fowle outrage doen by living men;
For all thy citties they shall sack and rase,
And the greene grasse that groweth they shall bren
That even the wilde beast shall dy in starved den "*

From Kilcolman also the poet took that most as-
tonishing " View of the State of Ireland," of
which we shall see more hereafter;—a most
practical view,—the view not of a bard but of an
undertaker, whereby we find, that however his
imagination may have bled for enchanted damo-
sels or elfin knights, suffering sentimental woes,
the *heart* of him, in dealing with mere living
wights, was harder than the nether millstone.

At last all the Munster and Leinster Irish
were broken and reduced, except the redoubtable
Fiach Mac Hugh of Wicklow; and during all
this long and inglorious war the only day of
which one can speak with pleasure, is the *day of
Glendalough.* Immediately on Lord Grey's arrival in Dublin—it was the summer of 1580—he
led a large force of horse and foot into the mountains, fully resolved to grapple with the fierce
O'Byrne in his own strongholds, and crush that
gallant sept for ever. When the army arrived
at the entrance of the valley, the cavalry under
command of Grey himself scoured the open

* " The very wolves, the foxes, and other like ravening
beasts, many of them lay dead, being famished."—Holin-
shed. See also Spenser's own horrible picture of this
famine.

ground while the foot were ordered to advance into the glen. The O'Byrnes allowed them to proceed into the silent recesses of the mountain, wondering that they found no enemy,—and then suddenly shouting their battle-cry, rushed from all sides upon the *sagums dearg*, and hewed them to pieces till their arms were weary with slaying. Grey and his horsemen could give no assistance, and had to retreat much more rapidly than they had advanced, leaving in that fatal glen eight hundred slain, and amongst them Sir Peter Carew, Colonel Moore, and Captains Audley and Cosby. Never, since black Monday at Cullenswood, had the sword of the Cullane mountaineer drank so deep of the stranger's blood.

But this was of no service to the luckless Desmond. He was hard pressed by his mortal enemies the Butlers. His Spanish auxiliaries were cut off, and the coast blockaded by Admiral Winter with the English cruisers. Most of the Munster lords were either weary of the war or in the ranks of England. His country was a howling wilderness,—himself an aged and homeless fugitive, and at last in a wood near Tralee, he fell by the hand of a common soldier, and his head was sent to the Queen of England, who caused it to be impaled in the usual manner upon London bridge.

Thus fell the great Earl of Desmond; and thus the fairest province of this island, wasted and destroyed by the insane warfare of the Irish themselves, lay ready for the introduction of the foreigner's law, civilization and religion; or, as Doctor Leland has it, "for effectually regulating and modelling this country upon the principles of justice and liberal policy."[*] And accordingly a parliament was soon held for the purpose of vesting in the Queen of England all the lands which had been inhabited by the kinsmen and adherents of Desmond. Letters were written to every county in England offering estates in fee to all " younger brothers" who would undertake the plantation of Munster ; each undertaker to *plant* so many families ; but " none of the native Irish to be admitted."[†] No specific mode of disposing of these poor native Irish seems to have been pointed out in any official document; but how the thing was *done* we know—they were simply starved to death ; and the end was attained more speedily than poet Spenser tells us he could even have hoped. " The end will (I assure me) be very short, and much sooner than can be hoped for ; although there should none of them fall by the sword, nor be slaine by the souldiours, yet thus being kept from manurance, and their cattle from running abroad, by this hard restraint they would quickly consume themselves and devoure one another."[‡] And so " in a short space there were none almost left, and a most populous and plentifull countrey suddainly left voyde of man and beast." And starvation being in some instances too slow, crowds of men, women, and children were some, times driven into buildings which were then set on fire. The soldiers were specially careful to

* Leland's History, vol. 2, p. 291.
† MS. in Trin. Coll. cited by Leland.
‡ Spenser's *View*, p. 166.

destroy all Irish infants—" for if they were suffered to grow up, they would become popish re.
bels" Women were found hanging upon trees,
with their children strangled in the mother's
hair."*——

But we turn from those fields of blood, and
come back to the North.

° Lombard, Comment. de Hibern. ap. Curry.

CHAPTER VI.

BEGINNING OF THE ULSTER CONFEDERACY.

A. D. 1584—1590.

The Antrim Scots had grown numerous and powerful during the Geraldine war. New bands of Islesmen had arrived from the Hebrides; and Tirlough of Tyr-owen being old and weak, and Baron Hugh absent in the South, there seemed some danger that Ulster would fall under their power. This ill suited the views of Hugh O Neill, who had designs of his own in that regard; and accordingly in this year, 1584, we find there was a powerful expedition to the North. Sir John Perrot, Hugh O'Neill, and his friend, the Earl of Ormond, with all the forces of the Pale, marched to Newry, separated their forces there, and prepared to attack the Scots both in Claneboy and Tyr-owen. Some English ships were sent round to Lough Foyle to intercept the communication with the isles; while Perrot and Ormond marched northward by the right shore of Lough Neagh and the Bann, and O'Neill and Norris on the left, driving the Scots before them and plundering their Irish allies. The O'Cahans of Arachty, (or, as it is now called, the " county of Londonderry,") were in league with the Scots;

and from them Norris drove a prey of two hundred head of cattle.   Dunluce Castle was besieged by Perrot and taken ; and at last the Scots
were forced to fly to the woods of Glancom-
keane ;* and their leader, Sorley buidhe Mac
Donnell, surrendered and gave hostages to the
deputy.   The troops then marched to Newry,
where Sir Henry Bagnal resided ; and here the
deputy received "submissions" from several chiefs
of Down and Armagh.

Hitherto Hugh O'Neill seemed to have answered the expectations of the English court in
promoting their designs against the liberty of
Ireland.   Ulster seemed about to yield its independence without even a struggle : and so well
assured was Perrot of the submission of the
North, that he forthwith divided the whole coun
try west of the Bann into seven new counties,
Armagh, Monaghan, Tyr-owen, Coleraine, Donegal, Fermanagh, and Cavan, for each of which
the English historians assure us "he appointed
sheriffs, commissioners of the peace, coroners,
and other necessary officers ;" an arrangement
most satisfactory to the deputy and his employ-
ers, if, indeed, it existed anywhere else than in
state papers,—a matter which needs some in-
quiry.

The truth then is, that in all these proceedings
Hugh O'Neill, while he seemed to be an instru

* This was an extensive forest on the north-west cor
ner of Lough Neagh, in Arachty O'Cahan.   Moryson,
with his usual inaccuracy, says it was a fastness near
Lough Erne.   It is correctly laid down in the map ac-
companying the *Pacata Hibernia*

ment in the hands of Perrot for reducing the North under foreign subjection, was, in fact, making use of the deputy and the forces of Elizabeth to establish his own power there.   By the aid of Perrot he humbled the Scots of Antrim (who had begun to rival the house of O'Neill,) and, in return, permitted that officer to imagine that he was making "shire-ground" of Ulster, although for a long time after this no agent of the queen dared to enter the borders of those seven counties or challenge jurisdiction there. Those sheriffs and coroners, like the queen's northern bishops, were merely titular; and Sir John Davies expressly informs us that in Perrot's time "the law was never executed in these new counties by any sheriffs or justices of assize, but the people left to be ruled by their own barbarous lords and laws,"*—pronouncing those laws "barbarous," as for an attorney-general of the Pale it was altogether professional to do.

And so long as the queen and her deputies ex ercised no power in Ulster, O'Neill's policy was (not like that wild Shane) to acquiesce most courtier-like in the nominal supremacy arrogated by the English monarch ;—a crafty policy, which the present writer is called upon only to state, not to defend by logics and ethics ; yet it is well to recollect, who were the men with whom he had to do,—for what base uses they had treacherously destined him,—what a cruel game they were playing with him and with his country.

For two years, we have little record of O'Neill's

"Discovery of the True Cause," &c.. p. 191.

life; but he was silently strengthening himself
in the North, and gaining the hearts of the clansmen of Tyr-owen. While the accomplished nobleman was growing in favour with Elizabeth
and her court, the Irish chieftain was gradually
getting recognized as the main hope and leader
of the Kinel Eoghain. Nay, he took a manifest
pleasure in sustaining those two characters; and
one can hardly say whether he was most at home
in the halls of Greenwich or Dungannon. In
the year 1587 we find him in London, where he
was ever a welcome visitor, soliciting the queen
(Ah! that " profound dissembling heart,") that
he might be admitted to the honours and estates
of Earl of Tyr-owen, under the " letters patent"
granted to his grandfather, Con the Lame. To
gain the favour of Elizabeth, it was always needful " to feign love and desire towards her, to address her in the style of passion ;"* and O'Neill,
with a tongue that " dropt manna," well knew
the art of flattery. Much affectionate advice he
gave the queen as to the good government of Ireland, and specially solicited that the law against
assuming the name of *O'Neill*, a most pestilent
and rebellious name, might be strictly enforced ;
so the letters patent were issued, and the queen
solemnly invested him with both lands and title,
(of which the former were not hers to grant, and
the latter his soul abhorred,) reserving, however,
a small piece of ground on the Blackwater, for a
fortress which was to be built there ; and with
certain stipulations for the benefit of old Tirlough

* See Hume—note in chap. 41

Lynnogh, who still held the nominal chieftaincy of the country.

Hugh returned to Ireland with his letters patent, a belted earl : and here, as a favoured courtier of the queen, the deputy was obliged to treat him with deference and honour ; while his increasing influence in Ulster gradually stripped Tirlough, the legitimate prince, of his power and numerous following ; and it became manifest that the grandson of the Dundalk blacksmith would soon predominate in the North. Those six companies of troops also that he kept on foot (in the queen's name, but for his own behoof) began to be suspicious in the eyes of the state : for it is much feared that he changes the men so soon as they thoroughly learn the use of arms, replacing them by others, all of his own clansmen, whom he diligently drills and reviews for some unknown service.—And the *lead* he imports,— surely the roofing of that house of Dungannon will not need all these ship-loads of lead ;—lead enough to sheet Glenshane, or clothe the sides of Cairntocher. And, indeed, a rumour does reach the deputy in Dublin, that there goes on at Dungannon an incredible casting of *bullets.* No wonder that the eyes of the English governor began to turn anxiously to the north.

Now it happened that O'Donnell, on the far north-west, was just then in high rage against "the foreigners of Dublin" by reason of some intimation conveyed to him by Perrot, that the ancient patrimony of the Kinel Conell was now "shire ground," and ought to admit a *sheriff.* And the chieftain's youthful son, the gallant Red

Hugh, then a fiery stripling of fifteen, was already known throughout the five provinces of Ireland, not only "by the report of his beauty, his agility, and noble deeds," but as a sworn foe to the Saxons of the Pale. Moreover, "the English knew," says the chronicler of Hugh Roe, "that it was Judith, the daughter of O'Donnell, and sister of the before-mentioned Hugh, that was the spouse and best-beloved of the Earl O'Neill."* And if this princely Red Hugh should live to take the leading of his sept,—and if the two potent chieftains of the North should forget their ancient feud and unite for the cause of Ireland;—then, indeed, not only this settlement of the Ulster "counties" must be adjourned, one knows not how long; but the Pale itself or the very Castle of Dublin might hardly protect her majesty's officers. These were contingencies which any prudent agent of the Queen of England must speedily take order to prevent; and we are now to see Perrot's device for that end.

Near Rathmullan, on the western shore of Lough Swilly, looking towards the mountains of Inishowen, stood a monastery of Carmelites, and a church dedicated to the Blessed Virgin, the most famous place of devotion in Tyrconnell, whither all the Clan-Conell, both chiefs and people, made resort at certain seasons to pay their devotions. Here the young Red Hugh, with Mac Swyne *of the battle-axes*, O'Gallagher of Bally-shannon, and some other chiefs, were, in the sum-

* MS. Life of Red Hugh O'Donnell in Litrauy of R. I. A., translated from the Irish by O'Reilly. p. 3.

mer of 1587, sojourning a short time, in part to pay their vows of religion ; but not without stag-hounds and implements of chase, having views upon the red-deer of Fanad and Inishowen. One day, while the prince was here, a swift-sailing merchant ship doubled the promontory of Dunaff, stood up the lough, and cast anchor opposite Rathmullan ; a " bark, black-hatched, deceptive," bearing the flag of England, and offering for sale, as a peaceful trader, her cargo of Spanish wine. And surely no more courteous merchant than the master of that ship had visited the North for many a year. He invited the people most hospitably on board, solicited them, whether purchasers or not, to partake of his good cheer, entertained them with music and wine, and so gained very speedily the good will of all Fanad.

Red Hugh and his companions soon heard of the obliging merchant and his rare wines. They visited the ship where they were received with all respect, and indeed with unfeigned joy ; des-cended into the cabin, and with connoisseur dis-crimination tried and tasted, and finally drank too deeply : and at last when they would come on deck and return to the shore they found them-selves secured under hatches ; their weapons had been removed ; night had fallen ; they were *prisoners* to those traitor Saxons. Morning dawned, and they looked anxiously towards the shore ; but, ah . where is Rathmullan and the Carmelite church? And what wild coast is this? Past Malin and the cliffs of Inishowen; past Ben-

more, and southwards by the shores of Antrim
and the mountains of Mourne flew that ill-
omened bark, and never dropped anchor till she
lay under the towers of Dublin. The treacherous Perrot joyfully received his prize, and "ex-
ulted," says an historian, " in the easiness and
success with which he had procured hostages for
the peaceable submission of O'Donnell."* And
the prince of Tyrconnell was thrown into " a
strong stone castle," and kept in heavy irons
three years and three months, " meditating,"
says the chronicle, " on the feeble and impotent
condition of his friends and relations, of his
princes •and supreme chiefs, of his nobles and
clergy, his poets and professors."† Where we
leave him for the present, to mingle vows of
deepest vengeance with those of many other
noble youths, " both Gadelians and Fingallians,"
fellow captives with him in those accursed towers.

Meanwhile, in Ulster, Hugh O'Neill was busy in
the task he had now resolutely imposed on himself,
striving to heal the feuds of rival chiefs, and out of
those discordant elements to create and bind together an Irish nation—a noble design, for which
perhaps the time was still unripe; yet somewhat he
did accomplish in that direction. With O'Cahan,
whose territories he had wasted with fire and
sword three years before, he now reconciled himself, and sent his infant son to be fostered by that
chieftain, and to learn speed and strength among
the hills of Glen-given, by the banks of the crys-

---

* Leland.
† MS. Life of O'Donnell, p. 8.

tal Roe, to back a-horse, and to chase the deer
of Arachty. With the Mac Donnells of Antrim
he renewed his friendship, and lent them on some
of their expeditions a body of his well-trained
galloglasses; not without promise of like help
from them, if need should be. Other chieftains
he encouraged to resist the intrusion of sheriffs
or garrisons for the Queen of England. It was
even said that he harboured " seminaries" and
foreign priests, than which nothing was then accounted more suspicious to a Protestant state.
Yet O'Neill was apparently no strict Catholic ;
and, while in Dublin, scrupled not " to accompany the Lord Deputy to the church and home
again, and to stay and hear service, though the
very nobles of the Pale," as Captain Lee declares,
" as soon as they have brought him to the church
door, depart as if they were wild cats."*   Indeed honest Lee has no doubt that, " with good
conference," he would even be *reformed*, "for
he hath only one little cub of an English
priest, by whom he is seduced for want of his
friends' access to him, who might otherwise
uphold him."   On the whole a most complying
conciliatory, and courteous man, " a special good
member," as one might hope, " of that common-
wealth ;" but still, no sheriffs, no bishops,† no
judges. North of Slieve Gullion, the venerable

* Lee's *Memorial.*
† There was however at this period, and for some time
before, a clerical person with the English garrison in
Lecale, really chaplain to that garrison, (the only Pro-
testants in his diocess,) but purporting to be Bishop of
Down, and even of Connor.

Brehons still arbitrate undisturbed the causes of the people ; the ancient laws, civilization and religion stand untouched. Nay it is credibly rumoured to the Dublin deputy that this noble earl, forgetful apparently of his coronet, and golden chain, and of his high favour with so potent a princess, does about this time get recognized and solemnly inaugurated as chieftain of his sept, by the proscribed name of *The O'Neill;* and at the rath of Tulloghoge, on the Stone of Royalty, amidst the circling warriors, amidst the bards and Ollamhs of Tyr-eoghain, " receives an oath to preserve all the auncient former customs of the countrey inviolable, and to deliver up the succession peaceably to his Tanist ; and then hath a wand delivered unto him by one whose proper office that is ; after which, descending from the stone, he turneth himself round, thrice forward and thrice backward,"—even as the O'Neills had done for a thousand years: altogether in the most un-English manner, and with the strangest ceremonies, which no garter king-at-arms could endure.

The foreign policy also of the Northern chiefs received some strength at this period. In the year 1588, the mighty remnants of King Philip's vast armada, storm-tost and sorely buffeted by the wild sea of the Orkneys and Hebrides, came sweeping past the northern coast of Ireland ; and the Clan-Conal beheld with wonder those portentous floating fortresses, such as the Fomorian and Phœnician navigators of the northern seas had never sailed. But as the Spaniards made the headlands of Antrim, a storm came upon them from the north-west ; and with the iron coast of Inishowen and Horn-head upon their lee, with grievous toil and danger, the poor mariners had to struggle westward and double those terrible cliffs. Many were dashed to pieces and utterly lost, both ships and men ; but some were driven into the harbours, and received from the neighbouring chieftains relief and hospitality,* until they found means to return into their own country. The O'Donnell, indeed, father to our imprisoned Hugh Roe, who seems to have been a weak old man, and much under the influence of two Englishmen, named Hovenden, whom he permitted to reside in his country, was led to regard the unfortunate Spaniards as enemies and invaders (forgetful that the enemies of England must needs be his friends), and when a large ship was driven into Lough Foyle and staved to pieces on the Inishowen rocks, O'Donnell and the Hovendens attacked the shipwrecked crew at Elagh near Derry, killed some of them and sent the rest as prisoners to the Deputy. (Oh! that Red Hugh had but been there!) But the Mac Swynes and other chiefs of Tyr-connell were more humane, or better knew their natural allies. A ship under the command of Don Antonio de Leyva was driven upon the coast between Sligo and Ballyshannon, and O'Ruarc, Prince of Breffni, afforded them not only an asylum, but protection against Bingham, an English officer who held some places in Connaught, and who presumed to demand from O'Ruarc his shipwrecked guests as the queen's prisoners.†

* Moryson.   † O'Sullivan.

But, above all, the O'Neill, who foresaw advantages to be derived from a Spanish alliance, was most distinguished for the kindness shown to those fugitives. He received them with honour at Dungannon, treated them with high consideration, conversed with them on the policy of King Philip and the Catholic powers; and doubtless explained to them, for the information of their master, the situation of the North ;—how the old Irish hated the Queen of England and hoped in King Philip—how the Spanish landing at Smerwick had proved unavailing by reason of the powerful English faction in Munster; and how differently a band of auxiliary Spaniards would be received amongst the aboriginal septs of the North.

And now the new Deputy, Fitzwilliam, assisted the views of O'Neill by his treatment of a northern chief who was weak enough to trust an English governor. Hugh Mac Mahon, on the death of his brother the chieftain of that sept, found himself opposed by several other branches of the family who also aspired to the chieftaincy. These were Patrick, son of Art, Ebhir, or Ever chief of Farney, and Brien of Dartry. Singly he could not cope with his powerful rivals, and applied, in an evil hour, to Fitzwilliam, requesting his alliance, and the assistance of the Pale to establish him in his *inheritance*, as he called it : for the deceased Mac Mahon had been one of those who surrendered his country to the queen and took a " re-grant" of it, by English tenure, to him and *his heirs*, with remainder, in default of heirs male, to his brother Hugh,[*] which was the reason of the threatened war; for Monaghan like Tyr-owen and Thomond, could not abide regrants, estates tail, or "English tenures." Mac Mahon's application was right welcome to the English who desired nothing so much as an opportunity of interfering between the Irish chiefs, and so of strengthening foreign influence at the expense of all the contending parties.

Fitzwilliam in the first place demanded a present of six hundred cows ("for such and no other," says Moryson, "are the Irish bribes,") and then the Deputy marched northwards pretending to consider the whole matter referred to his decision, and, that he might adjudicate with dignity, took possession of Monaghan which he garrisoned for the queen; and then awarded to his ally Mac Mahon the nominal chieftaincy over a small part of his territory, and to his rivals the exclusive rule over certain other portions: thus dividing, according to an immemorial English maxim, the following of a potent chieftain amongst several hostile claimants, and so breaking, as he hoped, the power of their resistance to foreign encroachment. Then poor Mac Mahon having failed in some part of the stipulated payment, (as feeling, perhaps, that he had not received value,) was arrested by order of Fitzwilliam, who immediately proceeded once more to Monaghan with considerable forces to "settle" that country finally A charge was soon found against the prisoner. He had lately raised his tribute in the usual man-

[*] Moryson.

ner from his refractory tributary of Farney, by
.eading thither a military expedition and driving
away the spoil ; which if it were not a levying of
war against the queen, the Deputy could not tell
what it was. Yet, not to condemn without hear-
.ng, or refuse a subject the benefits of English
law—and perhaps with a view of shewing the
northerns what was that happy system of polity
which they contumeliously rejected—a *jury* was
to be empanelled to try Mac Mahon—the first
jury in Ulster—the composition and arrangement
of which deserve study as affording a model in
that kind.

Spenser has informed us of the difficulties
which attended trial by jury in Ireland at that
time ; for "most of the freeholders," says Irenæus, "are Irish, which when the cause shall fall
betwixt an Englishman and an Irish, or between
the queen and any freeholder of that country,
they make no more scruple to pass against an
Englishman and the queen, though it bee to
strayn their oathes, than to drinke milke un-
strayned,"* the inconvenience of which he thus
laments :—"I dare undertake that at this day
there are more *attainted lands* concealed from
her majestie than she hath now possession of in
all Ireland ; and it is no small inconvenience ;
for besides that she looseth so much lande as
should turne to her great profite, she besides looseth
so many good subjects which might be assured
unto her as those lands would yeelde inhabitants
and living unto." And when Eudoxus suggests

* Spenser's *View*, p. 33.

that all this "might be much helped in the judges
and cheefe magistrates which have the choosing
and nomination of those jurors, if they would
have dared to appoint either most Englishmen or
such Irishmen as were of *the soundest judgment
and disposition*," Irenæus immediately objects—
"Then would the Irish partie crie out of par-
tiality and complaine, he hath no justice—he is
not used as a subject."

Now, in arranging this jury to try Mac Mahon,
it is too clear that the Deputy was not so
well acquainted with the delicate theory of
juries as subsequent officers became; yet in his
own rude way he attained the end very well.
Twelve soldiers were empanelled on the shortest
notice, of whom four, being Englishmen, were
suffered to go and come at pleasure, and the other
eight, being of Irish birth, by close confinement
and the simple process of starvation, were compelled to find the prisoner guilty.* And so
within two days after Fitzwilliam's arrival in the
country this unfortunate chief was indicted, ar-
raigned, convicted, and executed at his own
door. The deputy forthwith divided his country
amongst some English officers, of whom the principal were Marshal Sir Henry Bagnal and one
Captain Hensflower. "And the Irish," says Moryson, "spared not to say that these men were

* Moryson. This writer does not give these facts on
his own authority, which might have been construed as
bringing the English tribunals into contempt, but in
such cases always prefixes the words "The Irish say."
He does not contradict the statements, which besides are
incontrovertible on the authority of other historians.

all the contrivers of his death, and that every one was paid something for his share."* Those English officers did not indeed at that time enter upon the enjoyment of their Monaghan estates: for Mac Mahon's rival Brien, Lord of Dartry, a more active and resolute character, was elected by his sept the Mac Mahon and chieftain of Monaghan ; and held his country against the stranger for a time.

Space would fail us to recount all the villanies which both English and Irish historians tell of this greedy Deputy Sir William Fitzwilliam; how he made strict search, through such parts of the North as he dared to enter, for Spanish treasure, left there, it was said, by the shipwrecked Armada ; and how, finding no gold, he took means to seize upon two chiefs, Mac Toole and O'Doherty, and imprisoned them in Dublin castle, till O'Doherty bribed him, with many herds of cows, to release him. On the whole, his transactions with the North had little tendency to make Ulster in love with English laws or governors ; " rather, indeed, a loathing of English government," says Moryson, " began to grow in the northern lords, and they shunned as much as they could to admit any sheriffs or any English among them." So when the Deputy informed the Mac Guire of Fermanagh that his country, being now " shire ground," must prepare to admit a sheriff, to execute the writs of the Queen of England, to empanel juries and do other sheriff-duty there. " Your sheriff," said Mac Guire, " shall be wel-

* Moryson.

come, *but let me know his erick*, (how much his life is worth,) that if my people should cut off his head, I may levy it upon the country."

O'Neill, from his house in Dungannon, calmly regarded all these things; but his heart swelled secretly with hope and joy : for he knew that the time was not far off, when the banners of Tyrowen should wave in the van of the banded septs of Ulster, and the haughty battle shout of *Lamh dearg* affright those traitor deputies in Dublin castle.

CHAPTER VII.

O'NEILL AT COURT—BAGNAL'S SISTER—ESCAPE
OF O'DONNELL—TRINITY COLLEGE.

1590—1594.

HUGH NA GAVELOCH, son to Shane O'Neill by
O'Donnell's wife, appears now for a moment upon
the stage. He bore a deadly hatred against Hugh
of Dungannon as an usurper of the name and honours of O'Neill; and this year we find him de-
nouncing his chieftain to the Deputy and council,
as a traitor, informing them that certain noble
Spaniards from the fleet of Medina Sidonia, had
been entertained at Dungannon, had received
presents from O'Neill, and also letters for the
King of Spain, soliciting assistance against the
Queen of England, and promising support; all
which he, Hugh of the Fetters, would prove,
either upon the body of the accused by way of
combat, or by evidence on oath, as to the Deputy
should seem meet. Fitzwilliam prohibited the
combat, but set a day for the production of the
evidence, and prepared with much dignity to
hold solemn inquest upon so important a crimi-

nal.[*] But before that day arrived, O'Neill
had the prosecutor arrested as a foul conspirator
against his lawful chieftain, had him tried in
a most summary manner and condemned to be
strangled, a sentence which was forthwith executed, though not without difficulty; for no man
in all Tyr-owen would be the executioner of one
who bore the honoured name of O'Neill; and
Hugh himself, it was said, had to end the difficulty, and his prisoner's life together, with his
own hand. It would seem that the Prince of
Ulster was not a man to be given in charge to
the juries of an English Deputy.

But to dissipate these clouds of suspicion and
even direct accusation which began to blacken
his name in the court of England, O'Neill proceeded to London, in his Saxon character of earl;
and having left Ireland without leave asked of
the Deputy, (which it seems was uncustomary for
Irish peers,) he was on his arrival placed under a
kind of nominal arrest, as matter of etiquette:
but soon we find him high in favour as usual,
mingling with the court "at the Honour of
Greenwich," says Camden, "as noblemen use
to do," deliberating weighty affairs of state with
the chancellor, Sir Christopher Hatton, and en-
tering warmly, even eagerly, into all Elizabeth's
views for the civilizing of Ireland. As for the
territory of Tyr-owen, he would have it formed
into "a shire or two—with *gaols* for holding of
sessions;"[†] and for the name of O'Neill, if that

---

[*] O'Sullivan. This author says, Fitzwilliam summoned O'Neill *to Stradbally.*
[†] Moryson.

displeased so fair a princess, he would never bear
it more.

> " My name, dear saint, is hateful to myself,
> Because it is an enemy to thee."

He protested that he had assumed that name,
only to prevent some other of the tribe from
usurping it—and would surely renounce it; "yet
beseeching that he might not be urged to promise that *upon oath.*"* Amongst other articles
gravely agreed upon by O'Neill, as the basis of a
final settlement, were, that he should not foster
with any neighbouring chiefs; should give no
aid to the Scots, and receive none from them,—
should not harbour monks or friars, nor have intelligence with foreigners—nor levy *black rent*—
nor suffer his people to wear *glibbes*, or other
Irish apparel—and finally that he would live at
peace with old Tirlough Lynnogh and other
neighbouring chiefs; yet all this "upon condition that Tirlough and the other chiefs of Ulster
should in like manner engage themselves to keep
peace with him; lest when he was quiet and
thought no harm, he should be exposed to the
injuries of those turbulent persons."† Surely
one of the fairest conditions, which he seems to
have been well aware could not be complied with.

His old ally, the Earl of Ormond, and the Lord
Chancellor Hatton having become sureties for
O'Neill's performance of all he had undertaken,
he returned to Ireland, and was to enter into for-
mal indentures with the deputy, binding himself

---

* Moryson.   † Camden.   Queen Eliz.

to all these articles, by the first of August **in the** same year ; but as he steadily required that **all** the other chiefs of Ulster should come in and take on them similar engagements, the indentures were never executed ; the first of August came and passed ;—and the settlement of Ulster was indefinitely deferred " by many subtile shifts, whereof," says Moryson, " he had plenty."

He returned to prosecute his grand project of northern confederation, and to perfect the organisation of the Kinel-Eoghain. But matters were still unripe for an effectual effort against English power ; one main limb of the enterprize was wanting while the present feeble chief of Tyrconnell ruled that potent sept, and young *Beal-Dearg** O'Donnell still pined in the dungeons of Fitzwilliam. For the present he could only bide his time ; and for another year there is nothing to record, save an incident of a rather domestic and tender nature.

The marshal, Sir Henry Bagnal, and his English garrison in the castle and abbey of Newry, were a secret thorn in the side of O'Neill. They lay upon one of the main passes to the North, frowning over Iveagh and the O'Hanlon's country ; and he had deeply vowed that one day the ancient monastery, *De viridi ligno*, should be swept clear of this foreign soldiery. But in that castle of Newry the Saxon Marshal had a fair sister, a woman of rarest oeauty, whom O'Neill thought it sin to leave for a spouse to some churl

---

* Red mouth.

of an English undertaker.*—Besides, 'twas pity
so sweet a soul should sit in darkness of Protestant heresy;—rather than so, he would undertake
her conversion himself, and make her the bride
of an Irish chieftain. And, indeed, we next hear
of him as a love-suitor (with that persuasive
tongue of his) at the feet of the English beauty.
How or where he met, and wooed and won this
maiden, or by what legal or ecclesiastical process
he divorced his lawful wife to make way for her,
we have, unhappily, no record : but that he sped
in his wooing, and also in his divorce suit, is
plain ; for the lady fled from her brother's castle,
and was borne in triumph to Dungannon, where
she speedily became reconciled to the church, and
was duly wedded to the Prince of Ulster. Sir
Henry conceived his house dishonoured by this
alliance, because O'Neill, as he said, had another
wife alive,—putting little faith, as it seemed, in
the divorce. He had been sufficiently unfriendly
to the chief before ; but from that hour there
grew up the deadliest enmity between them ;
which afterwards bore fruit, as we shall see.

But the time had arrived when Red Hugh
O'Donnell was to see his native mountains once
more. A year before this, he had escaped from

---

* O'Sullivan is the only writer who tells of this lady's
beauty. "Tironus Bagnalis sororem fœminam formâ
conspicuam, speciei pulchritudine captus, rapuerat, ma-
trimonio sibi conjunxerat, et a Protestante converti ad
fidem Catholicam fecerat."—4to. 132. There is a novel
founded on this story, and entitled "The Adventurers,"
lively with incident, but wanting the colouring and character of the period

Dublin Castle with a noble Lagenian youth of
the O'Cavanaghs. They fled southwards, and
made for that "long extensive mountain, the
boundary between the Gathelians of the Lagenian province and the English of Dublin,"* traversed the hills all night, and before morning had
passed the " red mountain," hotly pursued. They
took refuge with Felim O'Toole, who was unable to protect them, and gave them up to the
English. For that time they had to return to
their dungeon, where O'Donnell was loaded with
" heavy iron fetters," and languished there for
another whole year, "until the feast of Chris-
mas, 1592, when it seemed," says the chronicle,
" to the Son of the Virgin time for him to escape."
Again he found an opportunity to fly, accompanied by Henry and Art, two sons of Shane
O'Neill, and made once more for the glens of
Wicklow. The mountains were covered with
snow and all that night the storm beat fiercely
upon them. They did not however again trust
themselves with the O'Tooles, but struggled still
southwards to reach the pass of Glenmalur,
(Gleann Maolughra,) where the gallant Fiach
Mac Hugh, victor of Glendalough, would be
sure to protect them against all the forces of the
Pale. Three days and nights they wandered
through the mountains, feeding upon leaves and
grass,† and famishing in the savage winter weather : and at last O'Byrne's people found two of
them (for poor Art had perished) stretched under

* MS. Translation of Life of O'Donnell, p. 10.
† O'Sullivan.

the shelter of a cliff, benumbed, and nearly life-less. The O'Byrne brought them to his house, and revived, and warmed, and clothed them, and instantly sent a messenger to Hugh O'Neill (with whom he was then in close alliance) with the joyful tidings of O'Donnell's escape. O'Neill heard it with delight, and sent a faithful retainer, Tirlough Buidhe O'Hagan, who was well acquainted with the country, to guide the young chief into Ulster. After a few days of rest and refreshment, O'Donnell and his guide set forth, and the Irish chronicler minutely details that perilous journey;—how they crossed the Liffey far to the westward of Fitzwilliam's hated towers, and rode cautiously through Fingal and Meath, avoiding the garrisons of the Pale, until they arrived at the Boyne, a short distance west of Inver Colpa, (Drogheda,) " where the Danes had built a noble city,"—how they sent round their horses through the town, and themselves passed over in a fisherman's boat; how they passed by Mellifont, a great monastery " which belonged to a noted young Englishman attached to Hugh O'Neill," and, therefore, met no interruption there,--rode right through Dundalk, and entered the friendly Irish country where they had nothing more to fear. One night they rested at Feadh Mor (the Fews,) where O'Neill's brother had a house, and the next day crossed the Blackwater at Moy, and so to Dungannon, where O'Neill received them right joyfully. And here " the two Hughs" entered into a strict and cordial friendship, and told each other of their wrongs and of their hopes. O'Neill listened, with such feelings as one can imagine, to the story of the youth's base kidnapping and cruel imprisonment in darkness and chains; and the impetuous *Beal Dearg* heard, with scornful rage, of the English deputy's atrocity towards Mac Mahon, and attempts to bring his accursed sheriffs and juries amongst the ancient Irish of Ulster. And they deeply swore to bury for ever the unhappy feuds of their families, and to stand by each other, with all the powers of the North against their treacherous and relentless foes. The chiefs parted, and O'Donnell, with an escort of the Tyrowen cavalry, passed into Mac Gwire's country. The chief of Fermanagh received him with honour, eagerly joined in the confederacy, and gave him " a black polished boat," in which the prince and his attendants rowed through Lough Erne, and glided down that " pleasant salmon-breeding river"* which leads to Ballyshannon and the ancient seats of the Clan-Conal.

We may conceive with what stormy joy the tribes of Tyrconnell welcomed their prince; with what mingled pity and wrath, thanksgivings and curses, they heard of his chains, and wanderings, and sufferings, and beheld the feet that used to bound so lightly on the hills, swollen and crippled by that cruel frost, by the crueller fetters of the Saxon. But little time was now for festal rejoicing, or the unprofitable luxury of cursing; for just then Sir Richard Bingham, the English leader in Connaught, relying on the irresolute nature of old O'Donnell, and not aware of Red Hugh's re-

* MS. Life of O'Donnell

turn, had sent two hundred men by sea to Donegal, where they took by surprise the Franciscan
monastery, drove away the monks, (making small
account of their historic studies and learned *annals*) and garrisoned the buildings for the queen.
Issuing out from thence, the soldiers made raids
into the country round about, spoiling the people,
driving away their sheep and oxen, and burning
their houses on the march. The fiery Hugh
could ill endure to hear of these outrages, or
brook an English garrison upon the soil of Tyr-
connell. He collected the people in hot haste,
led them instantly to Donegal; and commanded
the English by a certain day and hour, to betake
themselves with all speed back to Connaught and
leave behind them the rich spoils they had taken;
all which they thought it prudent, without further parley, to do. And so the monks of St.
Francis returned to their home and their books,
gave thanks to God, and prayed, as well they
might, for Hugh O'Donnell.*

In the following spring, on the third day of
May, there was a solemn meeting of the warriors,
clergy, and bards of Tyrconnell, at the rock of
Doune in Kilmacrenan, "the nursing-place of
Columkille." And here the father of Red Hugh
renounced the chieftaincy of the sept, and his impetuous son, at nineteen years of age, was duly
inaugurated by the Erenach O'Firghil, and made
the O'Donnell, with the ancient ceremonies of
his race. And surely it was time that the powers

* It was in Donegal Abbey the "Annals of the Four
Masters" were compiled.

† MS. Life of O'Donnell

of Tyrconnell should be wielded by a resolute hand.

Upon the eastern border of O'Donnell's country, 'where the two old rivers Finn and Mourne, which the Deluge left behind, mingle their waters,"* dwelt Tirlough Lynnogh O'Neill, in the town and castle of Strabane, holding such poor state as the Dungannon chief still permitted him. This foolish old Tirlough kept certain English troops in his country under the command of one Captain Willis; perilous auxiliaries for an Irish chief. And " it was a-heart break," says the chronicler, " to Hugh O'Donnell, that the English of Dublin should thus obtain a knowledge of the country." He fiercely attacked Strabane, drove back Tirlough and his Englishmen as far as Glengiven (Dungiven) and besieged them in O'Cahan's castle on the banks of Roa river. O'Cahan came forth to treat with O'Donnell, reminded him that he had been his foster-son, and that the fugitives were his guests, and so persuaded the young chief to refrain from violating the hospitality of a friendly roof. For that time O'Donnell retired; but he never rested, nor suffered Tirlough to rest, while those detested English were on his borders. The old chief was soon obliged to banish his outlandish allies, and accept the powerful friendship of O'Donnell in their place; and this is the last we hear of Tirlough. He died the next year.

Shortly after, we find this Captain Willis on

* MS Life of O'Donnell.

the scene again; Maguire, it seems, had made some kind of compact with Fitzwilliam that no English marauder, in name of a sheriff, should be sent into Fermanagh; and in consideration of this promise had given the corrupt Deputy a herd of three hundred cows. Yet in the year 1593, Willis having been driven out of Tyr-owen, is found in Maguire's country, purporting to be a sheriff there, and "having with him three hundred of the very rascals and scum of the kingdom;"* and all living, says Moryson, "upon the spoil of the country," until Fermanagh could endure the banditti no longer. Mac Guire and his people set upon Willis who had fortified himself, after the usual manner of the English, in a church, reduced him to extremity, and were on the point of destroying both sheriff and *posse comitatus,* when Hugh O'Neill interfered to save their lives, on condition of their instantly quitting the country.†

But Mac Guire did not lay down his arms. The English of Connaught were growing too strong to be endured as near neighbours; and the forces of Fermanagh being in the field, he led them southwards by the eastern shore of Lough Allen, and the base of the Iron mountain, through the south of Breffni O'Ruarc, through Corran, and over the bridge of Boyle abbey to the plains of Magh-ai. Bingham was then in camp upon a hill near Tulsk; and a body of his cavalry meeting with a party of Mac Guire's while patrolling at night, fled to the main body and were pursued

* Lee's *Memorial.*   † Moryson.

G

by the Irish with slaughter into their trenches.
William Clifford, who commanded the party,
was slain ;* and the primate Mac Gauran,† who
resided with Mac Guire, and had accompanied
him on the expedition, was among the slain on
the side of the Irish.

The Lord Deputy immediately dispatched a
"hosting" into Mac Guire's territory. A large
army of the Meath and Leinster forces under
command of Marshal Bagnall and Hugh O'Neill,
marched into Fermanagh from the east, and
Bingham's troops invaded it from Connaught.
Mac Guire boldly met them at the " ford of the
Lamb's corner," where the river issues from
Lough Erne and contested that passage stoutly ;
but O'Neill having crossed at the head of the
cavalry and charged the Irish in flank, Mac Guire
was obliged to retreat. In this charge the zealous O'Neill was wounded in the thigh ; and as
the Irish chronicler relates, " he thought this
well for him, because he was not suspected by
the English." The army proceeded through
Mac Guire's country wasting and plundering in
their march, and then departed, leaving a body
of troops with Conor Roe Mac Guire whom
the English set up as a rival to the lawful chieftain. This was the first *Queen's Mac Guire :*
and it was confidently hoped that civil war
would soon desolate the lands of Fermanagh and

* M.S. Life of O'Donnell. O'Sullivan calls the leader
who fell Guelford : and Camden tells us that the English gained a considerable victory here.

† " One Gauranus, a priest, whom the pope (forsooth)
had made primate of all Ireland."—Moryson.

leave it ready for English sheriffs in a year or two.

Young O'Donnell could ill endure this Saxon settlement on Lough Erne. To keep the English out of Ulster was the grand passion of his life: and his fiery spirit chafed at the strange policy of O'Neill, which we can well believe he did not understand. Yet hitherto he had acted by the advice of his cautious confederate, and refrained from joining Mac Guire ; but when Fitzwilliam, in the beginning of 1594, led another army to the North, took Enniskillen by surprise, and left an English garrison there, Hugh Roe could look on in silence no longer. He led the Clan-Conal into Fermanagh and laid close siege to Enniskillen, which he cut off from all communication with the country. The northern Irish were not skilled in the attack or defence of fortified places, and this siege seems to have been carried on entirely by way of blockade. All summer O'Donnell lay before it, and his troops scoured the country to the southward, burning and wasting the lands in possession of the English : until at last by the month of August the garrison had consumed all their provisions, and it was hoped must soon surrender from mere famine.

While Hugh Roe was here, a messenger came to him from the North, announcing that a force of Scottish auxiliaries whom he expected had arrived in the Foyle, under command of Donald Gorm Mac Donald, and Mac Leod of Ara. He hastened to Derry to meet them, found there an efficient and well-armed body of troops, and in

corporated them (as the Irish historian asserts*)
with the Irish forces: but this is improbable, as
in dress, arms, and manner of fighting the Scots
differed considerably from the Irish. Their principal weapon was the huge two-handled broad
sword, and they wore the tartan of their clans: while
the Irish infantry bore sharp battle-axes and short
swords, and were enveloped in long woollen cloaks
which in action they often wound round the left
arm.† But whatever may have been the organi-
zation of these Scots, or their place in battle,
they were a welcome aid to their brother Celts of
Ireland, and did good service in these wars
against the enemy.

While Red Hugh was absent from the camp,
the Clan-Conal and Mac Gwire, lying before Enniskillen, received news of a large army coming
upon them from Connaught, commanded by Sir
Edward Herbert and Sir Henry Duke, to raise
the siege and victual the garrison. Mac Gwire
prepared to meet them, and looked anxiously
northward for O'Donnell and the Scots. And
now the English had passed the mountains of
Leitrim, and he could see the smoke of their
devastating progress as they burned the country
in their march ; when most opportunely a body
of three hundred galloglasses and one hundred
cavalry, of the well-trained troops of Tyr-
owen, with Cormac O'Neill the chief's brother
at their head, arrived in the Irish camp. With

---

* MS. Life of O'Donnell.
  † Spenser. See also for dress of Irish and Scotch,
MS Life of O'Donnell, and Ware.

this reinforcement, and the troops of Fermanagh and Tyr-connell, Mac Gwire and Cormac
waited for the enemy at a ford near Enniskillen
and encountered them in a pitched battle. From
morning till night the English pressed on gallantly, and were as fiercely met, but at last their
whole army was utterly routed and pursued over
the river with such slaughter and havoc that the
baggage was left behind. All the stores of bread
intended to relieve Enniskillen were lost in the
river; and that battle-ground is called the *Ford
of Biscuits* unto this day.* Enniskillen was immediately surrendered to Mac Gwire. The English fled to Sligo through the mountains of
Breffni O'Ruarc, and Fermanagh was once more
cleared of foreign soldiery. O'Donnell was returning rapidly from Derry, when messengers
met him with the news of the victory : "and he
was sorry," says the chronicle, " that he had not
been in that battle as he would have prevented
the escape of so many of the English."

Deputy Fitzwilliam was about this time recalled to England. All historians† of both nations
concur in representing him as one of the most
flagitious, greedy, cruel, and corrupt governors
that an English monarch ever sent to Ireland.
To the nobles and people of the Pale he was as
odious as to the Irish enemy—for " he never
respected any man's necessity," says Lee, " in

* *Beal-atha-na riscoid.* See MS. Life of O Donnell,
and O'Sullivan. The latter calls the place *vadum-panum
biscoctorum.*

† See Camden, Moryson, Cox, Lee, O'Sullivan, Mac
Geoghegan

comparison of his own commodity;" and then, " he kept so miserable a Christmas," as Dublin had never seen before.* But his viceroyalty is famous for the founding of Dublin University. Perrot had some years before proposed to convert St. Patrick's cathedral into a college ; and the project was bitterly opposed by Archbishop Loftus, who had other uses for the revenues of his two cathedrals ; and " was particularly interested in the livings of this church," says Leland, " by leases and estates which he had procured for himself and his kinsmen"—being, in fact one of those rapacious bishops censured by Dr. Mant, who alienated the lands of the church, and reduced many bishoprics " as low as sacrilege could make them."† Nothing, therefore, was done for that time : but, after Loftus had procured the recal, disgrace, and death of Perrot (for he never could forgive that sacrilegious attempt in a layman) he determined to signalize his own zeal for education, and heartily co-operated with the queen in her renewed plan of a college. And instead of despoiling his churches for the purpose, he pointed out, as a convenient site, that " suppressed" monastery of All Hallows, then in the hands of the Dublin corporation. He convened a meeting, prevailed on the mayor and aldermen to give the ground and buildings for so meritorious an object; and to collect funds, circulars were addressed to the principal gentry of

* Lee's *Memorial.*
† Mant. " History of the Church of Ireland," p. 445

the Pale, entreating assistance by way of private contribution : but Dr. Mant gives the reply of one person to that application, and seems to infer from it that the proceeds thus obtained were very small :—" He had applied to all the gentlemen of the barony of Louth, whose answer was, that they were poor, and not able to give anything."

There were forfeited lands, however, in the south ; and some abbeys which had lately fallen into the hands of English rapacity ;—O'Dorney in Kerry, Cong in Mayo. Besides innumerable monasteries in Ulster, long since " suppressed," as we saw ; but where the monks still contumaciously did their alms-deeds ; and prayed for the souls of many an Irish chieftain who had endowed their houses to that end. Some of these a generous queen could bestow (in a certain anticipatory manner) upon her new Protestant college. The college, indeed, was long kept out of its northern property—" was frustrated," as Dr. Leland has it, " of the benefit of its *grants* by the wars in Ulster :" but being a true undertaking college, it took the " letters patent" in the meantime, and was content to wait, like other undertakers, and realize the queen's bounty by degrees, as the sword of her generals and the plots of her statesmen should extend English power in Ireland.

Thus was founded and endowed, by a Protestant princess, this great Protestant university, for strictly Protestant purposes—with Catholic funds, and upon the lands of a Catholic abbey.

CHAPTER VIII.

O'NEILL IN ARMS—CLONTIBRET.

A. D. 1594—1595.

It had become too plain that Hugh O'Neill was not likely to answer those politic ends for which Elizabeth's government had been so long protecting and cherishing, and, as they believed, educating him. His *ingratitude*, as English historians term it, had become too apparent. "Though lifted up," says Spenser, "by her majesty out of the dust to that he hath now wrought himself unto, now he playeth like the frozen snake." And nothing better, Spenser fears, would be the result if Shane O'Neill's sons could be taken out of the hands of this Hugh, and set up as rivals to his power—for "if they could overthrow him, who should afterwards *overthrow them ?*" Wherefore he infers "it is most dangerous to attempt any such plot."* However the queen's councillors, pondering these things with care, and believing that O'Neill was the main hope of the northern confederacy, advised the Deputy, as the best that could be done in the mean time, to offer O'Donnell "pardon," provided, says Moryson, "he would sever himself

* Spenser's *View* p. 180.

from O'Neill ;" a proposal which, it hardly needs
to be said, took no effect.   Imagine the haughty
Beal-Dearg receiving that offer of an English
pardon !

Private orders had been given to Sir William
Russell, the new Deputy, to make a prisoner of
O'Neill if ever he should have him in his power ;
of which the chief had immediate information
through a friend.   " It is credibly made known
unto him," says Lee, " that upon what security
soever he should come in, your majesty's pleasure
is to have him detained."   Yet, in contempt of
this base plot, O'Neill appeared in Dublin immediately on Russell's landing, where he found himself formally accused before the council, by his
mortal enemy, Bagnal, of various articles of treason—of confederating with the Northern chiefs,
of being The O'Neill, of harbouring priests, and
finally, of seducing the accuser's sister and carrying her off to Tyr-owen.   It was debated in
council whether the chieftain should be detained
a prisoner to answer these charges, notwithstanding a " protection" he had obtained : but the majority, either through scruples about violating
the protection, " or from some secret affection for Tyrone,"* declared that he ought in justice and honour to be dismissed.   Ormond, however, informed O'Neill privately that Russell
would obey his orders from England and arrest
him unless he speedily escaped from Dublin.
And no man better knew the treacherous devices
of English policy than this Earl of Ormond,

* Camden.   Queen Elizabeth.

whose indignant letter, in reply to the Lord
Treasurer Burleigh (when similar orders had
been sent to himself), is recorded by Carte :—
" My Lord, I will never use treachery to any
man, for it would both touch her highness's honour and my own credit too much ; and whoso-
ever gave the queen advice thus to write, is fitter
for such base service than I am. Saving my
duty to her majesty, I would I might have revenge by my sword of any man that thus per-
suadeth the queen to write to me." By advice
of his friend Ormond, O'Neill fled from Dublin,
made his way, with some risk, through the Pale,
for Russell had been drawing a *cordon* around
him, escaped to the North, and prepared to stand
on his defence.

It was about this time (594) that Captain Thomas Lee drew up the celebrated *memorial* addressed
to Queen Elizabeth, and intended to inform her
how her servants in Ireland executed the trust
committed to them. Lee had commanded some
troops himself in various posts on the frontiers of
Ulster during Fitzwilliam's administration ; and
he indignantly describes the many villanies and
cruelties of that officer and his creatures ; but the
most remarkable feature in the production is the
strong affection which the writer manifests for
O'Neill. O'Neill is his hero : in assertion of
O'Neill's loyalty and truth, honest Lee is ready
(perhaps rashly) to lay down his life. " If he
were so bad as they would fain enforce (as many
as know him and the strength of his country will
witness thus much with me,) he might very easily
cut off many of your majesty's forces which are

laid in garrisons, in small troops, in divers parts bordering upon his country; yea, and over-run all your English Pale to the utter ruin thereof; yea, and camp, as long as should please him under the walls of Dublin, for any strength your majesty yet hath in that kingdom to remove him.

" These things being considered, and how unwilling he is (upon my knowledge) to be otherwise towards your majesty than he ought, let him (if it so please your highness) be somewhat hearkened unto, and recovered if it may be, to come in unto your majesty to impart his own griefs, which no doubt he will do, *if he will like his security.* And then, I am persuaded, he will simply acknowledge to your majesty how far he hath offended you; and besides, notwithstanding his protection, he will, if it so stand with your majesty's pleasure, offer himself to the marshal (who hath been the chiefest instrument against him) to prove with his sword that he hath most wrongfully accused him. And because it is no conquest for him to overthrow a man ever held in the world to be of most cowardly behaviour, he will, in defence of his innocency, allow his adversary to come armed, against him naked, to encourage him the rather to accept of his challenge. I am bold to say thus much for the earl, because I know his valour, and am persuaded he will perform it."*

This cartel took no effect: but it was plain that O'Neill would soon have an opportunity of meeting his enemy, if not in listed field, yet in

* Lee's *Memorial.*

open *melee* of battle: for news arrived in the North, that large reinforcements were on their way to the Deputy from England, consisting of veteran troops who had fought in Bretagne and Flanders, under Sir John Norreys, the most experienced general in Elizabeth's service; and that garrisons were to be forced upon Ballyshannon and Belleek, commanding the passes into Tyrconnell, between Lough Erne and the sea. The strong fort of Portmore also, which O'Neill had permitted to be built on the southern bank of the Blackwater, was to be strengthened and well manned; thus forming, with Newry and Greencastle, a chain of forts across the island, and a basis for future operations against the Irish country to the North.

And now it was very clear that, let King Philip send his promised help, or not send it, open and vigorous resistance must be made to the further progress of foreign power, or Ulster would soon be an English province. The northern confederacy too, that great labour of O'Neill's life, was now strong and firmly united. Even Mac Gennis and O'Hanlon, two chiefs who had long been under the influence of Bagnal, were in the ranks of their countrymen, and O'Neill gave his daughter to the chieftain of Iveagh, his sister to him of Orier. In Leinster, the O'Byrnes, the O'Cavanaghs, and Walter Fitzgerald (surnamed *Riagh*) had entered into close alliance with O'Neill, and were already wasting the borders of the Pale: and O'Donnell and Mac Gwire were in arms, impatient for the chief of Tyr-owen to lift his banner and take his rightful post in the van of embattled Ulster.

At last the time had come; and Dungannon, with stern joy, beheld unfurled the royal standard of O'Neill, displaying, as it floated proudly on the breeze, that terrible *Red Right Hand* upon its snow white folds; waving defiance to the Saxon queen, dawning like a new Aurora upon the awakened children of Heremon.

With a strong body of horse and foot O'Neill suddenly appeared upon the Blackwater, stormed Portmore, and drove away its garrison, "as carefully," says an historian, "as he would have driven poison from his heart:" then demolished the fortress, burned down the bridge, and advanced into O'Reilly's country, everywhere driving the English and their adherents before him to the South, (but without wanton bloodshed, slaying no man save in battle; for cruelty is no where charged against O'Neill; and finally, with Mac Gwire and Mac Mahon, he laid close siege to Monaghan, which was still held for the Queen of England.

O'Donnell, on his side, crossed the Saimer at the head of his fierce clan, burst into Connaught, and shutting up Bingham's troops in their strong places at Sligo, Ballymote, Tulsk, and Boyle, traversed the country, with avenging fire and sword, putting to death every man *who could speak no Irish*;* ravaging their lands, and send-

* See Mac Geoghegan. Some writers say "all Protestants;" but as *all* the Protestants then in Connaught were foreigners, and *all* the foreigners were hostile in

ing the spoil to Tyr-connell. Then he crossed the Shannon, entered the Annally's, where O'Ferghal was living under English dominion, and devastated that country so furiously that " the whole firmament," says the chronicle, " was one black cloud of smoke."*

Not having sufficient force to meet the confederates in the field, Russell had recourse, for the present, to negotiation ; and while O'Neill lay before Monaghan he received intelligence that a certain Sir Henry Wallop, who was styled "treasurer at war," accompanied by Sir Richard Gardiner, the queen's chief justice, had arrived in Dundalk, as commissioners, to confer with the Irish chiefs. They summoned O'Neill, by his Saxon title of Earl of Tyr-owen, and the other leaders, according to their rank, to attend them at Dundalk, as English subjects, and state their "grievances" there. But O'Neill haughtily refused to see these commissioners, save at the head of his army, or to enter any walled town as a liege man of the Queen of England ; " For be it known unto thee, O Wallop, that the Prince of Ulster, on his own soil, does homage to no foreign monarch : and for your 'earls of Tyrone'—earl me no earls ;—my foot is on my native heath, and my name *The O'Neill.*† So they met in the

raders, it is invidious and unjust to designate the sufferers in these wars by their sectarian appellation.

* MS. Life of O'Donnell.

† " My foot is on my native heath. and my name is *Mac Gregor.*" The writer gladly acknowledges a plagiarism from the Red Gregarach : and further admits that the above may not have been the very words of O'Neill's message ; but it was to that effect.

cpen plain, in presence of both armies ; and O'Neill
demanded, as the first condition of a peace, that
no garrisons or sheriffs should for the future be
sent into any part of Ulster, save to Newry and
Carrickfergus ;—that no attempt at religious persecution, or, as the English called it, "reformation," should be made in the North ; and finally,
that Marshal Bagnal should be restrained from
encroaching upon the Irish territory, or the jurisdiction of its chiefs, and also be compelled to pay
him, O'Neill, one thousand pounds of silver, as a
marriage portion with the lady whom he had
raised to the digity of an O'Neill's bride. O'Donnell made the same demands, as to garrisons and
sheriffs, and freedom of religion ; and further
complained of his treacherous abduction and
severe imprisonment, and of a certain " Queen's
O'Donnell" who presumed to claim his chieftaincy by "English tenure." Their terms, in
short, were, that all pretence of English interference with the North should forthwith cease.[*]

The queen's commissioners pretended to consider some of these conditions reasonable : others
they "referred" to her majesty ; but when they
came to propose certain terms to the confederates,
as a kind of temporary arrangement, until the
queen's pleasure should be known,—as that they
should lay down their arms, beg forgiveness for
their "rebellion," discover their correspondence
with foreign states, and the like ; the chiefs rejected their proposals with scorn : in Moryson's
phraseology, " the rebels grew insolent ;" and the

* Moryson.

conference was hastily broken off, O'Neill having
agreed only to a short truce. The English deputy and his lawyers, seeing they could do no
better, on the 3rd of September in the same year
(1595) solemnly empanelled a *jury* to try O'Neill
and his allies, for what they termed " high treason." The chiefs of the North, in their absence,
were, with the utmost gravity, given in charge to
this tribunal, which speedily found them all
guilty : and O'Neill, O'Donnell, O'Ruarc, Mac
Gwire, and Mac Mahon were forthwith proclaimed " traitors."

O'Neill well knew that, notwithstanding the
overtures of peace, Norreys and Russell were
actively engaged in preparing for war. Bagnal,
about the beginning of June, had marched with
a strong force from Newry into Mac Mahon's
country, relieved Monaghan, and compelled the
Irish to raise the siege, and, shortly after, the
deputy and General Norreys made good their
march from Dundalk to Armagh after a severe
skirmish with some Irish troops at the Moyry
pass.*   On the approach of these forces, O'Neill
burned down Dungannon and the neighbouring
villages, and retired into the woods, hoping by
the show of terror and hasty retreat to draw the
enemy further into the difficult country, and destroy them at his leisure.   But Russell contented

* Near Mount-Norris, county Armagh. Norreys afterwards built a fort, to command this pass, and called it
by his own name. This district was at that time much
encumbered by woods and bogs, but it was the only prac-
ticable passage from Dundalk northward, except round
the coast at Carlingford

himself with stationing a garrison at Armagh, and returned to Dublin, leaving the Northern forces under the command of Norreys.

The castle of Monaghan, which had been taken by Con O'Neill, was now once more in the hands of the enemy, and once more was besieged by the Irish troops. Norreys, with his whole force, was in full march to relieve it; and O'Neill, who had hitherto avoided pitched battles, and contented himself with harassing the enemy by continual skirmishes, in their march through the woods and bogs, now resolved to meet this redoubted general fairly in the open field. He chose his ground at Clontibret,* about five miles from Monaghan, where a small stream runs northward through a valley enclosed by low hills. On the left bank of this stream the Irish, in battle array, awaited the approach of Norreys. We have no account of the numbers on each side, but when the English general came up he thought himself strong enough to force a passage. Twice the English infantry tried to make good their way over the river; and twice were beaten back, their gallant leader, each time, charging at their head, and being the last to retire.† The general and his brother, Sir Thomas, were both wounded in these conflicts; and the Irish counted the victory won, when a chosen body of English horse,

---

* *Cluain-tiburaid,* "the lawn of the spring."

† Regii bombardarii bis a Catholicis confutati sunt, reclamante Norrise, qui ultimus omnium pugnâ excedebat."—*O'Sullivan.* The Irish historians always do justice to the valour, good faith, and generosity of this general.

led on by Segrave, a Meathian officer, of gigantic
bone and height, spurred fiercely across the river,
and charged the cavalry of Tyr-owen, commanded
by their prince in person. Segrave singled out
O'Neill, and the two leaders laid lance in rest for
deadly combat, while the troops on each side
lowered their weapons and held their breath,
awaiting the shock in silence. The warriors
met, and the lance of each was splintered on the
other's corslet : but Segrave again dashed his
horse against the chief, flung his giant frame upon
his enemy, and endeavoured to unhorse him by
the mere weight of his gauntletted hand. O'Neill
grasped him in his arms, and the combatants
rolled together, in that fatal embrace, to the
ground :—

> " Now, gallant Saxon! hold thine own :—
> No maiden's arms are round thee thrown."

There was one moment's deadly wrestle, and a
death-groan : the shortened sword of O'Neill was
buried in the Englishman's groin beneath his
mail. Then from the Irish ranks arose such a
wild shout of triumph as those hills had never
echoed before :—the still thunder-cloud burst
into a tempest :—those equestrian statues became
as winged demons : and with their battle-cry of
Lamh-dearg-aboo, and their long lances poised,
in Eastern fashion, above their heads, down swept
the chivalry of Tyr-owen upon the astonished
ranks of the Saxon. The banner of St. George
wavered and went down before that furious
charge. The English turned their bridle-reins,
and fled headlong over the stream, leaving the

field covered with their dead, and, worse than all, leaving with the Irish that proud red-cross banner, the first of its disgraces in those Ulster wars.*   Norreys hastily retreated southwards, and the castle of Monaghan was yielded to the Irish.

Hugh Roe O'Donnell was by this time master of all Connaught, except a few forts : but George Bingham, who commanded for the queen in the castle of Sligo, knowing that the Mac Swynes were in O'Donnell's army, and that the coasts of Tyr-connell must be lying open to any sudden descent, and having heard of the riches of Rath-mullen priory, bethought himself of an expedition worthy of the pirate Danes from whom he derived his race. He fitted out two vessels, filled them with armed men, and leaving Sligo to be kept in his absence by Ulick Burke, sailed round the northern coast, entered Lough Swilly, plundered and destroyed the village of Rathmullan and the cloisters of the Carmelites, robbing the monks of their plate, their vestments, and sacred relics ;—then on his way back to Sligo he landed on Tory Island, " a place blessed," says a chronicler, " by the holy Columba," illustrious then with its seven churches and the glebe of the saint : and the English burned and ruined both houses and churches, plundered everything, according to their wont, carried off the flocks and

* "Circum Sedgreium octodecim equites splendidi regii succumbunt, et signum capitur."—*O'Sullivan.* For the mode of charging used by the Irish cavalry, with their lances poised over the right shoulder, see Spenser's *View.*

herds, and left no four-footed beast on the whole
island.   Tory never recovered from that hideous
wreck.   It is now a bare and dismal rock, lashed
by the howling Atlantic, and inhabited by a few
wretched fishermen ; but still. by the ruins of a
round tower, by its two stone crosses, and the
mouldering walls of its many churches, attests
the piety of the holy men who, in days of old,
made a sanctuary of that lonely isle.

The English pirate returned with his booty to
Sligo ; but the division of the spoil caused a jea-
lousy in the garrison between the English and
Irish ; which ended in Ulick Burke and his adherents falling upon and exterminating the Saxons and their leader, and then delivering up the
place to O'Donnell.   The castle of Ballymote
was about the same time taken by Red Hugh
from Sir Richard Bingham and given to its rightful owners, the Mac Donoughs ; so that, on the
whole, at the close of the year 1595, the Irish
power predominated both in Ulster and Connaught.

CHAPTER IX.

NEGOTIATIONS—TYRRELL'S PASS—DROM-FLUICH.

A. D. 1595—1597.

DURING the following winter the two parties remained inactive : and what we find chiefly interesting, is the warm attachment which General
Norreys conceived for O'Neill, the man whom he
had it in command to reduce by fire and sword.
He convinced himself that the chief had been
heavily wronged, recommended him to the favourable consideration of his government ; and would
answer it with his life that kindness and justice
would make this formidable chieftain one of the
queen's best subjects. The strange fascination
of O'Neill's character had captivated the soldier-
like and generous Norreys ; and instead of vigorously prosecuting the war, he was devising
means to bring about a reconciliation between
the revolted "earl" and his offended sovereign.
There is reason to fear that the politic Hugh misled
this straightforward soldier, to gain time for his
own projects and his negotiations with Spain ;—
a supposition which is strengthened by his dealings with the queen's envoys in the following
year.

For the English government, finding that no progress was made in reducing Ulster by force of arms, directed a commission to the general along with Sir George Bourchier, styled Master of the Ordnance, and Sir Geoffrey Fenton, commanding them to invite the Northern chiefs to a conference, and propose terms of peace. The commissioners wrote to O'Neill requesting a meeting at Dundalk; and though well aware that it was to his own successes he owed these friendly dispositions of the English court, which would last only until they had an army in the field able to cope with him; yet, having objects of his own to serve by delay, he proceeded to Dundalk, and declining, as usual, to enter a town, he held conference with the English negotiators across a small river, O'Neill standing on the north bank and the commissioners on the south. Here he assured them of his loyalty and his desire to be treated as a good subject of the queen, provided only that the laws, customs, and religion of the Irish country should remain inviolate; (a proviso which included precisely the old demands of exemption from sheriffs, bishops, judges, and " reformation ;") and upon those terms he protested that her majesty would have no more devoted subject than he.* As for holding com-

* Moryson would have us believe that both at this conference and several others O'Neill made the most abject protestations of repentance and submission, craving pardon on his knees for his "rebellion.' But no Irish historian says anything of this; and it is hardly probable that, after such brilliant victories he would so humble himself to those who were entreating for peace. The

munications with Spain, he denied it altogether; but he much feared that Hugh O'Donnell was a disaffected person, and engaged in some treasonable correspondence; for he was credibly informed that a ship had arrived from Spain in one of the ports of Tyr-connell.*

The commissioners were delighted by his zeal and candour, communicated with their government, and were immediately vested with full power to conclude a final peace with O'Neill upon easy terms; and then it was hoped they should soon be able, by his help, to deal with that pestilent O'Donnell. So they wrote again to O'Neill, appointing another meeting at Dundalk, on the second of April, which he "accepted," says Moryson, "with shew of joy;" but when the second of April arrived, and the commissioners waited for him at the place of meeting, he did not condescend to appear. Apparently his end had been answered, and he was not yet ready to assume his new character of a loyal subject. Yet, unwilling to abandon their mission, the English diploma-

Abbé Mac Geoghegan says, with some reason, "Les Anglois conviennent qu' on desiroit fort la paix avec O'Neill: mais ils ajoutent que ce Prince et les autres chefs des Catholiques Irlandois avoient coutume de demander pardon à genoux aux commissaires chargès de leur proposer la paix: Ceux qui sollicitent la paix sont ordinairement plus dans le cas de demander pardon que les autres."

* In this year, as we learn from the MS. Life of O'Donnell, Alonzo Copis came to that chief from Spain, bringing arms and ammunition: and Red Hugh sent him home with his ship well stored with "fat bucks and white-fleeced sheep."

tists once more plied him with letters, and appointed yet another day, the 16th of April; when they conjured him by all his hopes of pardon, and his duty to her most sacred majesty, that he should not fail to attend them. The 16th came, and the commissioners looked anxiously northward from Faughart hill, in vain ; the chief did not arrive ; but the next day, as if to make a scornful jest of their mean solicitation,* sent them his reasons, " justifying," says Moryson, " his relapse into disloyalty ;" for that the truce had not been duly kept with him and his people ; causes of offence had arisen at the Blackwater ; and moreover the Marshal had not restored some cattle which had been driven off the lands of a certain O'Neill. And under these circumstances, how could a prudent chieftain lay down his arms, or abandon the guardianship of his faithful clansmen ?

Possibly these reasons may have seemed frivolous to the commissioners ; more especially as it was notorious that O'Neill was improving the intervals of truce in arming and training more troops, in strengthening his alliances, and stirring up the Irish of Leinster to invade the Pale ; for at this time we find that " Fiach Mac Hugh," says Moryson, " breaking his protection, entered into acts of hostilitie ; and he, together with the O'Mores, O'Connors, O'Byrnes, O'Tooles, the Cavanaghs, Butlers, and the chiefe names of Connaught, animated by the success of the Ulster

* " A mean solicitation on the part of government to Tyrone."—*Leland.*

men, combined together, and demanded to have
the barbarous titles of O and Mac, *together with
lands they claimed,* to be restored to them, in
the meanwhile spoiling all the country on all
sides." These Leinster Irish were led principally by Owen O'More and Fiach O'Byrne.
Their inroads were fierce and bloody; the smoke
of their burnings darkened the air of Dublin;*
and there needed large forces to guard the frontiers of the Pale, and sleepless watch and ward
upon the city wall. But now the deputy resolved
to make another effort against the mountain septs
of Wicklow. In the month of May he penetrated with a strong force into the glens; took
the fort of Ballinacor by surprise, and put its inmates to the sword, including the gallant chief of
the O'Byrnes, who had so long held those fastnesses against the utmost efforts of English
power.   He left, however, two sons, Phelim and
Raymond, who received some troops from Hugh
O'Neill to assist them, joined with the O'Mores,
recovered the glens and mountains of their tribe,
and still kept the field against the stranger. At
this time, also, Hugh O'Donnell was pressing the
English hard in Connaught, detaching the chiefs
from foreign alliances, and combining them in the
national confederacy. Mac Dermot of Moy-luing
he compelled to make submission to himself as an
Uriaght or tributary chief; "as with those of his
place it was always customary."† And over Clan-

---

* "The village of Crumlin was plundered and
burned down, within two miles of the city."—*Cox.*

† MS. Life of O'Donnell. Moryson says "all Connaught was *in rebellion.*"

rickarde he reinstated the Mac William, who had
been supplanted by Theobald Burke, surnamed,
"of the Ships," supported by the English, and
claiming his chieftaincy by English tenure."

Armagh was still occupied by an English garrison : a strong force under command of Stafford
was stationed there ; and General Norreys, with
the main body of his troops, was encamped at
Killoter church.   On the expiration of the truce,
O'Neill attacked this encampment with desperate
fury ; and drove the English before him with
heavy loss till they found shelter within the walls
of Armagh.*   Norreys left here five hundred
men to reinforce Stafford, and himself retired to
Dundalk : leaving the whole country northward
in possession of the Irish.   O'Neill now resolved
to recover the city of Armagh.   He cut off all
communication between Norreys and the town,
sat down before it, and began a regular siege ;
but the troops of Ulster were unused to a war of
posts, and little skilled in reducing fortified
places by mine, blockade, or artillery. They better loved a rushing charge in the open field, or
the guerilla warfare of the woods and mountains ;
and soon tired of sitting idly before battlements
of stone. O'Neill tried a stratagem. General
Norreys had sent a quantity of provisions to relieve Armagh under a convoy of three companies
of foot and a body of cavalry ; and the Irish had
surprised these troops by night, captured the
stores, and made prisoners of all the convoy.
O'Neill caused the English soldiers to be stripped

* O'Sullivan.

of their uniform, and an equal number of his own men to be dressed in it, whom he ordered to appear by day-break, as if marching to relieve Armagh. Then having stationed an ambuscade before morning in the walls of a ruined monastery lying on the eastern side of the city, he sent another body of troops to meet the red-coated galloglasses; so that when day dawned, the defenders of Armagh beheld what they imagined to be a strong body of their countrymen in full march to relieve them with supplies of provisions: then they saw O'Neill's troops rush to attack these; and a furious conflict seemed to proceed; but apparently the English were overmatched: many of them fell, and the Irish were pressing forward, pouring in their shot, and brandishing their battle-axes, with all the tumult of a heady fight. The hungry garrison could not endure this sight. A strong sallying party issued from the city, and rushed to support their friends; but when they came to the field of battle all the combatants on both sides turned their weapons against them alone. The English saw the snare that had been laid for them, and made for the walls again; but now Con O'Neill and his party issued from the monastery and barred their retreat. They defended themselves gallantly, but were all cut to pieces, and the Irish entered Armagh in triumph. Stafford and the remnant of his garrison were allowed to retire to Dundalk, and O'Neill, who wanted no strong places, dismantled the fortifications and then abandoned the town. Soon after this, however, in O'Neill's absence, some English troops from Newry oc

Dundalk made their way to Armagh—fortified it again—and held it till after the battle of the Yellow Ford.

In May 1597, Russell was recalled from Ireland, and Lord De Burgh sent over as deputy. Norreys also was instantly dismissed from his northern command, and sent to govern the English forces in Munster; where he shortly after sickened and died, broken-hearted, it was said, at being superseded by De Burgh, who was his personal enemy; and also by the ill treatment to which he had been subjected by Russell; for this Deputy was jealous of the general's high reputation, and of the ample powers which had been vested in him; and never lost an opportunity of thwarting his plans and crippling his resources.*

The new Lord Deputy was a man of determination and experience in war, having commanded in the Netherlands against Spain, and done good service there.

The greater part of the island was now in the power of the Irish. In Ulster especially the English had not a foot of land save what was enclosed by the walls of seven castles, Newry, Carrickfergus, Dundrum, Carlingford, Greencastle, Armagh, and Olderfleet, (now called Larne,)† and De Burgh's instructions were to prosecute the northern war vigorously, to enter upon no conferences and listen to no terms. A truce, however, of one month was

* The Abbé Mac Geoghegan notes (as a judgment of heaven) that poor Norreys died, loaded with disgrace, in the very country which had given birth to St. Rumold, first bishop and patron of Malines, whose relics he had profaned in the Low Countries.

† Moryson.

agreed upon, and the time was used by the Deputy in collecting his forces and planning operations : neither was that interval altogether wasted
by O'Neill ; as we shall presently see.

At the close of the truce, attended by the
Earl of Kildare and Lord Trimbleston, the Deputy marched northwards by Newry and Armagh, while Sir Conyers Clifford, who now commanded for the queen in Connaught, was ordered
to penetrate into Ulster by the western shores of
Lough Erne. A thousand men of the Anglo-
Irish of Meath had assembled at Mullingar, and
were also destined for the North under command
of young Barnewall, a son of Lord Trimbleston :
and to prevent the junction of all these forces
was plainly the thing most desirable for O'Neill.
Now there was in the Irish army a gentleman of
English descent, by name Richard Tyrrell, of
Fertullagh, in the district of Meath, a zealous
Catholic, and one of O'Neill's most trusted friends
and bravest officers. He was instantly detached,
at the head of four hundred chosen men, to
watch the movements of the Meathians ; a service for which Tyrrell was well fitted by his ac-
tivity and knowledge of the country. Barnewall
and his troops marched from Mullingar ; and
when he heard of the small number of Tyrrell's
band, which was then posted in his neighbourhood, he resolved to attack it without delay and
sweep it from his path. Tyrrell retired before
him till he arrived at a defile winding between
thick woods, being precisely the spot which he
had marked out for the destruction of his enemy.
Here he placed a part of his band in ambush

under O'Connor, his lieutenant; and himself retreated still further to draw the English onward
into the pass. They rushed impetuously forward,
and the moment they had all passed the ambuscade, O'Connor sounded a charge and attacked
them fiercely in the rear, while Tyrrell on the
same instant wheeled round and engaged them
in front. The whole Meathian detachment was
hewn to pieces; and it is said that besides Barnewall, who was reserved as a prisoner for O'Neill,
only one man escaped through a neighbouring
bog, to carry the news to Mullingar.* O'Connor
so fiercely plied his sword that day, that his hand
swelled within the guard and had to be extricated
in the evening by means of a file. The place of
battle received the name of Tyrrell's-pass, and
still preserves the memory of that slaughter.

Tyrrell and O'Connor lost not a day in marching to join O'Neill: for by this time Lord De
Burgh was as far north as Armagh; and they
counted upon warm work at the Blackwater.

But before the two main bodies met, we have
to tell how it fared with Sir Conyers Clifford and
his Connaught levies. He set forth with seven
hundred men, and was to make his way northward by Ballyshannon and join the Deputy at
Portmore. But on that side the passes into Ulster were under the special care of Red Hugh
O'Donnell: and before Clifford had proceeded
far he found himself in front of a body of two
thousand of the Clan-Conal ("two thousand desperate rebels," as the English historians call

* Mac Geoghegan.

them), and perceiving that he was overmatched he thought it best to retire. For thirty miles he retreated through the mountains, in good order and with but little loss, and made good his way back to Connaught in the face of a superior enemy.* For that time he escaped the sword of Red Hugh: but, in a certain pass amongst those mountains of north Connaught, these two warriors were to meet once more, and there to do and suffer what their fate decreed. From pursuing Clifford, O'Donnell hastened back to join O'Neill where the brunt of battle was to be borne.

O'Neill knew that Lord De Burgh would direct his efforts to recover the fortress of Portmore, and therefore had entrenched a part of his army in a pass of the woods near the southern bank of the Blackwater, and right in the path of the English army, where, " to the natural strength of the place," says Moryson, " was added the art of interlacing the low boughs, and casting the bodies of trees across the way." De Burgh instantly attacked and forced this pass, drove the Irish northward across the river, took possession of Portmore fort, and garrisoned it. Their prayers and thanksgivings for this success were interrupted by calling to arms; and on the left bank of the river they saw the Irish issuing from their woods, and taking up a position between Portmore and Benburb,† as if bent to renew the battle. The Earl of Kildare was sent

* Moryson.
† *Beinn-Boirb*, the "Hill-brow."—Stuart's History of Armagh.

forward to attack them; and was shortly after
supported by De Burgh, with his whole army.
They pressed forward, and after some severe
skirmishes, had advanced a mile beyond Benburb, when they found themselves in front of the
chosen troops of Tyr-owen and Tyr-connell,
led by their chieftains in person, and supported
by the Antrim Scots under James Mac Donnell
of the Glynns; and it was now plain that O'Neill
had purposely decoyed them across the river that
he might engage them according to his wont, on
his own chosen battle-ground. The Lord Deputy,
however, attacked them gallantly, and was mortally wounded in the beginning of the conflict,
and carried off the field. Kildare took the command, but he also was struck down from his
horse, and his two foster-brothers, in rescuing
him from the press of battle were slain by his
side. The English were routed with terrible
slaughter: great numbers were drowned or cut
to pieces in their flight; and amongst the slain,
besides Lord De Burgh, were several officers of
distinction, Sir Francis Vaughan, brother-in-law
to the Lord Deputy, Thomas Waller and Robert
Turner. Kildare also died in a few days of his
wounds, or, as English historians will have it, of
grief for the death of his foster-brethren. That
battle-field is called Drumfluich; it lies about
two miles westward from Blackwater-town,
(Portmore); and Battleford-bridge marks the
spot where the English reddened the river in
their flight.*

* The authorities for this battle are O'Sullivan. Mac

The Queen's army retreated with all speed to Newry, and so to the Pale, leaving the garrison they had stationed in Portmore unsupported in the midst of a hostile country. Captain Williams, however, who commanded there, caused the defences to be speedily made up, and maintained himself bravely for a long time against all the efforts of O'Neill's troops.

Geoghegan, the MS. Life of O'Donnell, Moryson, and Camden. There is more than usual discrepancy in the several accounts, but all agree that Vaughan, Waller, and Turner, with many of the English troops, fell on the field; that De Burgh and Kildare died very soon after, having been wounded in the battle; and also that the English army retreated without attempting to penetrate further; though, as Moryson tells us, it was the express intention of De Burgh to march straight to Dungannon, a bold undertaking, he says, "which no other lord deputy had yet attempted." But the same Moryson, in describing the battle, coolly says, the English "prevailed against them." Leland tells us that De Burgh met with a "sudden death" on his way to Dungannon, and that Kildare died of "affliction,"—hardly a satisfactory account of the transaction. On the whole, the present writer prefers to rely upon the unanimous testimony of the Irish chroniclers.

CHAPTER X.

O'NEILL RECEIVES THE QUEEN'S GRACIOUS PAR-
DON—BATTLE OF BEAL-AN-ATHA-BUIDHE.

A. D. 1597—1598.

SHORTLY after Lord De Burgh's death, the civil
government of the Pale was committed to Loftus,
Archbishop of Dublin, and Chief Justice Gardiner. The Earl of Ormond, O'Neill's ancient
friend and ally, was made Commander-in-chief
of the queen's army, with the title of Lord Lieu
tenant. Ormond had instructions to conclude a
peace, if possible, with O'Neill; and a truce of
eight weeks was agreed upon between them in
the mean time. O'Neill and Ormond met at
Dundalk to arrange the terms of a peace, and
the chieftain stated the conditions on which he
and his allies would consent to lay down their
arms:—First, perfect freedom of religion, not
only in Ulster, but throughout the island; then,
reparation for spoil and ravage done upon the
Irish country by the garrisons of Newry and
other places; finally, entire and undisturbed
control by the Irish chiefs over their own territories and people.* These claims were to be transmitted to England; and during the truce O'Neill

Moryson, Mac Geoghegan.

was to hold no communication with Spain, to
suffer no outrage by his soldiers in violation of
the truce, to recall his troops from Leinster, to ——
give safe conduct to English officers in going to
and from the several castles, and to permit his
people to supply victuals to the fort of Portmoie.
And on the other hand, Ormond engaged that
the Northerns should be allowed free intercourse
with the Pale, and that none of O'Neill's troops
or confederates should be molested by the English without his consent.*   Moryson asserts that
O'Neill began this conference by making the
humblest professions of penitence, loyalty, and
submission to the queen; which cannot be true,
being not only unsupported by other authorities,
but altogether at variance with the chieftain's
haughty demands, and his contemptuous treat
ment of the queen of England and her officers
immediately after.   At the end of the eight
weeks' truce, authority arrived from the queen,
giving Ormond power to offer her "gracious pardon" to O'Neill, on his engaging to comply with
certain articles to the number of thirteen; of
which the principal were that he should break up
the Northern confederacy, disband his forces,
and send all foreigners out of his country; that
he should repair the Blackwater fort and bridge;
renounce the title of *O'Neill*, and all jurisdiction belonging to that chieftaincy; admit a sheriff
into Tyr-owen; pay a fine; deliver up all *traitors* (that is all who should presume to profess
the Catholic religion, or bear arms against the

* Moryson

English); that he should discover his negotiations with Spain; surrender into the hands of Ormond, Shane O'Neill's two sons (whom he had kept in prison for many years), and finally give his own eldest son as a hostage for due performance of his engagements.*

These were insolent terms to propose to a victorious sovereign prince at the head of his army; and he rejected them with scorn.   He could not think, he said, of abandoning his allies, nor would he send strangers out of his country, without safe conduct, nor deliver up those who sought refuge with him for conscience sake: as for Shane O'Neill's sons, they were his prisoners, not Elizabeth's; and for the name O'Neill, he would not nsist upon the authorities of the Pale addressing aim by that title; they might, if they pleased, call him Earl of Tyr-owen; but in Ulster he would, with their good leave, (or without it,) continue chief of his sept: and then the articles relating to English *sheriffs*, and the giving his son for a hostage, were wholly inadmissible: rather than be pardoned upon these terms he would dispense with pardon altogether.

Notwithstanding his contumacy, the gracious pardon was at Ormond's urgent entreaty duly made out and sealed with the great seal; and the Lord Lieutenant now pressed him to accept it upon any terms; the Irish should have all Ulster, north from Dundalk,† without hostages, without tribute, without sheriffs: it was all in vain; the truce was out, and O'Neill was pre-

---

* Moryson.   † MS. Life of O'Donnell.

paring to besiege Armagh and Portmore. Yet,
as a last resource, this notable "gracious pardon"
was sent, with its great seal, after him to th'
North: but the haughty chieftain manifested a
surprising indifference to the precious document,
and "continuing still his disloyal courses," says
Moryson, "never pleaded the same"—which it
seems it was needful to do—"so as upon his above-
mentioned indictment in September, 1795, you shall
find him after outlawed in the year 1600." Moryson is also precise as to the date of the pardon.
It passed the great seal upon the 11th of April, 1598

Indeed it must be acknowledged that all
these negotiations for peace and for pardon
were mere diplomacy on the part of O'Neil',
who was well acquainted with the rapacious
views of the English court, and only wished to
prolong the truce in hopes of receiving Spanish
succours he expected, that he might carry on the
war with greater vigour. In the month of April,
1597, a ship from Spain had arrived in Killybegs,
"on the west side of the glen blessed by the holy
Columba," as an Irish chronicler has it; and
O'Donnell had entertained King Philip's envoys
with distinction at Donegal, and presented them
with hounds and horses.* We have no account
of the arrangements made between them and the
northern chiefs; but it seems unaccountable that
Philip did not, about this time, give some efficient
support to O'Neill and O'Donnell, who were so
gallantly defending their country and religion
against their and his deadliest enemy; but some
Irish historians account for this by the rumours

MS. Life of O'Donnell.

which it was the policy of England to spread
abroad throughout the Continent, of the low condition to which O'Neill had been reduced, carefully concealing or denying the victories obtained
by him and his allies, and representing every
truce and conference as an abject "submission"
to the queen. An agent, they say,[*] was employed at Brussells to publish pretended submissions, treaties, and pardons; so that the Spanish
governor of Flanders might report to his master
that the power of the Irish Catholics was broken
and their cause wholly lost. And notwithstanding the frequent intercourse between Spain and
Ireland, it seems that such representations must
have had some effect; for O'Neill, during his
whole contest received no effectual help from
Spain; and the foolish expedition to Kinsale as
we shall see, was rather an injury to his cause
than an addition of strength.

In the summer of this year, however, he seems
to have thrown aside all reliance upon foreign
aid, and to have organized his countrymen for a
resolute stand, with all the powers of the Irish
against their enemy. And it is worth while to
know the proportions in which the various tribes
of Ulster contributed to their national army:—Of
the O'Neills, we find that Neal Bryan Fertough,
in Upper Claneboy, furnished eighty foot and
thirty horse; Shane Mac Bryan, of Lower Claneboy, sent eighty foot and fifty horse; Mac Rory,
of Kilwarlin, gave sixty foot-men and ten horsemen; Shane Mac Bryan Carogh, from the Bann

---

[*] Peter Lombard cited by Mac Geoghegan.

side, fifty foot and ten horse ; Art O'Neill, three
hundred foot and sixty horse ; Henry Oge
O'Neill, two hundred foot and forty horse ; Tur
lough Mac Henry O'Neill, of the Fews, had
three hundred foot and sixty horse ; Cormac
Mac Baron* (Hugh's brother) three hundred
foot and sixty horse ; O'Neill himself, of his
own household troops had seven hundred foot
and two hundred horse.   Then White's country (Dufferin in the district of Down) sent
twenty foot-men ; Mac Artane and Sliaght
O'Neill, also of Down, one hundred foot and
twenty horse ; Mac Gennis of Iveagh, brought
two hundred foot and forty horse ; Mac Mur-
tough, from the Mein water, sent forty foot-men ;
O'Hagan, of Tullogh-Oge, had one hundred foot
and thirty horse ; James Mac Donnell, son of the
yellow-haired Sorley, from the Route and the
Seven Glynns of Antrim, led four hundred foo
and one hundred horse ; Mac Gwire of Ferma
nagh, six hundred foot and one hundred horse
Mac Mahon and Ebhir Mac Coolye of Farney
(another Mac Mahon), contributed five hundred
foot and one hundred and sixty horse ; O'Reiliy
of Breffni O'Reilly, eight hundred foot and one
hundred horse ; and O'Cahan from the snores of
Lough Foyle and the banks of the Bann and Roe
led on five hundred foot and two hundred horse.
All these chieftains were tributary to O'Neill.†

* Son of the baron.   Irish names were sometimes
formed from the English titles of honour, as Mac an
Earlas, children of the Earl of Clanrickarde.
† The Mac Gwires and O'Reillys had formerly been
Uriaghts of O'Donnell.

From Tyr-connell, Red Hugh himself and his brother, brought three hundred and fifty foot, and one hundred and ten horse ; O'Dogherty of Inis howen led three hundred foot and forty horse ; Mac Swyne, five hundred foot and thirty horse ; O'Boyle one hundred foot and twenty horse ; and O'Gallagher of Ballyshannon two hundred foot and forty horse.* Hugh O'Neill and Red O'Donnell led these two great divisions ; they seem to have been of equal rank and authority, and to have acted independently of each other, but always in harmony, and their only contest was which should pierce deepest into the columns of the Saxon.

In the month of July O'Neill sent messengers to Phelim Mac Hugh, then chief of the O'Byrnes, that he might fall upon the Pale, as they were about to make employment in the North for the troops of Ormond ; and at the same time, he detatched fifteen hundred men and sent them to assist his ally, O'More, who was then besieging Porteloise,† a fort of the English in Leix. Then he made a sudden stoop upon the castle of Portmore, which, says Moryson, " was a great eyesore to him, lying upon the cheefe passage into his country," hoping to carry it by assault.

An eye-sore surely, brave O'Neill! and a heart-sorrow, is that accursed fortress of the Blackwater, bristling with Saxon spears—frown-

---

* Moryson is the authority for these numbers. He reckons in all of the Ulster troops 1,702 horsemen, and 7,220 foot-soldiers.

† Afterwards called Maryborough.

ing over the green vales of Tyr-owen ; the far-
thest step in the onward march of English power
towards the ancient territories of the Kinel
Eoghain. And by the souls of Heber and Heremon it shall be swept from the banks of that fair
river—razed and abolished from the face of the
earth, if there be right arms enough in all Ulster
to carry it away stone by stone.

Once and again he assayed to take it by
storm : but the fort was powerfully manned and
commanded by a skilful officer ; and without artillery or the science of attacking fortified places,
no progress could be made. The Irish assailed
the place with desperate bravery, and tried to
force their way by escalade : in vain ;—they
were shot down or flung headlong from the mound
and ramparts. The siege became a blockade ;
and day after day, week after week, the Irish lay
encamped around, and suffered nothing alive or
dead to enter or to leave the walls ; grimly waiting till famine and hardship should do their work
upon the garrison. In the mean time O'Neill
had also invested Armagh, and formed an encampment at Mullagh-bane, between that city and
Newry, to prevent all relief coming from the
South ; whilst his brother Cormac, with five hundred men, guarded the approaches near the beleagured walls.

Ormond now perceived that a powerful effort
must be made by the English to hold their ground
in the North, or Ulster might at once be abandoned to the Irish. Strong reinforcements
were sent from England ; and O'Neill's spies
soon brought him intelligence of large masses of

troops moving northward, led by Marshal **Sir
Henry** Bagnal, and composed of the choicest forces
in the queen's service. Newry was their place
of rendezvous; and early in August, Bagnal
found himself at the head of the largest and best
appointed army of veteran Englishmen that had
ever fought in Ireland. He succeeded in reliev-
ing Armagh, and dislodging O'Neill from his
encampment at Mullagh-bane; where the chief
himself narrowly escaped being taken; and then
prepared to advance, with his whole army, to the
Blackwater, and raise the siege of Portmore.
Williams and his men were by this time nearly
famished with hunger: they had eaten all their
horses, and had come to feeding on the herbs and
grass that grew upon the walls and in the ditches
of the fortress.* And every morning they gazed
anxiously over the southern hills and strained
their eyes to see the waving of a red-cross flag,
or the glance of English spears in the rising sun.

O'Neill hastily summoned O'Donnell and Mac
William to his aid, and determined to cross the
marshal's path, and give him battle before he
reached the Blackwater. His entire force, on
the day of battle, including the Scots and the
troops of Connaught and Tyr-connell, consisted
of four thousand five hundred foot and six hundred horse, and Bagnal's army amounted to an
equal number of infantry and five hundred veteran horsemen,† sheathed in corslets and head-
pieces; together with some field artillery, **in
which** O'Neill was wholly wanting. And **small**

* Moryson.   † O'Sullivan.

as these forces appear, they were the two largest armies, Irish against English, that had met upon this soil since Strongbow's invasion.   In Bagnal's ranks (a thing most unusual at that period) we find but one Irishman, Maelmorra O'Reilly, surnamed "the Handsome," a disloyal traitor, who fought against his country and his lawful chieftain, and was not ashamed to call himself *the queen's O'Reilly*.

Hugh Roe O'Donnell had snuffed the coming battle from afar, and on the 9th of August joined O'Neill with the clans of Connaught and Tyrconnell.   They drew up their main body about a mile from Portmore, on the way to Armagh, where the plain was narrowed to a pass, enclosed on one side by a thick wood, and on the other by a bog.   To arrive at that plain from Armagh the enemy would have to penetrate through wooded hills divided by winding and marshy hollows, in which flowed a sluggish and discoloured stream from the bogs ; and hence the pass was called *Beal-an-atha-buidhe*, " the mouth of the yellow ford."*   Fearfasa O'Clery, a learned poet of O'Donnell's, asked the name of that place, and when he heard it, remembered (and proclaimed aloud to the army) that St. Bercan had foretold a terrible battle to be fought at a yellow ford, and a glorious victory to be won by the ancient Irish.—Besides, are they not heretics, these English? and hath not Moran the son of Maoin said that "Nought prevails in battle so powerfully

* Or it may have been called *yellow* from the colour of the soil, which seems filled with ochre.

as the Truth?"* Even so, Moran, son of Maoin!
And for thee wisest poet, O'Clery! thou hast this
day served thy country well: for, to an Irish army,
auguries of good were more needful than a com-
missariat; and their bards' songs, like the Do-
rian flute of Greece, breathed a passionate valour
that no blare of English trumpets could ever
kindle.

Bagnal's army rested that night in Armagh;
and the Irish bivouacked in the woods, each warrior covered by his shaggy cloak, under the stars
of a summer night :—for to " an Irish rebell," says
Edmund Spenser, "the wood is his house against
all weathers, and his mantle is his couch to sleep
in." But O'Neill, we may well believe slept not
that night away ;—the morrow was to put to
proof what valour and discipline was in that
Irish army which he had been so long organizing and training to meet this very hour. Before
him lay a splendid army of tried English troops,
in full march for his ancient seat of Dungannon,
and led on by his mortal enemy. And O'Neill
would not have had that host weakened by the
desertion of a single man, nor commanded—
no, not for his white wand of chieftaincy—
by any leader but this his dearest foe. Ah!
never had he desired the love of Bagnal's
sister with fonder eagerness than now his soul
yearned for the heart's blood of her brother. He
watched the east and longed for the grey of morning.

The tenth morning of August rose bright and
serene upon the towers of Armagh and the silver
waters of Avonmore. Before day dawned, the
English army left the city in three divisions, and
at sun-rise they were winding through the hills
and woods behind the spot where now stands the
little church of Grange. The sun was glanc-
ing on the corslets and spears of their glitter-
ing cavalry; their banners waved proudly, and
their bugles rung clear in the morning air;*
when, suddenly, from the thickets on both sides
of their path, a deadly volley of musketry swept
through the foremost ranks. O'Neill had stationed here five hundred light-armed troops to
guard the defiles; and in the shelter of thick
groves of fir-trees they had silently waited for the
enemy. Now they poured in their shot, volley
after volley, and killed great numbers of the
English: but the first division, led by Bagnal in
person, after some hard fighting, carried the pass,
dislodged the marksmen from their position and
drove them backwards into the plain. The centre
division under Cosby and Wingfield, and the
rear-guard led by Cuin and Billing, supported in
flank by the cavalry under Brooke, Montacute
and Fleming,† now pushed forward, speedily
cleared the difficult country and formed in the
open ground in front of the Irish lines. " It was

"Sereno et grato die, vexillis explicatis, tubarum
clangore tibiarum concentu." &c. —*O'Sullivan.* He is
the only writer, Irish or foreign, who gives an intelligible account of O'Neill's battles; but he was a soldier as well as a chronicler.
† Camden Queen Eliz.

not quite safe," says an Irish chronicler, (in admiration of Bagnal's disposition of his forces) " to
attack the nest of griffins and den of lions in
which were placed the soldiers of London."*
Bagnal, at the head of his first division, and
aided by a body of cavalry, charged the Irish
light-armed troops up to the very entrenchments,
in front of which O'Neill's foresight had prepared some pits, covered over with wattles and
grass ; and many of the English cavalry rushing
impetuously forward, rolled headlong, both men
and horses, into these trenches and perished
Still the Marshal's chosen troops, with loud cheers
and shouts of " St. George, for merry England !"
resolutely attacked the entrenchments that
stretched across the pass, battered them with
cannon, and in one place succeeded, though with
heavy loss, in forcing back their defenders. The
first the main body of O'Neill's troops was
brought into action ; and with bagpipes sounding
a charge, they fell upon the English, shouting
their fierce battle-cries, Lamh-dearg ! and O'Donnell Aboo ! O'Neill himself, at the head of a body
of horse, pricked forward to seek out Bagnal
amidst the throng of battle ;† but they never
met: the marshal, who had done his devoir that day
like a good soldier, was shot through the brain
by some unknown marksman : the division he
had led was forced back by the furious onslaught
of the Irish, and put to utter rout ; and, what

* MS. Life of O'Donnell.
† " Tyrone pricked forward with rage of envy and
settled rancour."—*Moryson.*

added to their confusion, a cart of gunpowder exploded amidst the English ranks and blew many of their men to atoms. And now the cavalry of Tyr-connell and Tyr-owen dashed into the plain and bore down the remnant of Brooke's and Fleming's horse: the columns of Wingfield and Cosby reeled before their rushing charge— while in front, to the war-cry of *Bataillah-Aboo !** the swords and axes of the heavy-armed galloglasses were raging amongst the Saxon ranks. By this time the cannon were all taken ; the cries of " St. George " had failed, or turned into death-shrieks ; and once more, England's royal standard sunk before the Red Hand of Tyr-owen.

The last who resisted was the traitor O'Reilly : twice he tried to rally the flying squadrons but was slain in the attempt : and at last the whole of that fine army was utterly routed, and fled pell-mell towards Armagh, with the Irish hanging fiercely on their rear. Amidst the woods and marshes all connexion and order were speedily lost ; and as O'Donnell's chronicler has it, they were " pursued in couples, in threes, in scores, in thirties, and in hundreds," and so cut down in detail by their avenging pursuers. In one spot especially the carnage was terrible, and the country people yet point out the lane where that hideous rout passed by, and call it to this day the " Bloody Loaning." Two thousand five hundred English were slain in

* "The cause of the noble Staff." War-cry of the Tyr-connell galloglasses, whose hereditary leader was one of the Mac Swynes.— *Ware Antiq.*

the battle and flight, including twenty-three superior officers, besides lieutenants and ensigns.
Twelve thousand gold pieces, thirty-four stan-
dards, all the musical instruments and cannon,
with a long train of provision waggons, were a
rich spoil for the Irish army. The confederates
had only two hundred slain and six hundred
wounded.*

Fifteen hundred English found shelter in the
city,·which was forthwith closely invested by the
victorious Irish, and "for three days and three
nights nothing passed in or out."† On the fourth
day they surrendered the place; and although
some of the chieftains would have taken cruel revenge upon these unfortunate survivors of the
battle, O'Neill's voice prevailed, and they were
disarmed and sent in safety to the Pale. Portmore was instantly yielded and its garrison dismissed with the rest.

"Thus," says Camden, "Tyr-owen triumphed
according to his heart's desire over his adversary." All Saxon soldiery vanished speedily
from the fields of Ulster, and the Bloody Hand
once more waved over the towers of Newry and
Armagh

---

* O'Sullivan. See also Mac Geoghegan and MS. Life
of O'Donnell. Moryson admits on the part of the English only 1,500 slain. The Irish piously buried all the
dead.—*Irish Annals* cited by Curry.
† MS. Life of O'Donnell.

CHAPTER XI.

MUNSTER TAKES HEART.—RED HUGH IN CON-NAUGHT.

A. D. 1598—1599.

HIGH harping in Dungannon, and in the halls of Tyr-connell ;—and throughout broad Ulster from the Glynns to Ath-Seanagh, from Dundalk to Derry-Calgach, there was feasting and jubilee, and the triumph-song of many a bard. Surely, ye sweet singers of Ulladh ! the second Hector— the heaven-sent Moses of your prayers, has at length arisen :—the children of the Scythic Eber Scot have returned ; and old Ireland is yet fated to rise out of the dust and ashes of Saxon-land.*

The fame of this victory over the detested English was instantly spread abroad through all the island ; and O'Neill was celebrated every-where as the deliverer of his country and most zealous champion of the Catholic religion. In this

---

* See the song of Fearflatha O'Gnive, a poet of Clan-hugh-buidhe, in Walker's Irish Bards.—" Is there no Hector left for the defence, for the recovery of Troy ?— It is thine, oh ! my God, to send us a second Moses :— thy dispensations are just: and unless the children of the Scythian Eber Scot return," &c. A translation of it by Callanan appears in the "Ballad Poetry of Ireland," 121.

letter character he drew into the confederacy many
lords of old English race, but Catholic in faith,
who never would have been found in the Irish
ranks, save to defend themselves from Elizabeth's
persecuting Reformation. These two elements of
resistance, therefore, national feeling and religious
zeal, united against the queen of England :—the
one party could not endure her political usurpation, her judges, lords president and sheriffs ;—
the other abhorred her forced " Reformation,"
and her undertaking bishops. But every enemy
of England, from what motive soever, was now
O'Neill's sworn brother, and looked to the victorious Northern chieftain as the sword and shield
of their cause. All Leinster was in arms under
O'Cavanagh, O'Byrne, and Owen Mac Rory
O'More of Leix, who had by this time, with the
aid of O'Neill's auxiliary troops, expelled all Eng
lish undertakers from his ancient territory (which
they had prematurely named " the King's
county,") and now his clansmen, with the mountain septs of Wicklow, were ranging through the
Pale unopposed and levying tribute from the very
valley of the Liffey, while Ormond's English
troops, utterly panic-stricken, shut themselves up
in their forts and strong-holds, raised draw-bridge,
and pointed cannon from battlement and bastion,
and far from assailing their enemy, lived in
continual fear, by day and by night, of surprise
and slaughter.

Munster also began to breathe after the terrible agony of that Geraldine war, and to look

with hope and joy to the dawn that was rising on them from the North. And, though there was in the South a strong English army under the " Lord President," Sir Thomas Norreys, yet the settlers who had been lately "planted" in the fairest tracts of Munster began to fear for the security of their ill-gotten wealth.* A powerful Catholic gentleman of Limerick, named Pierce Lacy, a close ally of O'Neill, sent messengers to the North and to Owen Mac Rory O'More, praying that a band of the victorious Irish of Ulster or Leinster under some active leader might be sent southward, where, so soon as the national standard should be unfurled, all the oppressed Catholics and plundered Irish of Munster would rush to join it in the name of liberty and holy church. O'Neill immediately detached Richard Tyrrell of Fertullagh at the head of a chosen band from the Northern army to join O'Moore ; and the chief of Leix, leaving his brother to command in Leinster during his absence, and taking with him the renowned victor of Tyrrell's Pass, marched rapidly through Ormond, entered Desmond, and was forthwith joined by the remnants of the unfortunate Geraldines. The Knight of Glyn, and the White Knight, Fitzmaurice Baron of Lixnaw, the Knight of Kerry, Dermod and Donogh Mac Carthy, the O'Donoghoes, Roche, Viscount Fermoy, and two powerful kinsmen of Ormond himself, Thomas Butler, Baron of Cahir, and Richard Lord Mountgarret, who was married to O'Neill's daughter, besides the O'Sullivans, O'Driscols,

* Camden

O'Donovans, and O'Mahonys of Carbry, all took arms in the common cause. Norreys, after shutting up a part of his force in garrison at Kilmallock, retreated with the remainder to Cork, with O'More close upon his rear: while the English undertakers were on all sides ejected from those lands which their queen had so lately taken it upon herself to grant them. Their castles were taken and dismantled, their houses burned down and razed to the ground: we hear of no wanton cruelty done upon the settlers but they were all driven away and forced to find refuge in the cities and garrisons, and resume those swords which had carved them out estates before.* Amongst those burnt-out adventurers, one cannot much grieve to find the gentle poet of Kilcolman, now sheriff of Cork. He had but lately finished that " View of the state of Ireland," of which we have already seen somewhat, and from his retreat on " Mulla's" banks had also issued the *Faërie Queene,* which he had dutifully presented, with a mellifluous copy of verses, to the Earl of Ormond, then the queen's Lord Lieutenant and natural patron of all undertakers.† He

* This transaction in Munster seems to have been precisely similar to the resumption of plundered estates in Ulster in 1641.

† " Receive, most noble lord, a simple taste

Of the wilde fruit which saluage soyl hath bred," &c.

When one reads of Spenser's expulsion from Kilcolman, and the burning of his furniture and effects, it is not easy to forget the mode of treatment he had suggested for his brother bards of Ireland, who were always regarded by the English government, and with reason, its natural enemies—" I would wish," says he, " that a was driven from both house and bailiwick, left Ireland as poor as he had entered it twenty years before, and died in London the following year *for lack of bread!** Ah! poor Spenser! Those " barbarian" Irish, with their genial nature and poetical temperament, better knew how to honour their inspired poets than these proud English. Not a " lewd barde" of them all but had a better reward than *this.*

So passed the winter of 1598, and by the beginning of the following year no English force was able to keep the field throughout all Ireland. The Geraldines and their adherents had recovered their power and possessions in the South ; and as they had yet no Earl of Desmond there to take the leading of their tribe (a thing unknown in Munster for many an age) O'Neill had to take order for supplying one. And as the kings of England had sometimes presumed to confer Irish chieftaincies and estates, to be held by " English tenure," even when they had no power of securing to their grantees the benefit of those

Provost Marshal should be appointed in every shire, which should continually walke about the countrey with halfe a dozen or halfe a score horsemen to take up such loose persons as they should finde thus wandering, whom he should punish by his own authority with such paines as the person shall seem to deserve : for if hee be but once so taken idly roguing hee may punish him more lightly, as with stocks or such like ; but if hee be found againe so loytering he may scourge him with whippes or rodds ; after which, if hee be againe taken let him have the bitternesse of marshall law."—*View of the State of Ireland.*

* Ben Johnson's Letter to Drummond of Hawthornden

gifts ; so the prince of Ulster, seeing he *had* the power, knew no reason why he should not create an earl, to hold his earldom by *Irish* tenure. There had been queen's O'Donnells, queen's Mac Gwires, queen's bishops ;—there should now be an O'Neill's Count Palatine of Desmond. Earl Gerald, the last of that title, had left a son who was delivered in his youth to the English as a hostage, and had now, for seventeen years, lain a prisoner in the Tower of London. This was the true claimant of the earldom according to English law : but O'Neill, having regard rather to the Irish custom of Tanistry than to Saxon descents and inheritances, sought out among the Geraldines a fit man to bear the weight of leadership in Munster, and James, the son of Thomas the Red, and nephew to Gerald, was duly invested (by what sort of official document or ceremonial we are not informed) with the dignity, estates and ancient privileges of Earl of Desmond ; stipulating to hold the same as a vassal and tributary to the prince of Ulster.* And so having established Irish power once more in Munster, the Northern troops were recalled.

While O'Neill was thus predominating over all Ireland, exercising sovereign powers, and cooping up the queen's troops within their fortifications, one is hardly prepared to find him making more "submissions :" but if Lord Mountjoy's secretary is to be believed (which the present writer thinks he is *not*) this victorious chief

* " On condition that (forsooth) he should be vassal to O'Neill."—*Moryson.*

was now craving pardon of his beaten enemy, and tendering abject allegiance to the foreigner: " May you hold laughter," says that singular historian, "or will you think that Carthage ever bred such a fœdifragous, truce-breaking wretch, when you shall reade, that even in the middest of these garboyles, whilst in his letters to the King of Spaine he magnified his victories, beseeching him not to believe that he would seeke or take away any conditions of peace, yet, most impudently, he ceased not to entertain the Lord Lieutenant with letters and messages, with offers of submission." Yet Moryson was not the inventor of this falsehood : such rumours were really spread at the time, to impose upon Catholic powers on the Continent, to conceal from them the true nature and magnitude of the Irish war and prevent them from sending troops here : " And to the same purpose,"* suggests Sir Francis Bacon, "nothing can be more fit than a treaty, or a shadow of treaty, of a peace with Spain ; which methinks should be in our power to fasten, at least *rumore tenus*, to the deluding of as wise a people as the Irish."

O'Donnell, in the meantime, had cleared the plains of Connaught of all Englishmen, and adherents of England, and had driven Sir Conyers Clifford once more into garrison. He kept his

---

* That is " the cutting off the opinion and expectation of foreign succours."—See Bacon's *Considerations touching the Queen's Service in Ireland.* This is the same Bacon who was afterwards discoverer of a " Novum Organon Scientiarum," and also Lord Chancellor of England.

Christmas piously in Ballymote : then led his
troops into Clanrickarde, plundering the country
and compelling the western clans to acknowledge
the jurisdiction of his newly created Mac William.   Athenree was taken by his fierce assault ;
its English garrison put to the sword, and all the
plunder of the enemy, clothing, arms, and many
herds of cattle, sent home to Tyr-connell.   The
whole of Connaught had now been over-run by
the Kinel-Conal, except only Thomond : and
Red Hugh's army had a month's repose ; when
the fiery chief began " to think it long that they
were at rest"* and prepared to invade the territory of the Dal-Cais, where Donogh O'Brien,
Earl of Thomond, and the Baron of Inchiquin,
still retained their base titles and preserved a
shameful "loyalty" to the Queen of England.
Thomond was doomed to plunder and slaughter ;
but "because it would be encountering," says
O'Donnell's chronicler, " certain opposition and
battle to assail the noble race who dwelt therein,
the tribe of Cas, son of Conal, of the swift steeds,
descended from Brian Boroihme, son of Ken-
nedy," the chieftain took care to gather a powerful force of all his tributaries and allies.   He
summoned the clans to Ballymote, and was
speedily attended by his three brothers, Rory,
Manus, and Cathbar, by Hugh Oge O'Donnell,
O'Boyle, O'Dogherty, and the Mac Swynes,
with all the troops of Tyr-connell : Mac Gwire
with the clans of Fermanagh, also attended this
rendezvouz ; and of the tribes of Connaught

* MS. Life of O'Donnel.

O'Ruarc and Mac William, with O'Dowd, Mac Donough, O'Hara, O'Kelly, and Mac Dermott. We find also in that army, holding high command under his chieftain, a certain Niall Garbh O'Donnell—a name accursed—of whom we are to hear more in the course of this story.— O'Donnell's Irish chronicler is very minute in his detail of this expedition: how Red Hugh marched southwards silently and rapidly, through Clanrickarde, and halted in the evening at the Red beach between Kilcolgan and Ardrahan; how they bivouacked in the woods, lighted fires, and took food and wines of Spain: how, at midnight, they all arose as one man, continued their silent march, and by the dawn of day arrived at Clancy's wood: then how O'Donnell "as the light of day prevailed over the stars, advanced to Corcomroe, and thence to Kilfenora, sending out strong parties to scour the country and ravage the lands of all those who were friendly to the stranger, or owned the sway of Saxon earls and barons; how Mac Gwire attacked and took the castle of Conor O'Brien, Baron of Inchiquin, and made the baron prisoner. while other bands ranged through Thomond, burning, slaying, and ravaging; how they drove all the cattle to Kilfenora; and how the whole northern army, having feasted and regaled themselves, turned their faces homewards, each party driving its own allotted prey, and the hills of Burren could hardly be seen by reason of the multitudes of sheep and cattle that trooped over them, wending their way to the pastures of Connaught and Tyr-connell.

Now there was a certain poet in Thomond, by
the name of Maoilin Oge, and whilst he was absent from home, some of the northern forayers
had driven away his cattle, not knowing that it
was to one of the honoured race of bards those
sheep and kine belonged: and Maoilin Oge,
when he came to know his loss, having heard of
the generosity of this noble Red Hugh, and how
reverently he cherished and protected the bards
and Ollamhs of the North, took his harp and
hastened after the host of O'Donnell: and being
introduced into the chieftain's presence, he
shewed him, out of ancient writings, " that it was
no shame to the Dal-Cais to be plundered by one
bearing the name of Hugh O'Donnell;"—and he
touched his harp and sang how the holy Colum-
kille had foretold this very event—" that a certain Hugh, of the Kinel-Conal should come to
revenge on the Dal-Cais the destruction of that
royal seat of Aileach and the carrying away of
the stones thereof by Murkertach O'Brien."*—
' My wood, my grove!" (so ran the prophecy
of the blessed saint,) "Ah! my dwelling and my
school: alas! oh God, a multitude of men. He
who will revenge my Aileach: the Hugh of

* This was six hundred years before. The sovereignty
of Ireland had been disputed between Mac Lochlin, chief
of the Hy-Niall and the O'Briens of Thomond. The
Ulster chieftain had invaded Munster, wasted Limerick,
and burned the great palace of Kincora. A few years
after, in revenge, O'Brien led a great army to the North,
levelled the famous royal residence of Aileach, four miles
from Derry, and caused his clansmen to carry off each
man one stone of it to Thomond.

ftεεcεs of rough roads, the polished body, fame
without reproach, long hair in ringlets." And
asssuredly " *he* was that Hugh ;" and this plunder of the tribe of Cas was indeed heaven's vengeance granted to the prayer of the patron saint
of Tyr-connell. Then O'Donnell was well pleased
both with the poet's song and with Columba's
prophecy : and he restored to Maoilin Oge all his
herds and cattle, and the bard went on his way
rejoicing, and left his benediction with the
princely chief.

One must admit that all the expeditions of this
wild leader, though daring and dashing, resem-
bled more the cruel and predatory raids of a
horde of savages, or of the border clans of Scotland a century before, than any more regular military movements : but an intense hatred of the
Saxons and of all Saxon usages was Red Hugh's
master passion : his whole life was vowed to vengeance : those cruel fetters of Perrot had worn
his young flesh—had burned into his proud heart
his crippled feet yet bore the shooting pangs of
frost that had benumbed him while he lay perish-
ing, in his flight, upon the snowy mountains:
and his daily thoughts, his dreams by night, were
of rooting out and utterly exterminating those
treacherous foes of his race, and all who held
with them. The smoke of their blazing towers
was pleasant as incense to his soul, and he deemed
a hecatomb of their slain the offering most grate-
ful to heaven.

Hugh O'Neill who was now the recognized
leader, the head and the heart of our national
confederacy, and directed its operations every-

where throughout the land, at length saw foreign power totally prostrated in Ireland, its military resources annihilated or defeated, its Irish adherents either crushed, or, what was better, brought over to the cause of patriotism and honour : but still he omitted no means of strengthening the league : he renewed his intercourse with Spain, planted permanent bodies of troops on the Foyle, Erne, and Blackwater, engaged the services of some additional Scots from the Western Isles, improved the discipline of his own troops, and on every side made preparation to renew the conflict with his powerful enemy. For he well knew that Elizabeth was not the monarch to quit her deadly gripe of this fair island without a more terrible struggle than had yet been endured.

CHAPTER XII.

ESSEX—O'NEILL AT HOLY-CROSS.

A. D. 1599—1600.

BAGNAL's death, and the signal disaster of the Yellow Ford, frightened and enraged Queen Elizabeth's government and people. The military prowess of this formidable Northern chief was even exaggerated in their estimate ; and Moryson himself tells us that " the generall voyce was of Tyrone amongst the English after the defeat of Blackwater, as of Hannibal among the Romans after the defeat of Cannæ." The queen was highly enraged against her Lord Lieutenant for remaining idly in Leinster, engaged in petty contention with the O'Mores and O'Byrnes, whilst he had intrusted to Marshal Bagnal the leading of those fine troops which she had sent him, to end, as she hoped, these Irish wars at a blow. Yet it was by no means clear that Ormond's commanding the army in person would have ensured a victory. An enemy was now to be dealt with such as England had never encountered upon Irish soil before ; and it was plain that the amount of forces hitherto employed in Ireland would no longer suffice. De Burgh and Kildare, Norreys and Bagnal had been successively hurled back from the frontiers of Ulster with ignominious rout and overthrow ; each campaign only strengthening O'Neill, wasting the power and ruining the reputation of English government, until at length a time had come when either the Queen of England must at once yield up her footing upon Irish ground, or put forth all the powers of an empire to retain it.

Two thousand men under Sir Samuel Bagnal were hastily sent over to strengthen Ormond's garrisons in the mean time. And Robert Devereux, Earl of Essex, then the most powerful subject in England, the queen's prime favourite, and son to that Essex who had made the unfortunate attempt to plunder, convert, and colonize the North, was selected as Lord Lieutenant and commander-in-chief of the splendid army now destined for Irish service. Some dark intrigues there were connected with his appointment—malignant contrivances of his enemies at court—self-seeking machinations of his friends at court—a whole net-work of court intrigue ; which may be found in English historians, but in which we do not here concern ourselves. Essex had commanded with some distinction against the Spaniards, and ardently coveted this Irish service as a sphere in which he might arrive at still higher fame ;— might crush the dreaded O'Neill ; and, as his friend and councillor Sir Francis Bacon expressed it, " refound and replant the policie of that nation." " Which design," continues Bacon, " as it doth descend to you from your noble father who lost his life in that action though he paid tribute to nature and not to fortune, so I hope your lordship shall be as fatal a captain to this war as Africanus was to the war of Carthage, after that both his uncle and his father had lost their lives in Spain in the same war."*

* Letter from Sir Francis Bacon to Essex.—*Scrinia Sacra*. This celebrated person, who was afterwards Lord Chancellor of England, and (being one of the basest of mankind) sold his judgments to the highest bidders, was about this time much occupied in devising methods of reducing and governing Ireland for behoof of his friend and patron Essex. His thoughts on the subject are conveyed in the "Considerations touching the Queen's Service in Ireland," cited before, and in two or three letters to Essex himself. A passage from the "Considerations" will indicate the general nature of his plans:—"One of the principal pretences whereby the heads of the rebellion have prevailed both with the people and the foreigner hath been the defence of the Catholique religion: and it is that likewise hath made the foreigner reciprocally more plausible with the rebel. Therefore a toleration of religion *for a time not definite*, except it be in some principal towns and precincts after the manner of some French edicts, seemeth to me to be a matter warrantable by religion, and in policie, of absolute necessity. Neither if any English Papist or recusant shall for liberty of his conscience transfer his person, family, and fortunes thither, do I hold it a matter of danger, but expedient to draw on undertaking and to further population." Upon which fraudulent and cruel suggestion the English government really acted; for in the last years of Elizabeth, and first of James, no interference was made with Catholic worship in Ireland; some monasteries were repaired, priests appeared without disguise, and the mass was celebrated openly. But the toleration was "for a time not definite;" and, in 1605, King James issued that famous proclamation commencing—"Whereas his majesty is informed that his subjects of Ireland have been deceived by a false report,

Under such auspices, with such high hopes, and with twenty thousand men at his back, the Earl of Essex set forth for Ireland, and landed in Dublin on the 15th of April, 1599.* His instructions were to neglect, in a great degree, all chiefs of lesser note, and to strike at the head of the Irish confederacy by stationing strong garrisons at Lough Foyle and Ballyshannon,† and then, having barred O'Neill's country from its communications with Connaught and Scotland, to grapple with the chieftain in his fastnesses of Tyr-owen. The plans were unexceptionable the means furnished to carry them out were enor-

that his majesty was disposed to allow them liberty of conscience, and the free choice of a religion : he hereby declares to his beloved subjects of Ireland, that he will *not* admit of any such liberty of conscience as they were made to expect by such report." And upon that declaration he most strictly acted. The same Bacon, in one of his private letters to Essex (*Scinia Sacra*) suggests for Ireland what he calls the "princely policie," "*to weaken by division and disunion.*" Oh, sage Sir Francis ! Thou hast indeed found the true *Organon* of Irish government :—these golden rules of thine,—to deceive by treacherous conciliation,—to weaken by division,—are to be the soul and marrow of English policy in Ireland for ever :—and for this thou shalt sit, robed in purest ermine, on the highest judicial seat of thy country, and shalt keep the conscience of a king !

* Besides the large army which had been prepared for him he demanded, when about to leave England, that two more regiments of old soldiers should be placed at his disposal ; which was immediately complied with.— "He had an army assigned him," says Moryson, "as great as himself required, and such for number and strength as Ireland had never yet seene."

† Camden.

nuous: but it soon became apparent that the Man was a-wanting.

O'Neill and his confederates were not dismayed at the arrival of this great army and its magnificent leader. They did not now, what had been too frequent in Ireland, and what appears to have been looked for in the present case, vie with each other in proffering submissions and suing for pardons. O'Neill had, in Ulster, six thousand veteran and victorious troops; no landing of foreigners was likely to be made in Lough Foyle without stern resistance; and the chief himself, with his main body occupied the passes north of Dundalk, calmly watching for the first movement of his enemy. O'Donnell with four thousand men, was holding Connaught, and guarding the defiles near Lough Erne; O'More had greatly increased his forces in Leinster; and, in the South, the Geraldines, headed by O'Neill's Earl of Desmond, were once more in arms and eager to wipe away the shame of their former defeats. Ireland had never been so strong, so proud, or so united. Foreign nations also, when they saw her so well able to help herself, began to offer their assistance; and, early in June, a ship arrived from Spain in the bay of Donegal, carrying arms for two thousand men, all which O'Donnell divided into two equal parts, one for himself, and the other, says his chronicler, " he sent to Hugh O'Neill, as was becoming."

Lord Essex soon showed what mettle was in him. Instead of marching in force upon the North, he began to waste his strength by petty expeditions into Munster, and against O'More.

L

He gave the command of all his cavalry to his friend Lord Southampton ; conferred the honour of knighthood and an office of high trust upon one John Harington, a trifling courtier and devoted slave of his own ; then led his vast army to besiege Cahir castle, a fortress of the Butlers situated on the Suir ;* but, before he reached it, whilst he marched through Leix, five hundred of the O'Mores waited for him in a defile, fell upon his rear-guard, slew many of his men, and shore so many waving plumes from the high-crested cavalry of England that the place was afterwards named by the Irish, Bearna-na-cleite, the *Pass of Plumes.*† Essex, however, held on his way to Cahir ; invested the castle, battered it with cannon, and after ten days' stout resistance, and some hard fighting with Desmond and Redmond Burke who came to relieve the place, succeeded in taking it. Then, having received submissions from Lords Cahir and Roche, he advanced into Limerick, but near Crome was encountered by the Geraldines and Mac Carthys. Sir Thomas Norreys, Lord President of Munster, was slain in the battle,‡ and the English army was totally defeated and forced to retire with heavy loss and

---

* Moryson.　　　　　† O'Sullivan.

‡ O'Sullivan. The English chroniclers make no mention of this battle : they always suppress as far as possible whatever is unfavourable to her majesty's arms : but the author of the *Pacata Hibernia,* as if incidentally, speaks of the " unfortunate death of Sir Thomas Norris, lately slaine by the *rebels* ;" and also tells us that, at this time, the same " rebels" were "swollen with pride by reason of their manifest victories, which almost in all encounters they had lately obtained."

disgrace towards the Pale, closely pursued for six days by the victorious Irish. When Lord Essex arrived in Dublin, stung by defeat and shame, he found that a body of six hundred men whom he had stationed on the borders of the O'Byrne's country, had been set upon by the Irish mountaineers and utterly routed with terrible carnage. Essex chose to impute this disaster to misconduct : he subjected the officers who had commanded that detachment to a trial by court-martial ; and, with the ferocious cruelty that belongs to a coward, decimated the surviving soldiers.

Soon after that, finding that the queen was impatient of that petty warfare, and displeased that he had not yet measured swords with O'Neill, he wrote her majesty a long letter,* describing the many difficulties he had to contend with, the powerful and disciplined troops of the Irish, consisting, as he says, of men with stronger bodies and more perfect in the use of arms than her majesty's forces : and he tells the queen that to subdue these Irish their priests must be hunted down ; that Bacon's policy of division and disunion must be resorted to ; and that all purpose of establishing English law, sheriffs and the like, throughout the island must be well concealed until the military power of the chiefs should be ruined. Then he developes a systematic plan for reducing the North : to guard the coasts, to plant garrisons, to lay waste the country :—most judicious devices for the purpose, not one of which he ever attempted to carry into effect, being indeed wholly incompetent for such a service. And the letter concludes, as was usual in all communications from Elizabeth's courtiers, with expressions of passionate admiration for her majesty's person, and constancy eternal.

All this did not satisfy the imperious queen; and at last Essex, for very shame, was obliged to announce his purpose of marching northwards against O'Neill; then suddenly another urgent occasion arose, that he should first go to Leix and O'Fally against the O'Mores and O'Connors, whom, says the historian, " he brake with ease:" and after that, finding his army much weakened, he asked for a reinforcement of one thousand men before he could venture upon O'Neill. These were speedily sent to him : and now at length he seemed resolved upon the northern war, and actually sent orders to Sir Conyers Clifford to attack Belleek on the Saimer, so as to cause a diversion on that side, while he should himself penetrate Ulster by Dundalk and Newry. But once again he changed his mind, and, the summer being nearly wasted, wrote again to England that he could do no more this year, except draw his forces towards the borders of Ulster.* The truth seems to be, that this courtier-general had no stomach for the North ; he trembled to encounter the conqueror of far abler leaders than himself, and his craven heart melted within him at the very name of *Blackwater*.

Sir Conyers Clifford, however, who was a ve-

* Moryson

teran soldier, and not a courtier, having received
his orders from the commander-in-chief, set forth
to execute them at the head of two thousand men,
consisting of fourteen hundred infantry and Lord
Southampton's horse, with some auxiliary cavalry
supplied by Clanrickarde, and commanded by
Lord Dunkellin. Long before Clifford was ready
to march, O'Donnell and O'Ruarc had intelligence of the intended movement, and were already
waiting for him in the mountains of Sligo and
Breffni, "chasing wild deer" to pass the time
until nobler game should come.* Clifford left
Boyle and marched northward by the passes of
the Corsliabh mountains, till he arrived at a
wooded gorge, which the general thought it prudent to explore first with the infantry, leaving
his baggage, cavalry and artillery on the plain.

He led the troops himself into the defile, and
when he had advanced so far as to make retreat
perilous, the bagpipes of the Irish were heard
both in front and on every side: the cry of
O'Donnell-aboo! rung through the hills; and,
almost before the English saw an enemy, with
the rush of a winter torrent the Clan-Conal was
upon them. Clifford's soldiers fought bravely,
and sustained the charge like men who knew that
to turn their backs was death: but nothing
could stand against the fierce onset of O'Don
nell's clansmen : Clifford himself and Sir Henry
Ratcliffe were slain, and their whole force was
soon totally routed and driven back with slaughter into the plain. The cavalry, under Jephson,

* MS. Life of O'Donnell.

having now ground where they could act, dashed
amongst the Irish and charged them up to the
very skirts of the wood: but after a severe
struggle the cavalry also yielded, and the whole
army retreated, or rather fled, to Boyle abbey,
pursued for three miles by the victorious Irish.*
Next day a council of war was held in Boyle by
the surviving officers, Jephson, Lord Dunkellin
and Sir Arthur Savage; and, as they heard that
O'Donnell's entire force was at hand, they thought
it best to abandon the whole expedition and with-
draw their troops into garrison.†

This battle of the Corsliabh mountains‡ was
followed by the surrender of Sligo to O'Donnell.
That place had been held for the English by
Theobald Burke "of the Ships" and O'Connor
Sligo: but now Burke made sail, with all his
ships, for Galway; and O'Connor, having submitted to O'Donnell, was reinstated in his chieftaincy, on engaging to assist his countrymen
against the English.

Another royal army scattered, like chaff, upon
the borders of Ulster: another veteran general
slain: the months of summer trifled away: the
army wearied by driftless expeditions, disheart-
ened by defeat, and thinned by the Irish battle-
axes: these had been hitherto the net result of
an enterprize of such pith and moment as the

---

* Moryson; Mac Geoghegan. The latter states the
numbers killed on the side of the English at 1,400, the
former at 120. Moryson also excuses the flight of Jephson's horse, for that their powder, he says, was spent.
† Moryson.
‡ Generally miscalled " the Curlews."

expedition under Lord Essex. Having failed, however, in his military operations, we are next to see his lordship trying negotiation. On O'Neill's invitation he met the chief at the old place of parley, near Dundalk : they were both on horseback at opposite sides of the "ford Ballaclinch ;"[*] and O'Neill, ever the flower of courtesy, spurred his horse into the middle of the stream while Essex stood upon the opposite bank. First they had a private conference, in which Lord Essex, won by the chivalrous bearing and kindly address of the chief, became, say English historians, too confidential with an enemy of his sovereign,[†] spoke without reserve of his pretensions, his daring hopes and most private thoughts of ambition ; until O'Neill had sufficiently read his secret soul, fathomed his poor capacity and understood the full meanness of his shallow treason. Then Cormac O'Neill and five other Irish leaders were summoned on the one side ; on the other Lord Southampton and an equal number of English officers ; and a solemn parley was opened in due form. On this occasion the demands of O'Neill seemed to have been precisely what he had always required before—freedom of religion— exemption from English government—restitution of plunder, (or in English phraseology, of *forfeited estates :*) and Essex, it seems, protested on his part that he thought those terms altogether just, and promised to use his influence with the queen to have them agreed upon as the basis of

* Moryson.   † Camden; Moryson.

a peace. For the present the conference ended in the parties agreeing to a six weeks' truce, each retaining a right to begin hostilities again, upon giving notice to the other fourteen days before.*

This notable truce had scarcely been concluded until Essex, taking violently to heart a severe rebuke contained in a letter from the queen, and fuming like a peevish child, suddenly, in the month of September, threw up his Irish command, left all powers of government in the hands of Archbishop Loftus and Sir George Carew—hurried to London, attended by his creature Harington and some others, and flung himself at the feet of her majesty—a place better suited to him than an Ulster hill-side, with dark woods around him, and the Bloody Hand of O'Neill beckoning him onward. How he was received at Greenwich; how the virago queen ordered him into instant arrest; how she stormed and swore at his presumption in daring to quit his post in Ireland without leave asked, what treasons were alleged against him, and how it fared with him thereafter;—all this belongs to English history, not to Irish. Yet one reads with pleasure how the queen spurned from her presence the foolish knight Harington as he kneeled at her feet and sought to excuse his unfortunate master :—" She catched at my girdle when I kneeled to her," says Harington, " and

* For this conference, see Camden, Moryson. It was one of the treasons afterwards charged against Essex that he had entertained these proposals, and engaged to support them.

swore, 'By God's Son I am no Queen: that man
is above me.'" Then she demanded of Harington
a journal which he had been ordered to keep of
the transactions in Ireland; and on reading the
record of disgrace, said fiercely, "By God's Son
ye are all idle knaves and the Lord Deputy
worse"*—in which sentiment of her majesty there
are few that will not probably concur.

But to return to Ireland: Hugh O'Neill had
not been idle. He had renewed his intercourse with Spain; and King Philip the Second
having died in this very month of September, his
successor, who appears to have been impressed
with a higher idea of the importance of the religious war in Ireland, instantly despatched two
envoys to O'Neill—Don Martin de la Cerda, and
Mattheo of Oviedo, the latter of whom was an
ecclesiastic and appointed by the pope to the
archbishopric of Dublin. They brought to Ireland papal indulgences for those who should fight
against English heresy; and presented O'Neill
with a "phœnix plume," blessed by his holiness,
and, what was more useful, with 22,000 pieces of
gold.†

The six-weeks' truce made with Essex had
expired: and O'Neill sent warning to the queen's
council that in fourteen days he would take the
field again. In the mean time he marched through
the centre of the island, at the head of his troops,
to the South;—a kind of royal progress, which

* Harington's *Nugæ Antiquæ*, cited by Lingard
† O'Sullivan; Moryson.

he thought fit to call a pilgrimage to Holy Cross:
for he was aware that religion was the bond of
union amongst his adherents in Munster, and accordingly appeared there, not in his character of
a Celtic chieftain, but rather as the pope's champion and leader of the Catholic cause.   He held
princely state at Holy Cross, concerted measures
with the Southern lords, and distributed a mani-
festo, announcing himself as the accredited Defender of the Faith.   Those chiefs whom he
found zealous in the cause he strengthened and
encouraged : "from such as he held doubtful,"
says Stafford,* " he took pledges, or detained
them prisoners ;" put in irons the White Knight
and his son-in-law, Donogh Mac Cormac Carty,
whom he found trafficking with the enemy ; dis-
placed Donal Mac Carthy from the chieftaincy
of Clan-Carrha, and advanced to that dignity Florence Mac Carthy, who was more devoted to the
good cause.   Those who still held back from the
national confederacy, and could not be moved by
persuasion, he treated as enemies, wasting their
lands and pursuing them with fire and sword,—
that so they might be brought to a better mind.
One of the most powerful of these refractory
lords was the Viscount Barry. O'Neill therefore
let loose a body of troops upon his country, took
some prisoners, and drove away a spoil of three
thousand cows and four thousand horses ;—and

* Or rather Carew :—author of the Pacata Hibernia.

then, having given him so intelligible a warning, reasoned with him earnestly by letter :*—

"My Lord Barry,—Your impietie to God, crueltie to your soule and bodie, tyrannie and ingratitude both to your followers and country are inexcusable and intolerable. You separated yourselfe from the unitie cf Christ's mysticall bodie, the Catholicke Church. You know the sword of extirpation hangeth over your head as well as ours, if things fall out other wayes than well: you are the cause why all the nobilitie of the South (from the east part unto the west) you being linked unto each one of them, either in affinitie or consanguinitie, are not linked together to shake off the cruell yoake of heresie and tyrannie, with which our soules and bodies are opprest. All those aforesaid, depending of your resolution, and relying to your judgment in this common cause of our religion and countrey; you might forsooth with their helpe, (and the reste that are combyned in this holy action,) not only defende yourselfe from the incursion and invasion of the English, but also (by God's assistance, who miraculously and above all expectation gave good successe to the cause principally undertaken for his glorie, exaltation of religion, next for the restauration of the ruines and preservation of the countrey,) expel them and deliver [them and] us from the most miserable and cruell exaction and subjection, enjoy your religion, safetie of wife and children, life, lands, and goods, which all are in hazard through your folly.—Enter, I beseech you, into the closet of your conscience, and like a wise man weigh seriously the end of your actions, and take advise of those that can instruct you and informe you better than your owne private judgment can leade you unto. Consider and reade with attention and settled mind this discourse I send you; that it may please God to set open your eyes and graunt you a better minde. From the campe this instant, Tuesday, the sixt of March, according to the new computation. I pray you to send me the papers I sent you as soon as your honour shall reade the same.

"O'Neill."

* Pacata Hibernia.

Lord Barry's answer was spirited : he reminded O'Neill, that he, an Anglo-Irish baron, was altogether differently circumstanced with respect to the Queen of England, from the ancient Celtic race ;—which indeed was true :—" for you shall understand," he says, "that I hold my lordships and lands, immediately under God, of her majestie and her most noble progenitors, by corporall service, and of none other, by very ancient tenour ; which service and tenour none may dispense withal but the true possessor of the crowne of England, b .ing now our sovereign lady Queen Elizabeth." He then demands " restitution of his spoyle and prisoners ;—and after," he continues, " unless you be better advised for your loyalty, use your discretions against mee and mine, and spare not if you please, for I doubt not, with the helpe of God and my prince to bee quit with some of you hereafter, though now not able to use resistance. And so wishing you to become true and faithful subjects to God and your prince, I end, at Barry Court, this twenty-sixe of February, 1599"—1600.

It does not appear that O'Neill used any further severity towards Barry or his people in consequence of this obstinacy.

All this time the English forces in Munster lay closely shut up in Cork, and a few other garrisons, not daring to keep the field. Sir Warham Saint Leger and Sir Henry Power were now the queen's commissioners for the government of these southern troops until a new Lord President of Munster should be appointed instead of Sir Thomas Norreys : but while O'Neill was in the South their dominion was bounded by the walls of Cork.

One day, in this same month of February, 1600, "Tyrone with his hell-hounds," as an English historian has it, "being not far from Corke," these two functionaries were riding out to take the air, about a mile from the city, accompanied by some officers and gentlemen and a guard of horsemen. Suddenly they were confronted by Mac Gwire at the head of a patrolling party of O'Neill's cavalry; and, on the instant, Sir Warham discharged a pistol at the chieftain of Fermanagh and wounded him mortally; but Mac Gwire, before he fell, struck Saint Leger so crushing a blow with his truncheon upon the head, that he also fell dead from his horse. Save these two, not a blow was struck on either side.* The English betook themselves to the city, and ventured abroad more cautiously afterwards.

"The intent of O'Neill's journey," as Moryson tells us, "was to set as great combustion as he could in Munster, and so, taking pledges of the rebels, to leave them under the command of one chief head." And now having accomplished his mission there, he turned his face homeward; marched through Ormond,—through Westmeath between Athlone and Mullingar, and arrived in his dominions of Ulster without meeting an enemy; although there was then in Ireland a royal army amounting, after all the havoc made in it during the past year, to 14,422 foot, and 1,231 horse,† well provided with artillery and all military stores.

* Pacata Hibernia.
† Moryson. Before O'Neill's wars we hear of no English force employed in Ireland amounting to more than two or three thousand men.

CHAPTER XIIL

EXPEDITION TO DERRY—TREACHEROUS POLICY OF MOUNTJOY.

A. D. 1600.

WHILST the prince of Ulster was awakening and organizing the South, a new English deputy had arrived in Dublin, a more formidable enemy by far than any whom O'Neill had yet encountered.   Charles Blount, Baron Mountjoy, who was not only an experienced officer, but a nobleman of much learning and taste, a " bookish man," as his secretary describes him,—a powerful theologian and confuter of Papists, arrived in February to take the command in Ireland.   He had strict instructions to establish at once powerful garrisons in Derry and Ballyshannon ;* and to effect this paramount object, additional troops were to be poured into Ireland and placed at the governor's disposal ;—a fleet of transport ships was to be provided.— No toil, or peril, or blood ; no fraud, corruption, or treasure, was to be spared which might become necessary for the reduction of this re-

Camden.

nowned Northern chieftain and his gallant Ulster septs under the sway of England.   Not tnat
the queen of that country had any claim to the
North, or any subjects there, or any just quarrel
with the inhabitants or their chiefs; but English
undertakers lusted after the broad lands of Ulster ;—English divines longed to *undertake* the
rich livings, the fertile carucates, ballyboes, and
plow-lands wherewith Catholic piety had endowed that Northern church.   And besides, an
Irish annalist tells us, " it was great vexation
of mind to the queen and her councils in England and Ireland, that the Kinel Conal, Kinel
Eoghain and all Ulster, besides those chiefs that
were confederated with them, had made so long
and successful a defence against them.   They
also remembered, yea, it secretly preyed like a
consumption upon their hearts, that so many of
their people had been lost and so much of their
money and wealth consumed in carrying on the
Irish war."*   So the preparations of England
were on a larger scale than ever : another desperate effort was determined upon ; and the ablest
·man in the queen's dominions was sent to conduct it.

Mountjoy had not been a week in Ireland when
news reached him that O'Neill was on his march
northward, and intended to pass through Westmeath.   He instantly drew together all his available force and set forth from Dublin to intercept

---

* Cited in the admirable historical sketch of Derry in
the Ordnance Memoir.

him :* but O'Neill had advanced so rapidly that
when Mountjoy arrived in Westmeath the Irish
were already in O'Reilly's country: he did not
follow them into the North, but returned to the
Pale to take counsel with the other English
officers, on the operations of that grand campaign
which was now meditated against every province
of the Island.

In the same ship that carried Mountjoy to Ireland came Sir George Carew, to whom the queen
gave the title of "President of Munster," and
assigned a body of three thousand foot and two
hundred and fifty horse, for serving in that province. About the same time a powerful armament, destined for Lough Foyle, embarked at
Chester and sailed to Carrickfergus bay, where
it was joined by a thousand additional troops
drafted from various garrisons in Ireland. Sir
Henry Docwra was chosen to command it; and
on the 7th of May he set sail from Carrickfergus,
with a fleet of sixty-seven sail, carrying four
thousand infantry and two hundred horse,† besides
the seamen. They took with them, according to
Sir Henry's own account, "a quantitie of deal-
boards and spars of timber, 100 flocke bedds,
with other necessaries to furnish an hospitall
withall; one piece of demy cannon of brass, two
culverins of iron, a master-gunner, two master-
masons, and two master-carpenters, allowed in

---

* Pacata Hib.

† It is an instance of Moryson's uncandid practice of
falsifying numbers, &c., that he officially states Docwra's
cavalry at 100 men; when Sir Henry himself admits he
had twice that number.

pay, with a great number of tooles and other utensils, and with all victuall and munition requisite."* On the 14th this strong force entered Lough Foyle.

During those same days that Docwra's fleet was coasting round the headlands of Antrim, Lord Mountjoy with another army was marching northwards in order to draw away the attention of O'Neill and O'Donnell from the Foyle. On Whit-Sunday morning he passed the Moyry, and by the 16th of May had occupied the country around Newry. On the 17th Lord Southampton and Sir Oliver Lambert were to form a junction with him; and Mountjoy sent Captain Edward Blaney with five hundred foot and fifty horse to secure their passage through the dreaded Moyry defile, where O'Neill had often before turned back the tide of invasion. O'Neill was in the neighbourhood watching all these movements at the head of fourteen hundred men. Blaney was suffered to pass unmolested towards Dundalk; and then the Irish took up a position at the " four-mile-water," where there was a ford all environed by woods in the very middle of the pass. The English soon appeared, with Southampton, Lambert and Blaney, commanding a force much greater than O'Neill's. The Irish however fought every foot of ground, and, though finally forced back, retired in good order and with but little loss.†

---

* " A narration of the services of the army ymployed to Lough Foyle under the leading of me Sir H. Docwra, Knight."
† Moryson.

v

Mountjoy received his reinforcements; but as the troops of O'Neill and O'Donnell were now collecting in great force, and occupied every pass and position north of Newry; and as he calculated that Docwra had by this time effected his landing in the North, the deputy hastily withdrew his army towards the Pale, without having penetrated even so far as Armagh. He stationed however strong detachments in garrison at Newry, Carlingford, and Dundalk.

On the day of the fight at Moyry Pass, Docwra's fleet was lying at Culmore, where the river Foyle expands itself into the broad "lake of Feval, the son of Lodan." The troops disembarked and began to build a fort there;* while the O'Doghertys of Inishowen and O'Cahans of Arachty, though fully able to repel any invasion, such as had ever been attempted before, were totally unprepared for so vast an armament as this, and looked on in astonishment. Most of the available forces were beyond Armagh, with O'Neill and O'Donnell; and no resistance was offered to the enemy until they had finished their fort, landed their whole army, taken Aileach, a castle of O'Dogherty's, and finally made themselves masters of the hill of Derry, which Docwra describes as "a place in manner of an iland, comprehending within it forty acres of ground, wherein were the ruines of an old abbay, of a bishopp's house, of two churches, and at one of the ends of it an old castle, the river called Lough Foyle, encompassing it all on one side,

* Docwra's "Narration."

and a bogg most commonlie wett, and not easilie passable, except in two or three places, dividing it from the maine land." These ruins were the remains of Randolph's fortification, and of the churches he had turned into castles, and which had never been repaired since his men were driven from that post in Shane O'Neill's time.

Docwra began with energy to fortify the hill, and lay out a town there. He sent ships along the shores of Lough Foyle, to pull down all houses near the beach, and bring away the timber for building; and as there was a fine wood, containing abundance of old birch trees, lying on the other side of the river, in O'Cahan's country, he sent daily parties of woodcutters, with a guard of soldiers, to hew it down, and "there was not," he says, "a stick of it brought home but was first well fought for."*

When Mountjoy had withdrawn to Dublin, O'Neill and O'Donnell, hearing of this new enemy on the Foyle, once more turned their faces northward, and suddenly appeared with five thousand men before Derry, hoping to take it by surprise. They attacked a party of horsemen whom they found early in the morning, patrolling outside the entrenchments, drove them in to the foot sentinels, and "made a countenance," says Docwra, "as if they came to make but that one day's work of it; but, the alarum taken, and our men in arms, they contented themselves to attempte no further; but seeking to draw us forth into the country, where they hoped to take us at

* Docwra's "Narration."

some advantages ; and finding we stood upon **the** defensive onlie, after the greatest parte of **the** day spent in scrimish, a little without our campe, they departed towards the evening, whither did wee think it not fitt to pursue them."

Docwra's instructions were, so soon as he should have established himself in Derry, to detach one thousand foot and fifty horse, and send them by sea to Ballyshannon, under Sir Matthew Morgan, to effect another landing there ; but he very soon found that it would need all the force he had to hold his ground in Derry. Morgan's expedition was therefore deferred : and although Docwra had, between soldiers and seamen, a larger force than the whole Irish army of Ulster, yet the garrison of Derry for several months attempted no military operations in the country : they found they must "sitt it out all winter:" and besides, Docwra says, " the country was yet unknown to us ; and those we had to deal with were such as I am sure would chuse or refuse to feight with us as they saw their own advantage."

But it was not on battle-field that the main part of the new Deputy's work was to be done. Elizabeth's government had now fully adopted that policy which is contained in the two memorable precepts of Bacon : to weaken the Irish by disunion—and to cheat them by a temporary indulgence of their worship. A relaxation of the penal code would at once, it was hoped, detach the Anglo-Irish race from O'Neill's standard, and even break the strongest bond of union amongst **the** old Irish tribes themselves ; and with that

view, Lord Essex had already begun to discourage prosecutions in the High Commission Court,
had connived at the illegal celebration of mass,
and set at liberty several priests then imprisoned
for religion.* Mountjoy also, from the day of
his coming over, acted with similar forbearance ;
and we find, passing between this deputy and
Queen Elizabeth's council, a correspondence displaying all the liberality, all the tenderness, for
Irish Catholics, that a British minister has never
failed to assume, when a storm of Irish wrath
was to be weathered, or the hope of Irish nationhood to be crushed. "Whereas," says the Deputy, "it hath pleased your lordships in your last
letters to command us to deal moderately in the
great matter of religion, I had, before the receipt
of your lordship's letters, presumed to advise
such as dealt in it, for a time, to hold a more restrained hand therein." And again : " We should
be advised how we do punish in their bodies or
goods any such for religion as do profess to be
faithful subjects to her Majesty, and against
whom the contrary cannot be proved."† Thus
the act of Uniformity being for a time suspended,
all the Irish, even in the cities, where they had
been compelled by pains and penalties to attend
upon the Queen's clergy, (for they were *all* Catholics still,) immediately abandoned the reformed churches, and set the churchwardens at
defiance.‡

* Mac Geognegan.   † Moryson.
‡ "They be all Papists by profession."—*Spenser*.
The zealous reformers of that day treated the govern-

This policy, however, could hardly operate in the North, where the war was national, not religious; and where Reformation and persecution were still unknown. For the North, therefore, another artifice was used: the ambition of certain members of ruling families was excited by secret offers of English support, if they would

ment policy of temporising with what they called "idolatry" much as a similar policy has been received by the corresponding class in later times. The illustrious James Ussher was leader of that extreme section; and "his spirit," in the words of Dr. Mant, "was strongly stirred within him by this new condition of things." "He availed himself," continues the bishop, "of a special solemnity, when it was in his course to preach before the government at Christ Church, for delivering a remarkable sermon, in which he plainly expressed his sense of the recent proceeding: choosing for his text the 6th verse of the 4th chapter of Ezekiel, where the prophet, by lying on his side, was to 'bear the iniquity of the house of Judah forty days: I have appointed thee a day for a year'—a prophecy which he noted to signify the time of forty years to the destruction of Jerusalem, and that nation for their idolatry; and then, making direct application to his own country, in relation to its connivance at Popery, in these impressive words: From this year will I reckon the sin of Ireland, that those whom you now embrace shall be your ruin, and you shall bear their iniquity. This application of the prophecy was made in 1601, and in 1641 broke out that rebellion which was consummated in the massacre of many thousands of its Protestant inhabitants by those whose idolatrous religion was now connived at."

Dr. Mant is a Christian bishop, of eminent piety and profound learning. He has written an able, an erudite, and, as the present writer heartily believes, an honest book, upon the history of Irish Protestantism; yet *this* is the light in which he, for his part, views the war of '641, and the causes that led to it.

revolt against their chiefs. and aspire to the leading of their respective septs; and, accordingly,
in the course of this summer arose three preten-
ders to northern chieftaincies. Niall O'Donnell,
surnamed *Garbh,* "the Rugged," one of the
ablest leaders of Clan-Conal, and whose name
was distinguished in the Thomond expedition,
oasely sold himself to the enemy; and upon pretence of some injustice done him by the O'Donnell, entered into communication with Docwra,
gained over many of the clansmen to his side, revolted against his lawful prince, and received an
English garrison into the castle of Lifford. In
Tyr-owen, Art, the son of Tirlough Lynnogh,
and who probably still held his father's castle of
Strabane, became, by favour of Queen Elizabeth, Sir Arthur O'Neill, and encouraged by the
near neighbourhood of an English army, dared
to claim the chieftaincy of his sept. Both these
traitors became close allies of Sir Henry Docwra,
and by their assistance he was soon enabled to
push his operations somewhat farther up the river.
He built the fort of Dun-na-long, six miles from
Derry, and stationed eight hundred men there;
while the rebellious Irish were wasting and plundering the country of their kinsmen on both sides
of the Foyle. On the southern frontier of Ulster, also, Connor Roe MacGwire, having been
in like manner tampered with by the Deputy,
took arms against his country in the character of
" Queen's MacGwire."

It is plain that these revolted Irish did not aid
the Queen's forces from any servile " loyalty" to
a foreign princess; but rather accepted the prof-

fered aid of Docwra and Mountjoy, to further, as they fondly imagined, their own schemes of weak ambition.* They were treated by those officers, *for the present*, as allies and independent Irish chiefs—were addressed by them, for a time, as *the O'Neill* and *the O'Donnell*,† and afterwards fared as we shall see.

In Munster, Sir George Carew was at this time shut up in Cork, as Docwra was in Derry; and wrote to the council in Dublin that he could for the present do nothing in the field, with his three or four thousand men. " Yet," says his secretary, " relying upon the justnesse of the warre, more than upon the number of his forces, he resolved to try the uttermost of his witt and cunning, without committing the matter to the hazard of fortune;" and " the President discerning the warre in Mounster to be like a monster with many heads, or a servant that must obey divers masters, did thinke thus : that if the heads themselves might be set at variance t'ey would prove the most fit instruments to ruine one another."‡

The two most powerful leaders of the national army in Munster were James, Earl of Desmond, and Dermot O'Connor, who commanded fourteen hundred *Bonnoghts*, or mercenary troops, con-

---

* Pacata Hib.

† " Eadem *principatus affectatio* incitavit Nellum O'Donnellum, cognomento Asperum, ut adversus O'Donnellum belligerando, Tirconnellæ excidium afferret."— *O'Sullivan*. He pronounces them, as he well may, *worse than heretics*

‡ Pac. Hib.

sisting of northerns and Connaughtmen, as
O'Neill's lieutenant in the south. O'Connor was
married to a Geraldine lady, daughter of the late
Earl Gerald, and sister to the present heir of
that title, who was still a prisoner in the Tower,
while his dignity and estates were usurped by
O'Neill's Desmond. Here were elements of intrigue, incentives and materials for treachery,
which English statesmanship was not long in
turning to account. Carew, " in a very secret
manner, provided and sent a fit agent to sound
the inclination of the Lady Margaret, and, finding her fit to be wrought upon, the conditions
should be propounded—namely, that if her hus-
band would take Desmond prisoner, and deliver
him into the hands of the President, he should
incontinently receive one thousand pounds ster-
ling; and that he should have a company of men
in pay from the Queene, and other conditions of
satisfaction to herself and her brother."*   This

---

* Pac. Hib. Another part of the preparation for this
villanous transaction was a letter written by the President to Desmond, in which he pretends to treat with the
earl for the betrayal of Dermot O'Connor: this letter
was placed in O'Connor's hands; and he was to pretend
that he had intercepted it, and so was obliged, in self
defence, to seize upon his secret enemy. The letter was
as follows: " Sir, your last letters I have received, and
am exceeding glad to see your constant resolution of re-
turne to subjection, and to leave the rebellious courses
wherein you have long persevered. You may rest assured that promises shall bee kept; *and you shall no
sooner bring Dermond O'Connor to me, alive or dead,
and banish his Bownoghs out of the countrie, but you
shall have your demand satisfied,* which I thanke God I
am both able and willing to performe. Beleeve me, you

president's secretary and historian details with much candour, rather indeed as matter of triumph, many other dark machinations of his crafty master; how he suborned one Nugent to assassinate his officer, John Fitzgerald, brother to the earl; how he practised with Florence MacCarthy, and by his means got hold of O'Sullivar More; how showers of English gold, a net-work of English intrigue and perfidy, covered the land, until the leaders of the confederacy in Munster knew not whom to trust, or where they were safe from treason and assassination. Nugent's story

have no better way to recover your desperate estate than by this good service, *which you have proffered;* and therefore I cannot but commend your judgment in choosing the same to redeeme your former faults: and I do the rather beleeve the performance of it by your late action touching Loghguire, wherein your brother and yourself have well merited; and, as I promised, you shall find mee so just as no creature living shall ever know *that either of you did assent to the surrender of it.* All your letters I have received, as also the joint letter from your brother and yourselfe. I pray lose no time, for delays in great actions are subject to many dangers. Now that the Queen's armie is in the field, you may worke your determination with most securitie, being ready to releeve you upon a day's warning. *So praying God to assist you in this meritorious enterprize, I doe leave you to his protection this twentie ninthe of May.* 1600.

There might be some difficulty in believing that the English commanders in Munster resorted to these base tricks, unknown to all honourable warfare; but that the authority for it is Carew himself, writing under the name of his secretary Stafford. He describes the whole plot minutely, and publishes the letter " to manifest the invention."

may serve as an example of this policy of **Carew**, and is told with much coolness by his secretary: " Nugent came to make his submission to the President, and to desire pardon for his faults committed; answer was made, that for so much as his crimes and offences had been extraordinary, he could not hope to be reconciled unto the state, except he would deserve it by extraordinary service, which, saith the President, if you shall perform you may deserve not only pardon for your faults committed heretofore, but also some store of crownes to releeve your wantes hereafter. Hee presently promised not to be wanting in any thing that lay in the power of one man to accomplish, and in private made offer to the president, that if hee might bee well recompensed, hee would ruine within a short space either the Sugan earle, or John Fitzthomas, his brother. And indeed very likely he was both to attempte and perform as much as he spake—to attempte, because he was so valiant and daring, as that he did not feare anything; and to execute, because by reason of his many outrages before committed, the cheefe rebels did repose great confidence in him. The President having contrived a plot for James Fitzthomas, (as is before shewed,*) gave him in charge to undertake John, his brother." Shortly after the secretary continues : " Whilst these things were in handling, Nugent (whose promises to the President before

---

* He alludes to the plot formed with Dermot O'Connor's wife.

we recited) intending no longer to deferre the enterprize, attempted the execution in this sort. The President being past Loughgwire, John Fitzthomas riding forth of the iland towards the fastness of Arloghe, where most of his men remained, with one other called John Coppinger, whom he (Nugent) had acquainted with the enterprise, and, as he thought, made sure to him, he attended this great captaine, and being now passed a certain distance from all companie, permitted John Fitzthomas to ride a little before him, minding, (his backe being turned,) to shoote him through with his pistoll, which for the purpose was well charged with two bullets: the opportunitie offered, the pistoll bent, both heart and hand ready to doe the deed, when Coppinger, at the instant, snatched the pistoll from him, crying treason; wherewith John Fitzthomas, turning himself about, perceived his intent. Nugent, thinking to escape by the goodnesse of his horse, spurred hard: the horse stumbled, and hee taken, and the next day after examination and confession of his intent, hanged. This plot, although it attained not fully the desired successe, yet it proved to be of great consequence; for now was John Fitzthomas possessed with such a jealous suspicion of every one, that he durst not remaine long at Loughgwire, for feare of some other like attempte."

Dermot O'Connor, the traitor who undertook to betray Desmond, succeeded somewhat better He took an opportunity to arrest him and confine him in Castlelishin; but would not give him up to the President until he should first be paid a thousand pounds.* His wife, the Lady Margaret, was to meet Carew at Kilmallock, and receive the money ; but before these pecuniary matters could be fully arranged Desmond was rescued by his kinsmen and Pierce Lacy of the Brough. Carew, however, was not deterred by one failure. "There was no man of account," says his secretary, "in all Mounster whom the President had not oftentimes laboured about the taking of the reputed earl, promising very bountiful and liberal rewards to all, or any such as would draw such a draught, whereby he might be gotten, alive or dead." At last the White Knight, a Geraldine, and kinsman of his own, was fortunate enough to draw the successful draught, delivered up the earl in safety to Carew, and received his thousand pounds.† The unfortunate " Suggawn earl" was confined in Shandon castle for a time, and then forwarded to London, where he died in the Tower.

O'Neill, who was kept fully employed in Ulster by Mountjoy, began to perceive that the national party in the South was fast breaking up. The religious toleration (though *for a time not definite*) by removing the common terror of persecution, had allowed the ancient national animosities to revive ; and the nobles of Anglo-Norman descent were plainly not to be counted upon as faithful to the cause of Irish nationhood.‡   On

---

* Pac. Hib.   † Pac. Hib.
‡ "Of one thing I thinke good to give you particular notice, which is, not to put any confidence in any of

Florence Mac Carthy, whom he had made chief of Clan-Carrha, seems to have been placed O'Neill's greatest reliance :—" Our commendations to you, Mac Carthy More," thus he writes to Florence, " I send shortly unto you according .o our trust of you, that you will doe a stout and hopefull thing against the pagan beast ; and thereupon our armie is to goe into Mounster.   *   *
And since this cause of Mounster was left to you (next under God) let no weakeness or imbecillitie bee found in you; and the time of help is neere you and all the reste.   From Donganon, the sixth of February, 1601.

" O'Neill."

But Mac Carthy More's wife was also trepanned into the English interest. " She refused," says Stafford, " to come to his bed until he had reconciled himself unto her Majestie." This lady was a daughter of the former Earl of Clancarty; and " she knew," she said, "in what manner her father had that earldome from her highnesse ; and though she be not pleased to bestow the same wholly upon her, yet she doubted not to obtain some part thereof; but if neither of these could be gotten, yet was not she minded to goe a begging either unto Ulster, nor into Spaine."* And we soon find this chief trafficking and bargaining with the President, until Carew, having made

* Pac. Hib.

Mounster, of the English nation : for whatsoever they professe or protest unto you, they meane not to deale faithfully with us, but will forsake us in our greatest need." *Letter of Cormac Carty to O'Neill. Pac. Hib.*

use of him so far as he could, at length seized his person, had an accusation of high treason preferred against him, and sent him a prisoner to England, along with the Earl of Desmond.*

Carew having thus "tried the uttermost of his witt and cunning" to set at variance the heads of the southern confederacy, and so to destroy them by each other's means ; and besides, being steadily supported throughout by the Lords Clanrickarde, Thomond, Barry, and other Anglo-Irish families, was soon enabled to overrun all Desmond, and to reduce, by force or treachery, the castles of Askeaton, Glynn, Carrig-a-foyle, Ardart, Liscaghan, Loughgwire, and many others, everywhere driving off the cattle, and burning the houses and corn stacks ; so that by the month of December there was not one castle in all Munster held against the queen ; nor, in the language of Moryson, " any company of ten rebels together."

During the summer of 1600 Mountjoy himself had traversed Leix and O'Fally, with a numerous army, burning the country, until the 23d of August. He had the good fortune to kill O'More, of Leix, in a skirmish, and, after cutting down all

---

* Pac. Hib. Moryson. Carew had strict commands from his government to get Florence into his hands ; " which," he says, " without some temporising could not yet conveniently be performed." He therefore wrote to him to say, that the " state was well persuaded of his loyaltie and innocencie," and requested him earnestly to visit him, that he might have his advice about affairs of state. But all this was in vain until the lady was taken into the plot.

the green corn of the district, returned to Dublin.
His biographer calculates that in this expedition
he destroyed *ten thousand pounds worth of corn ;*
and, at the same time, by the usual contrivances, he detached some Leinster chiefs from
the cause of Ireland, and introduced treachery
and distrust into their councils.

O'Neill and O'Donnell now fully understood
the nature of the contest in which they were to
be engaged with this new Deputy.   Fraud, perfidy, and assassination were to take the place of
open battle ; the chink of gold was to be heard,
instead of clashing steel ; and the swords of these
false Saxons were to be turned into sickles, to
prostrate the unripe grain, and so to war against
women and children as well as fighting men.
But the northern chiefs had still a gallant army
at their backs, and were yet able to keep the
English garrisons imprisoned within their walls
and moats.   They were in daily expectation of
succour from King Philip, and hoped full soon to
cut asunder the meshes of this traitor policy with
their good swords.

CHAPTER XIV.

THE WAR IN ULSTER—THE SPANIARDS AT KIN-
SALE—DEFEAT OF O'NEILL AND O'DONNELL.

A. D. 1600—1601.

THE powerful garrison of Derry, with the forts
of Culmore, Dun-na-long, and Lifford, all in the
hands of the English, and the revolted Niall
Garb O'Donnell, with his adherents, gave abun-
dant employment to the chieftain of Tyr-Connell,
and effectually prevented him from joining
O'Neill, with all the powers of his clan, as he
had formerly been wont to do. Early this year,
having defeated Dockwra, in a severe skirmish
near Derry, and left a part of his force to watch
the motions of that officer, the fiery chief himself suddenly turned his face southward, traversed Connaught rapidly and silently, and once
more swept all Thomond, from Corcomroe to
Loop-head, covering with wreck and ruin the
wide domains of that degenerate Dalcassian who
styled himself Earl of Thomond.* He had
hardly driven off the spoil to Tyrconnell, before
he learned that treachery and corruption were

* O'Sullivan. Pac. Hibernia.

N

doing their work in Inishowen, the northernmost
corner of his territory. The O'Dogherty was
dead, and many of that clan had declared for
Docwra, who was supporting a pretender to the
chieftaincy of Inishowen, in opposition to the
rightful claimant. O'Donnell flew to Inishowen,
but before he could do any thing effectual there
he learned that the revolted Niall Garbh, with
the help of a body of English, had taken possession of the Franciscan monastery of Donegal,
driven out the friars, and fortified the buildings.
Red Hugh instantly marched to Donegal; and
laid siege to the abbey; three months he sat before it; and at last, the buildings having taken
fire by night, the garrison were obliged to fly
from the raging flames and crashing roofs, upon
the swords of their not less furious besiegers.
Hundreds of the English troops and revolted Irish
perished in the fire or the battle, (amongst others,
Conn O'Donnell, brother of Niall Garbh,) and
in the morning Red Hugh found himself master
of the smoking and blackened ruins of that beautiful and illustrious abbey.*

To guard the southern frontier of Ulster was
Hugh O'Neill's own peculiar care, and all the
efforts of the Deputy were bent to penetrate that
frontier by way of Dundalk and Armagh. On
the 15th of September, he encamped at Faughart, three miles north of Dundalk, with an

* This abbey was never repaired; and its rifted walls
and fast-decaying arches, the once-famous library and
cloisters of the *Four Masters*, are now a grey and lonely
ruin, at the head of the lovely bay of Donegal.

army of 2,400 foot and 300 horse,* intending so
soon as the weather would permit, to make a
grand attempt upon the Moyry Pass. O'Neill
had the pass entrenched, fortified with palisades,
and strongly manned,† and was waiting patiently
in the woods for the approach of Mountjoy.   At
last on the 9th of October the English army advanced, and after some severe fighting and heavy
loss on both sides. Mountjoy forced his way
through. He then cut down the woods and
cleared the country all round that difficult pass
and made his way to Newry. His chief object
was to regain Armagh ; and on the 2nd of November he marched from Newry about eight
miles to the north-west ; and then finding the
country that lay between him and Armagh too
difficult and too well guarded by O'Neill, to be
attempted in that season, he determined to build
a fort on the place where he then was, being the
very entrance of the dangerous Moyry Pass, so
as to secure the ground he had won, and effectually open up that way into Ulster for the
English armies.   This work was not effected
without daily alarms from O'Neill's men ; but,
at length the fort was built.   The Deputy called
it Mount Norris, in honour of Sir John Norreys,
his former master in the art of war, left 400 men
under Captain Blaney, to garrison it, and retired to Newry on his way to the Pale.‡
  Before leaving Ulster, Mountjoy solemnly made
proclamation of a great reward for the head of
O'Neill—two thousand pounds to the man who

* Moryson.   † Camden.   ‡ Moryson.

should bring in that "arch-rebel" alive—**one** thousand for his dead body; and then the **De-puty** marched by Fatham and Carlingford **to-**wards Dundalk.   At the "Pass of Carlingford," however, (probably at Glenmore or Riverstown,) O'Neill was upon him again.   A bloody battle ensued.   Mountjoy himself, Sir Henry Danvers, and many other officers were severely wounded,[*] and with heavy loss the English made good their way to Dundalk.   Mountjoy proceeded to Dublin and made no further attempt upon the North that year, the sole achievement of the campaign being the stationing of Blaney's garrison upon the Moyry.   Armagh, Portmore, and all the open country north of Newry were still in the hands of the Irish.

That winter was spent by Mountjoy in vain efforts to crush or capture the gallant Tyrrell, who still held a great part of Meath for O'Neill. The Deputy marched to Trim and Athlone, burning and wasting the country on all sides, and having offered large rewards for Tyrrell's head, returned to Dublin.[†]

The following spring saw the indefatigable Deputy once more at the Moyry.   On the 8th of June, he led his army through the pass, and, having erected some additional works at the "Three-mile-water," proceeded to Newry; then harried Iveagh, the country of Mac Gennis, took Downpatrick, and returned to Newry on the 21st.   A powerful force under Sir Henry Dan-vers, was then detached and sent against Armagh,

---

[*] Moryson.   [†] Ibid.

with orders to take possession of the city, and
abbey, and garrison them for the queen. O'Neill,
however, had all the passes manned, and gave
Danvers such a reception that he was fain to
take shelter behind the works of Mount Norris,
and wait there till the Deputy joined him.[*]
When Mountjoy came up, the English army advanced northward in force; and O'Neill after
some skirmishing in the woods, retired before
the enemy and fell back upon the Blackwater,
resolving to give them battle on the banks
of that illustrious river. Mountjoy, however,
had no intention of penetrating farther for that
time; he contented himself with making a minute survey of the battle-ground of *Beal-an-
atha-buidhe*, where the blood of Sir Henry
Bagnal and many a gallant Englishman had
" manured the reeking sod" three years before;
spent a considerable time, one can hardly tell
with what object,[†] in examining the various positions around that memorable plain, and on the
southern bank of the Blackwater (which the
English, says O'Sullivan, called Black by reason
of their many defeats sustained there,) then di-

---

[*] Moryson.

[†] Unless it were that this "bookish" general desired
to fancy himself a second Germanicus, and to imitate
that leader when he penetrated the woods of north Ger-
many, and discovered the spot where Arminius had destroyed the Varian legions, on the banks of the Elbe.
There were indeed some points of resemblance—" Medic
campi albentia ossa, ut fugerant, ut restiterant, dis-
jecta vel aggerata: adjacebant fragmina telorum, equo-
rumque artus"—"hic cecidisse legatos: illic raptas aqui-
las; primum ubi vulnus Varo adactum," &c.

rected his march upon Armagh, which was abandoned by the Irish on his approach; stationed there 750 foot and 100 horse under Danvers, and returned by Mount Norris to Newry.

Shortly after, Mountjoy advanced again to the Blackwater, made himself master of the dismantled fortress of Portmore, repaired it, and stationed three hundred and fifty men there, under Captain Williams, the ancient defender of that dangerous post. The several garrisons now occupying northern forts (exclusive of Dockwra's large army in the north-west), are thus stated by an English historian. In Newry there were four hundred foot and fifty horse, under Sir Francis Stafford; in Lecale (Down) three hundred foot, under Sir Richard Moryson, brother to the Deputy's secretary and historiographer; Sir Arthur Chichester held Carrickfergus, with eight hundred and fifty foot and one hundred and twenty-five horse; in Mountnorris were six hundred foot and fifty horse, commanded by Sir Samuel Bagnal; eight hundred foot and one hundred and twenty-five horse, under Danvers, garrisoned Armagh; and Williams, with three hundred and fifty men, kept Portmore. These strong parties, entrenched behind their fortifications, abundantly supplied with artillery, ammunition, and provisions, were well able to withstand any attacks of the impetuous, but unskilful and impatient Irish, and occasionally sallying into the country, burned the houses, drove off the cattle, cut down and trampled the corn, cleared passages through the woods, and betook themselves to their strong places again, when threatened by a superior force.

Next to establishing these garrisons, Mountjoy's care was to cut away and clear the woods which encumbered all the passes lying between Newry and the Blackwater, so as to secure a better passage for his troops. In this dangerous service he employed a great part of his army for many days; and on the 24th of August, having strengthened and revictualled the forts of Portmore and Armagh, he once more withdrew towards the Pale.

O'Neill was continually in the field, flying from place to place, cutting off the English working parties in the woods, and bands of their cruel reapers in the corn-fields; often his fierce war-cry scared the builders from their unfinished walls; and often, with rout and havoc, the brigand forayers of England were pursued by his avenging sword home to their very entrenchments.* Yet it must be admitted that English arms and English policy were at length making some way in this northern land. Ten thousand British troops upon the soil of Ulster—numerous garrisons and castles on both the Foyle and Blackwater—the sleepless energy, masterly dispositions, and hateful policy of Lord Mountjoy, had indeed begun to tell; and darkness once more seemed to brood over the cause of old Ireland. Still, the cause could not seem hopeless to the Ulster chieftains. The Spaniard, they trusted, was even then off Cape Clear; or if no help from King Philip, the ancient standard of the Bloody Hand still floated free over the hills of Tyr-owen; the proud river-frontier of the Blackwater was still inviolate.

Spanish negotiators had been with O'Neill and O'Donnell for some months. Matthew of Oviedo, the Archbishop of Dublin, made a visit to the North to confer with the chiefs, and afterwards set sail for Spain to hasten the embarkation; and it was now well known both to friend and foe that a powerful armament had been prepared in the ports of Spain, and was under orders for Ireland. In August came a letter from Sir Robert Cecil, the English Secretary of State, to Sir George Carew, apprising him "that certaine pinnaces of her Majestie's had met with a fleete of Spaniards, to the number of fiftie sale, whereof seventeene were men of warre, the rest transporting ships:" they had been descried at the Scilly islands, "and could not bee," said Sir Robert, "but for Ireland."*

On the twenty-third day of September, Lord Mountjoy and the President Carew were sitting in council in Kilkenny, with the Earl of Ormond, Sir Richard Wingfield, Marshal of the Queen's army, and Sir Robert Gardiner, the Chief Justice, "advising what course should be taken if the Spaniards should lande." Suddenly a letter arrived from Sir Charles Wilmot, then

* Pac. Hib.

commanding in Cork, to announce that a fleet
had been seen off the harbour of Cork; and
again, before their council broke up, another
hasty messenger from Wilmot brought news that
the Spaniards were at anchor in the harbour of
Kinsale. Instantly couriers were despatched by
Lord Mountjoy through Leinster and the North,
to draw together most of the troops scattered in
various garrisons, and concentrate the whole
English force upon Munster. Letters were sent
to Sir Charles Wilmot with instructions, and
despatches to England with urgent demand of
new reinforcements.

The Spanish fleet when it weighed anchor
from the Tagus mouth, consisted of forty five small
vessels, carrying about six thousand men. Of
their ships, only seventeen carried guns; eleven
of these were small, and only six of the class
called Galleons, the St. Paul, the St. Peter, the
St. Andrew, and three others whose names are
not given. The troop-ships were mostly of one
hundred and one hundred and fifty tons burthen;
and fifteen hundred Biscayan sailors manned the
whole fleet.* Even this force was much shattered
and diminished by a storm, which drove a squa-
dron of their ships ashore at Coruña; and by the
time they landed in Kinsale, there were but three
thousand four hundred soldiers, and many of
these *Besognies* who had never handled arms;†

---

* These particulars are contained in an official statement, sent by Sir Robert Cecil's correspondent in Lis-
bon, and transmitted by Cecil to the Lord President.—
Pac. Hib.

† Pac. Hib.

so that on the whole, it was a much smaller armament than O'Neill had reason to expect, inferior both in numbers and strength even to Sir Henry Dockwra's fleet and army in Lough Foyle, and wholly inadequate to the important service it was destined for.

What was even worse than this, Don Juan D'Aguila, the general to whom Philip had entrusted the command, seems to have been unequal to such an enterprize. He had commanded a Spanish force in Bretagne in 1594, and is charged with having tamely allowed the French and English to capture Morlaix and Quimper, without an effort to relieve them ; and at Crodon, a fort which defended the mouth of Brest harbour, after exposing a brave garrison to destruction through his incompetence and cowardice, he yielded that most important position which he had ample means to defend ;*—a mournful omen for unhappy Ireland.

Immediately on disembarking, Don Juan sent messengers to the two northern princes advising

---

* Matthew O'Conor (*Military Memoirs of the Irish Nation*) gives this story at length, out of Davila. He also censures Don Juan severely for landing in Munster, instead of making for some northern or western port ; but this charge is not well founded. It was evidently with the concurrence of O'Neill and O'Donnell that a southern port was selected. The Irish chiefs were probably themselves deceived as to the strength of their party in the south, and the faithfulness of their allies. O'Neill relied much upon the Clan Carrha and Florence Mac Carthy, and could hardly anticipate that so powerful a confederacy would be dissolved so soon by mere fraud, treachery, and bribery, without a blow struck.

them of his arrival, and requesting them to come
and join him without delay; and in the mean
time the Spaniards marched into Kinsale with
five and twenty colours flying; the English garrison retired to Cork; and the sovereign of the
town threw open the gates, went to meet the
strangers, and proceeded to billet them; " more
ready" says Stafford, " than if they had been the
queene's forces."   To set the town's people at
ease, Don Juan issued the following proclamation.   " WEE Don Juan De Aguila, Generall of
the Armie to Philip king of Spaine, by these
presents doe promise that all the inhabitants of
the towne of Kinsale shall receive no injury by
any of our retinew, but rather shall be used as
our brethren and friends, and that it shall be lawful for any ol the inhabitants that list to transport, without any molestation in body or goods,
and as much as shall remain, likewise without any
hurt.   Signed Don Juan De Aguila."* He then
took possession of the forts which protected the
entrance of Kinsale harbour, called Rincorran,†
and Castle-ne-parke; fortified and garrisoned
them, and expected to be immediately joined in
great force by the Irish of all the surrounding
country.

But national feeling had nearly gone out of
Munster.   All the Anglo-Irish lords, and most
of the ancient Irish had made their submission
to the President: the chiefs and leaders were

* Pac. Hib.
† A *scythe blade.* It was built on a tongue of land
resembling a scythe in shape.

either corrupted by English gold, or intimidated, or disgusted by the treachery of their allies, or imprisoned in the dungeons of London. In truth, O'Neill's noble effort to make a nation out of the miserable materials which Munster afforded him to work with, was a total failure. National honour, religious zeal, even thirst for vengeance, was dead amongst them:—one is forced to believe that these southern Irish, " were pigeon-livered, and lacked gall, to make oppression bitter;" the chivalrous Spaniards began to conceive a boundless contempt for them;— they thought, for their parts, that " Christ had never died" for such a people as this.

Of all the Munster Irish, only O'Sullivan Beare, O'Connor Kerry, and O'Driscol, declared openly for Ireland and King Philip; Carew and Mountjoy were marching upon Kinsale, with all their forces: three thousand one hundred fresh troops arrived from England; a fleet of ten ships of war. under admiral Sir Richard Leviston, appeared upon the coast, and disembarked two thousand more at Cork; all the towns of Munster, when called upon by Carew, contributed with alacrity their quotas to the queen's forces.* the earls of Thomond, and Clanrickarde, with their numerous Irish following, lifted their ban-

---

* Dr. Curry, strangely enough, notes this circumstance as a *merit* in the Irish towns. He says, " It is worthy of notice that all the cities and towns in the kingdom. though chiefly inhabited by the Catholic natives, continued *loyal to the queen* during this war."— *Review of the Civil Wars.* Nearly two-thirds of Mountjoy's army consisted of Irishmen.

ners on the same side; and in the month of
November, the Deputy and President sat down
before Kinsale, commanding a mixed English and
Irish army, fifteen thousand strong.

News of the Spanish landing soon reached
Ulster; and suddenly, with one consent all military operations were suspended on both sides;—
siege and foray, fortifying and ambuscading, all
stood still; every eye turned to Munster; every
nerve was braced for the trial of this mighty
issue at Kinsale. Don Juan's messengers found
Red Hugh O'Donnell besieging his own noble
castle of Donegal, which had been in his absence,
surprized by the "queen's O'Donnell," Niall
Garbh, and his Saxon allies. Without one
hour's delay, he arose with all his clan, left the
castle to its fate for that time and marched into
Connaught. At Ballymote he halted, and summoned all his tributaries and adherents to attend
him there, and range themselves under the standard of Tyrconnell. From Inishowen and Kilmacrenan,—from Breffni and Sligo, Hy Fiachra,
Hy Maine and Coolavin, the clans came trooping;
—O'Ruarcs and Mac Swynes, O'Dogherty's,
O'Boyles, Mac Donoughs, Mac Dermots, O'Connors, O'Kellys, and many another warlike north-
western tribe; and on the second of November,
he set forth for Munster at the head of two thousand five hundred men.

O'Neill instantly drew off his forces from the
petty skirmishing upon the Blackwater; sent to
Antrim for the Mac Donnells, to Down for Mac
Gennis and Mac Artane, and was speedily on his
march southward with between three and four

thousand troops. O'Donnell and he were to have
met at Holy-Cross in Ormond; and the army of
Tyrconnell being first at the rendezvous, encamped in a place where they were protected on
all sides by woods and bogs.* The Deputy now
detached Carew with a strong force against
O'Donnell, hoping to engage him before O'Neill
should come up. Red Hugh was not prepared
to give battle; and he soon found that he must
either retreat northwards again and abandon the
Spaniards, or make a forced march over the
mountains of Slieve Felim, which lay between
him and Limerick. There had lately been heavy
rains; and the mountains were so wet and boggy,
that no horses or carriages could pass. The President and his army lay at Cashel, and thought
they had effectually checked O'Donnell's advance; when, one night, a sharp frost occurred,
which he knew would harden the surface of
the earth and make the mountains passable for
a time. So soon as darkness came on, the whole
Irish army suddenly arose, traversed the rugged
country all that night, and by day-break were
more than twenty miles from Holy Cross. Carew made great exertions to intercept him before he should reach Kinsale; but in vain. He
seems to have been amazed at the expedition of
" this light-footed generall;" and computes that
one day's march from O'Magher's country to
Crome," at above two and thirty Irish miles,
" the greatest march, with carriage," he says,

---

* " A strong fastnesse of bogg and wood, which was
on every quarter plashed."—*Pac. Hib.*

" that hath been heard of."* O'Donnell then made a circuit to the westward, marched through Muskerry, to stir up the southern clans, and arrived at Castlehaven in time to form a junction with seven hundred Spaniards, who had arrived in that port and were destined to reinforce D'Aguila in Kinsale.†

Many of the Irish of West Munster who had been hitherto inactive, when they saw the northern forces, and heard of the new landing of Spaniards, at length bestirred themselves. Donogh O'Driscol at once received a Spanish garrison into his castle of Castlehaven which commanded that harbour ; Sir Finnan O'Driscol admitted a hundred and twenty Spaniards into his castles of Donneshed at Baltimore, and Donnelong on Inisherkan island, which between them completely defended the harbour of Baltimore ; and Donal O'Sullivan received two hundred Spanish auxiliaries under his command, declared for Ireland and King Philip, and manned and strengthened his castle of Dun-buidhe situated on Beare-haven.

In the mean time Lord Mountjoy and Carew were vigorously pressing the siege of Kinsale. Cannon were planted against the castle of Rincorran ; and after an obstinate defence, it was at

* Pac. Hib.

† The transport ships which had carried this reinforcement were attacked by the English fleet, under Leviston. in the harbour of Castlehaven, and after a sharp fight, some of them were taken or sunk. But the Spanish batteries from the shore handled the English ships so roughly that the admiral's own ship was riddled " through hulke, maste, and tackle," and returned much shattered to Kinsale.—*Pac. Hib.*

length yielded, and its garrison taken prisoners and sent to Cork. When the royal fleet arrived under Admiral Leviston, they began to batter Castle-ne-parke from their ships; but at first without success. A few days after, however, this out-work was also taken, its defenders having rendered it up on promise of their lives : and then Don Juan was confined entirely to the walls of Kinsale. It was resolved by the English commanders in a council of war not to attempt making a breach until they should first have destroyed the houses in the town by bombardment ; and with this view the trenches were drawn closer; cannon were placed in various positions near the walls, and a tremendous fire kept up for several days. A trumpeter was then sent to summon the place to surrender, who was not suffered to enter the town, but received his answer at the gate :— " Don Juan held that town, first for Christ, and then for the King of Spain, and so would defend it against all their enemies." Once more the English artillery thundered upon the walls. Several desperate sorties were made by the Spaniards, and many men were killed on both sides. The English pressed the siege with greater vigour than ever, because they had intelligence that O'Neill and O'Donnell had at length formed a junction, and were approaching Kinsale from the north-eastern quarter upon the left bank of Bandon river, and on the 19th of December the vanguard of O'Neill's army, were seen upon a hill about a mile distant from Mountjoy's camp.

By desperate exertions O'Neill had collected nearly four thousand men. had fought his way through West Meath, and, joined by the indefatigable Tyrrell, had traversed Leinster and Ormond by forced marches. At Bandon he met with O'Donnell and the Spaniards who had landed in Castlehaven; and now at length he found himself on the scene of action, and beheld the beleagured town of Kinsale, and the powerful fleet and army which invested it by sea and land. On the 21st O'Neill so disposed the Irish forces as to cut off all communication between Mountjoy and that part of the country from whence he was accustomed to receive his supplies. The whole force under O'Neill and O'Donnell amounted to no more than six thousand foot and five hundred horse,* and with so small an army O'Neill had no intention of immediately risking a general engagement. The English army was fast weakening by sickness and desertion: the soldiers of Irish race were leaving Mountjoy's ranks by troops; the Spaniards were still strong in Kinsale; and he hoped that the severity of the season, aided by privation and continual skirmishing would soon so waste and wear down the enemy that he might choose his own time for falling upon them and finishing their ruin. O'Donnell, indeed, with his usual impetuosity, burned to let loose the Clan-Conal upon Mountjoy's camp; but yielding to his more experienced ally he restrained himself and acquiesced in the more cautious policy.

"Our artillery," says Stafford, "still played upon the towne (as it had done all that while)

* Pac Hib

that they might see wee went on with our busi-
nesse as if wee cared not for Tyrone's comming :
but it was withall carried on in such a fashion as
we had no meaning to make a breach, because
we thought it not fit to offer to enter, and so put
all in a hazard untill we might better discover
what Tyrone meant to doe, whose strength was
assured to bee very great; and we found by letters of Don John's (which wee had newly intercepted) that hee had advised Tyrone to sett upon
our campes, telling him that it could not bee
chosen, but our men were much decayed by the
winter's siege, and so that wee could hardly bee
able to maintain so much ground (as wee had
taken) when our strength was greater, if wee
were well put to, on the one side by them, and
on the other side by him, which hee would not
faile for his parte to doe soundly."*

Such was indeed Don Juan's counsel; but
O'Neill was resolved to let Kinsale and the Spaniards bear the brunt of the siege a little longer ;
to rest and refresh his troops after their severe
marching ; and to persist in his policy of besieging the besiegers in their own entrenchments.
until circumstances should arise to make a change
of plan advisable.†

The Irish, however, had been but three days
before Kinsale, when an accident brought on a
general engagement, before there was time to
concert measures with the Spaniards in the town.
It is far from being clearly explained how this
battle of Kinsale came to be fought, without pre-

* Pac. Hib.   † Moryson.

meditation as it seems on the part of the commanders on either side :* but, before dawn in the morning of the 24th, Sir Richard Graham, who commanded that night the guard of horse, sent word to the Deputy that the scouts had discovered the matches of the Irish† flashing in great numbers through the darkness, and that O'Neill must be approaching the camp in force. Instantly the troops were called to arms: messengers were dispatched to the Earl of Thomond's quarter with orders to draw out his men. The Deputy now advanced to meet the Irish whom he supposed to be stealing upon his camp: and seems to have effectually surprised them, while endeavouring to prevent a surprise upon himself. The infantry of O'Neill's army retired slowly about a mile farther from the town, and made a stand on the banks of a ford where their position

* The author of the *Pacata Hibernia* says that Brian Mac Hugh Oge Mac Mahon, one of O'Neill's trusted officers, entered into communication with Carew on the previous day; that he cautioned him to be on his guard the following night; for that it had been determined in the Irish council of war, where he was present, that on the next night, shortly before day-break, a simultaneous attack should be made upon the English camp by the Spaniards in front, and by the Irish army in the rere; that this Mac Mahon was induced to give the information because his son had once been brought up in Carew's family as a page; and that the attack was made, or about to be made, in strict accordance with the warning. But in fact the Spaniards did not sally from the walls at all during the battle, and hardly seem to have been aware of it until all was over, which could not have been the case if it had been brought on by previous concert.

† The fire-arms of that period were matchlocks.

was strengthened by a bog in flank. Wingfield, the Marshal, thought he saw some confusion in their ranks, and entreated the Deputy that he might be allowed to charge. The Earl of Clanrickarde joined the Marshal, and the battle became general; but O'Neill's cavalry repeatedly drove back both Wingfield and Clanrickarde, until Sir Henry Danvers, with Captains Taaffe and Fleming came up to their assistance; when at length the Irish infantry fell into confusion and fled. Another body of them, commanded by Tyrrell was still unbroken, and long maintained its ground upon a hill; but at length seeing their comrades routed, they also gave way and retreated in good order after their main body. The northern cavalry covered the retreat; and O'Neill and O'Donnell, by amazing personal exertions, succeeded in preserving order and preventing it from becoming a total rout.

The Spaniards who had joined O'Donnell at Castlehaven, refused to leave the ground, and were nearly all cut to pieces; their commander, Del Campo, was taken prisoner with two of his officers, and about forty soldiers: but the Irish troops although to them no quarter was given,* retired with comparatively little loss. According to Carew's statement there were, of the Irish army, twelve hundred killed and eight hundred wounded;

---

* The most merciless of all Mountjoy's army that day was the Anglo-Irish and Catholic Earl of Clanrickarde. He slew twenty of the Irish with his own hand, and cried aloud to spare no "rebels." Carew says that "no man did bloody his sword more than his lordship that day." *Pac. Hib.*

and of his own, but six or seven persons in all; a disparity which in itself proves that O'Neill's troops were taken by surprise and had not intended to fight that day. But it avails little to plead surprise in excuse for a lost battle:—the battle *was* lost: the Irish camp was in the hands of the enemy: their plans were completely deranged, and most of their colours, arms, and baggage captured. It was now the depth of winter, and too late to prepare for a new campaign that year: and O'Neill was reluctantly compelled to order a retreat to the North, leaving Kinsale and Don Juan to their fate.

On the last day of December Don Juan sent Mountjoy proposals for a capitulation;[*] obtained honourable terms; agreed to surrender all the castles upon the coast into which Spanish garrisons had been admitted, and shortly after set sail for Spain; carrying with him all his artillery, treasure and military stores.

O'Neill and the remainder of his army set out on their homeward march; but Red Hugh

---

[*] In his negotiations with Mountjoy Don Juan affects to speak most contemptuously of O'Neill and O'Donnell, and the whole Irish nation; but if he had better known the country, he would have been aware that the exertions of the northern chiefs to relieve him, when shut up in Kinsale, at such a distance from Ulster, were almost superhuman. Besides, he ought to have remembered the terms of the requisition upon which the Spaniards came to Ireland—"*If the aides were sent to Ulster, then Tyrone required but fower or five thousand men: if the king did purpose to send an army into Mounster, then he should send strongly, because neither Tyrone nor O'Donnell could come to help them.*"—*Pac Hib.* p. 456.

O'Donnell, stung to madness by defeat, indignant at the conduct of this most ill-judged enterprise, and impatient of King Philip's dilatory councils and petty expeditions, gave the command of his clan to his brother Roderick; and three days after the battle, flung himself into a Spanish ship at Castlehaven, and, attended by Redmond Burke, Hugh Mostian, and seven other Irish gentlemen, set sail for Spain. He disembarked at Coruña, was received with high distinction, by the Marquis of Caraçena and other nobles, "who evermore gave O'Donnell the right hand; which, within his government," says Carew, "he would not have done to the greatest duke in Spaine." He travelled through Gallicia, and at Santiago de Compostella was royally entertained by the archbishop and citizens; but in bull-fighting, or the stately Alameda, he had small pleasure. With teeth set and heart on fire, the chieftain hurried on, traversed the mountains of Galicia and Leon, and drew not bridle until he reached Zamora, where Philip was then holding his court. With passionate zeal he pleaded his country's cause; entreated that a greater fleet and stronger army might be sent to Ireland without delay, unless his Catholic Majesty desired to see his ancient Milesian kinsman and allies utterly destroyed and trodden into earth by the tyrant Elizabeth; and above all whatever was to be done he prayed it might be done instantly, while O'Neill still held his army on foot, and his banner flying; while it was not yet too late to rescue poor Erin from the deadly fangs of those dogs of England. The king received him affectionately, treated him with high consideration, and actually gave orders for a powerful force to be drawn together at Coruna, for another descent upon Ireland.*.

But that armament never sailed; and poor O'Donnell never saw Ireland more; for news arrived in Spain, a few months after, that Dun-buidhe castle, the last strong-hold in Munster that held out for King Philip, was taken; and Beare-haven, the last harbour in the South that was open to his ships, effectually guarded by the English: and the Spanish preparations were countermanded: and Red Hugh was once more on his journey to the court, to renew his almost hopeless suit; and had arrived at Simancas, two leagues from Valladolid, when he suddenly fell sick; his gallant heart was broken, and he died there, on the 10th of September, 1602. He was buried by order of the king, royal honours, as betitted a prince of the Kinel-Conal; and the stately city of Valladolid, holds the bones of as noble a chief and as stout a warrior as ever bore the wand of chieftaincy, or led a clan to battle.

* Pac. Hib.

CHAPTER XV.

FIRE, FAMINE, AND SLAUGHTER—O'NEILL AT MELLIFONT.

A. D. 1602—1603.

After another severe winter journey, O'Neill gained his own territory ; he knew that he might shortly expect Mountjoy once more at the Black-water ; and employed the interval in disposing his men, so as best to guard the passes of the woods, and preparing for this last fierce struggle ; for he determined to dispute every foot of ground, and to sell life and land dear.

Mountjoy spent that spring in Munster, with the President, reducing those fortresses which still remained in the hands of the Irish, and fiercely crushing down every vestige of the national war. Richard Tyrrell, however, still kept the field ; and O'Sullivan Beare held his strong castle of Dun-buidhe, which he wrested from the Spaniards after Don Juan had stipulated to yield it to the enemy.* This castle commanded Ban-

---

* "Among other places, which were neither yielded nor taken to the end they should be delivered to the English, Don Juan tied himself to deliver my castle and haven, the only key of mine inheritance, whereupon

try Bay, and was one of the most important fortresses in Munster; and therefore Carew determined, at whatever cost, to make himself master of it. Dun-buidhe was but a square tower, with a court-yard and some out-works, and had but 140 men; yet it was so strongly situated, and so bravely defended, that it held the Lord President and an army of four thousand men, with a great train of artillery and some ships of war, fifteen days before its walls. After a breach was made, the storming parties were twice driven back to their lines; and even after the great hall of the castle was carried, the garrison, under their indomitable commander, Mac Geohegan, held their ground in the vaults underneath for a whole day, and at last fairly beat the besiegers out of the hall. The English cannon then played furiously upon the walls; and the president swore to bury these obstinate Irish under the ruins. Again a desperate sortie was made by forty men—they were all slain: eight of them leaped into the sea to save themselves by swimming; but Carew, anticipating this, had stationed Captain Harvey, "with three boats to keepe the sea, who had the killing of them all;" and at last, after Mac Geohegan was mortally wounded, the remnant of the garrison laid down their arms. Mac Geohegan lay. bleeding to death, on the floor of the vault;

the living of many thousand persons doth rest, that live some twenty leagues upon the sea-coast, into the hands of my cruell, cursed, misbelieving enemies."--Letter of Donal O'Sullivan Beare to the King of Spain. *Pac. Hib.*

yet when he saw the besiegers admitted, he raised
himself up, snatched a lighted torch, and stag-
gered to an open powder-barrel—one moment,
and the castle, with all it contained, would have
rushed skyward in a pyramid of flame, when
suddenly an English soldier seized him in his
arms : he was killed on the spot, and all the rest
were shortly after executed.   " The whole number of the ward," says Carew, " consisted of one
hundred and forty-three selected men, being the
best choice of all their forces, of which not one
man escaped, but were either slain, executed, or
buried in the ruins ; and so obstinate a defence hath not been seen within this kingdom."
Perhaps some will think that the survivors of
so brave a band deserved a better fate than
hanging.

But we must leave this ferocious Carew and
his willing assistants, Wilmot and Harvey, to
their terrible vocation.   Space would fail us to
recount what castles they took, what priests they
hanged : how they laid waste the lands, and destroyed the corn, and covered Munster with ashes
and blood, and smoking ruins.*   The war had
once more rolled northward

* O'Sullivan and Tyrrell still kept the field, and made
themselves masters of some castles.   They were encouraged by Owen Mac Egan, the apostolic vicar ; by letters from O'Neill, and the hope of O'Donnell's return
with help from Spain.   But when news came of O'Donnell's death, O'Sullivan, with four hundred men, set out
for the north, intending to take refuge with O'Neill.
They crossed the Shannon in *corraghs*, covered with the
hides of their own horses, fought their way through the
hostile country of Thomond and Clanrickarde, and at

Early in June Lord Mountjoy marched by Dundalk to Armagh, and from thence, without interruption, to the banks of the Blackwater, about five miles to the eastward of Portmore, and nearer to Lough Neagh.* He sent Sir Richard Moryson to the north bank of the river, commenced the building of a bridge at that point, and a castle, which he named Charlemont, from his own Christian name, and stationed a garrison of one hundred and fifty men there, under the command of a certain Captain Toby Caulfield.†

The Deputy then led his whole army across the river, and set out on his march for Dungannon; but long before he reached it he could plainly see both town and castle on fire. O'Neill found himself unable to cope with his enemy in the field; and, as he had once before done, when threatened by Sir John Norreys, burned his castle to the ground, and betook himself to the forests and mountains which occupied the centre of his territory.‡

There is a wide tract of moor and mountain, extending from the Foyle near Strabane, in a south-easterly direction to the shores of Lough Neagh, where it ends in the broad-backed Slieve Gallen. It thus intersects the whole district of ancient Tyr-

length, reduced to thirty-five men, they found shelter it Leitrim castle.

* Moryson.

† The founder of a noble family, which has held that spot from that day to this; but which afterwards (as is usual with settlers in Ireland) became more Irish than many of the Irish themselves.

‡ Moryson.

owen, and covers a large area which is now included in the two modern counties of Tyrone and Londonderry. To this tract, and the eastern part of Arachty lying on the lower Bann, O'Neill was now confined : hard pressed on the west and north-west by Sir Henry Docwra and his own traitor kinsman ; cut off by their chain of posts (which they had lately pushed southward as far as Omagh) from all communication with Tyrconnell ; enclosed on the Antrim side by Sir Arthur Chichester and his powerful forces ; and on the south, blockaded by Mountjoy and his numerous garrisons, and his thrice-accursed Queen's Maguires and Queen's O'Reilly's—he yet maintained himself at Castle Roe ; corresponded with the national chiefs throughout the island, had his agents in Munster and Connaught, held still aloft his noble Red Right Hand, and defied both the arms and the treachery of Elizabeth's crafty deputy. It is now that Mountjoy writes to the Lords of the Council in England, excusing himself for "that notwithstanding her Majesty's great forces, O'Neill doth still live," describing, and even exaggerating the difficulties of the country, and complaining that gold and treachery had not yet been so potent in the North as they had been found in Munster. The proclamations of high reward for O'Neill's head, it seems, had not tempted any of his clansmen or allies to assassinate him, as was expected : and Mountjoy cannot conceal his surprise. "It is most sure" says he, "that never traytor knew better how to keep his own head than this; nor any subjects have a more dreadful

awe to lay violent hands on their sacred prince,
than these people have to touch the person of
their O'Neales;—and he that hath as pestilent
a judgement as ever any had, to nourish and to
spreade his owne infection, hath the ancient
swelling and desire of liberty in a conquered
nation to work upon," &c.*

The deputy finished his fort and bridge of
Charlemont, and even built and garrisoned another on the shores of Lough Neagh, which he
called Mountjoy; and after he had left garrisons
in these he sent another party to take possession
of Augher, so that his posts now communicated
with those of Docwra, and completely encircled
O'Neill, both on the west and south.

He then sent orders to Sir Henry Docwra, Sir
Arthur Chichester, and Sir Richard Moryson,
that they should all be in readiness within twenty
days to penetrate O'Neill's country at once by
different routes ; and in the mean time, upon the
19th of July, he marched westward to Monaghan
and Fermanagh, left some troops there under St.
Lawrence, Esmond, and Conor Roe Mac Gwire,
wasted and burned the country, and returned to
co-operate in the grand combined effort against
central Ulster.

It was high summer; the fertile valleys of
Tyr-owen were waving with green corn, and the
creaghts abounded upon a thousand hills; when the
armies of the stranger were let loose upon that
doomed land; and never, since first a sword was
drawn upon this earth, did such a storm of demo-
niac wrath and unheard of atrocity burst upon a

* See this letter in the Appendix.

nation. Not the heathen Danes in their most frightful excesses ;—not the ferocious Tartar of Ghizni, when he swept over the plains of India like Azräel the Death-angel ;—not the bastard Norman when he fell upon North-Humber-land in his wrath, and left no man or beast alive from Tyne to Humber—ever spread abroad ruin and wreck so unsparing, so systematic, as this viceroy of the queen of England visited upon the ancient territory of the Hy Nial.

Chichester marched from Carrickfergus, and crossed the Bann at Toome : Docwra and his Derry troops advanced by way of Dungiven ; and Mountjoy himself by Dungannon and Killetrough :*—and wide over the pleasant fields of Ulster trooped their bands of ill-omened, red-coated reapers, assiduous in cutting that saddest of all recorded harvests. Morning after morning the sun rose bright and the birds made music, as they are wont to do of a summer's morning " on the fair hills of holy Ireland :"—and forth went the labourers by troops, with their fatal sickles in their hands ; and some cut down the grain, and trampled it into the earth, and left it rotting there ; and some drove away the cattle, and either slaughtered them in herds, leaving their carcases to breed pestilence and death, or drove them for a spoil to the southward ; and some burned the houses and the corn-stacks, and blotted the sun with the smoke of their conflagrations ; and the summer song of birds was drowned by the wail of helpless children and the shrieks of the pitiful women. All this summer

* Morvson.

and autumn the havoc was continued, until from O'Cahan's country, as Mountjoy's secretary describes it, " we have none left to give us opposition, nor of late have seen any but dead carcases merely starved for want of meat."

The Deputy had taken Magherlowny and Ennislaughlin, two principal forts and arsenals of O'Neill's, and now about the end of August he penetrated to Tullogh-oge, the seat of the clan O'Hagan, and broke in pieces that ancient stone chair in which the princes of Ulster had been inaugurated for many a century.* Castle-Roe also soon became untenable ; and O'Neill retiring slowly, like a hunted beast keeping the dogs at bay, retreated to the deep woods and thickets of Glan-con-keane,† the name of that valley through which the Moyola winds its way to Lough Neagh, then the most inaccessible fastness in all Tyr-owen. Here, with six hundred infantry and about sixty horse, he made his last stand, and actually defied the armies of England that whole winter. His western allies were still up in Connaught, and Bryan Mac Art O'Neill in Claneboy—and a favourable reverse of fortune was still possible ; or the Spaniards might still remember him ; and in any event he could ill brook the thought of surrendering.

But the winter's campaign in Connaught was fatal to the cause in that quarter. In the North

* Stuart, the historian of Armagh, says that some ragments of the O'Neill's stone chair used to be shewn upon the glebe of the parish of Desert-creight, county Tyrone.

† *Glann-cin-cein*, the " far head of the glen."

O'Cahan gave in his submission to Docwra, and Chichester and Danvers reduced Bryan Mac Art; so that early in the spring of 1603, O'Neill found that no chief in all Ireland kept the field on his part, except O'Ruare, Mac Gwire, and the faithful Tyrrell. He had heard too of Roderick O'Donnell's submission, and Red Hugh's death, and that no more forces were to be hoped from Spain. Famine also and pestilence, caused by the ravage of the preceding summer, had made cruel havoc among his people. A thousand corpses lay unburied between Toome and Tullogh-oge; three thousand had died of mere starvation in all Tyr-owen; and "no spectacle," says Moryson, "was more frequent in the ditches of towns, and especially of wasted countries, than to see multitudes of the poor people dead, with their mouths all coloured green, by eating nettles, docks, and all things they could rend up above ground." It was this winter that Chichester and Sir Richard Moryson, returning from their expedition against Bryan Mac Art, "saw a horrible spectacle—three children, the eldest not above ten years old, all eating and gnawing with their teeth the entrails of their dead mother, on whose flesh they had fed for twenty days past." Can the human imagination conceive such a ghastly sight as this?—Or picture a winter's morning, in a field near Newry, and some old women making a fire there; "and divers little children driving out the cattle in the cold mornings, and coming thither to warm them, are by them surprised and killed and eaten." Captain

Trevor "and many honest gentlemen lying in the Newry" witnessed this horror—a vision more grim and ghastly than any weird sisters that ever brewed hell-broth upon a blasted heath.

And at last the haughty chieftain learned the bitter lesson of adversity : the very materials of resistance had vanished from the face of the earth. and he humbled his proud heart, and sent proposals of accommodation to Mountjoy. The Deputy received his instructions from London, and sent Sir William Godolphin and Sir Garret Moore as commissioners to arrange with him the terms of peace. The negotiation was hurried, on the Deputy's part, by private information which he had received of the Queen's death, and fearing that O'Neill's views might be altered by that circumstance, he immediately desired the commissioners to close the agreement and invite O'Neill, under safe conduct, to Drogheda, to have it ratified without delay.

On the thirtieth day of March (alas! the day) Hugh O'Neill, now sixty years of age—worn with care and toil and battle, and in bitter grief for the miseries of his faithful clansmen—met the Lord Deputy in peaceful guise at Mellifont, and, on his bended knees before him, tendered his submission ; and the favourable conditions that were granted him, even in this his fallen estate, show what anxiety the councillors of Elizabeth must have felt to disarm the still formidable chief. First he was to have full " pardon" for the past ; next to be restored in blood, notwithstanding his attainder and " outlawry," and **to be reinstated in his dignity of Earl of Tyr-**

P

owen; then he and his people were to enjoy full
and free exercise of their religion; and new
" letters patent" were to issue, re-granting to
him and other northern chiefs the whole lands
occupied by their respective clans, save the
country held by Henry Oge O'Neill and Tur-
lough's territory of the Fews. Out of the land
was also reserved a tract of six hundred acres
upon the Blackwater; half to be assigned to
Mountjoy fort, and half to Charlemont.

On O'Neill's part the conditions were, that he
should once for all renounce the title of " The
O'Neill," and the jurisdiction and state of an
Irish chieftain; that he should, now at length,
sink into an Earl, wear his coronet and golden
chain like a peaceable nobleman, and suffer his
country to become " shire-ground," and admit
the functionaries of English government. He was
also to write to Spain for his son Henry,* who
was residing in the court of King Philip, and
deliver him as a hostage to the King of England.

And so the torch and the sword had rest in
Ulster for a time; and the remnant of its inhabitants, to use the language of Sir John Davies,
" being brayed as it were in a mortar with the
sword, famine, and pestilence together, submitted themselves to the British government, re-

---

* This Henry appears to have been the only son of
O'Neill and his first wife; and he had been living for
some years in the court of King Philip. O'Neill had
four wives in succession—first, a daughter of one of the
O"Tooles, then Hugh O'Donnell's sister, then Sir Henry
Bagnal's sister; and last, a lady of the MacGennis family, of Down.

ceived the laws and magistrates, and gladly embraced the King's pardon." That long bloody war had cost England many millions of treasure,* and the blood of tens of thousands of her veteran soldiers ; and from the face of Ireland it swept nearly one-half of the entire population.

From that day, the distinction of " Pale" and " Irish Country" was at an end ; and the authority of the Kings of England and their Irish parliaments, became, for the first time, paramount over the whole island. The pride of ancient Erin—the haughty struggle of Irish nationhood against foreign institutions, and the detested spirit of English imperialism, for that time, sunk in blood and horror ; but the Irish nation is an undying essence, and that noble struggle paused for a season, only to recommence in other forms and on wider ground—to be renewed, and again renewed, until—— Ah! *quousque, Domine, quousque ?*

* "In the year 1599 the queen spent six hundred thousand pounds in six months on the service of Ireland. Sir Robert Cecil affirmed that in ten years Ireland cost her three millions four hundred thousand pounds."— *Hume.* These were enormous sums at that period.

CHAPTER XVI.

THE CHIEFTAIN BECOMES AN " EARL."—ARTFUL CECIL.—THE END.

A. D. 1603—1616.

It now seemed as if the entire object of that tremendous war had been, on the part of England, to force a coronet upon the unwilling brows of an Irish chieftain, and oblige him in his own despite to accept "letters patent" and broad lands " in fee." Surely, if this were to be the " conquest of Ulster," if the rich vallies of the North, with all their woods and waters, mills and fishings, were to be given up to these O'Neills and O'Donnells, on whose heads a price had so lately been set for traitors ; if, worse than all, their very religion was to be tolerated, and Ulster, with its verdant abbey-lands and livings, and termon-lands, were still to set "Reformation" at defiance; surely, in this case, the crowd of esurient undertakers, lay and clerical, had ground of complaint. It was not for this they left their homes, and felled forests, and camped on the mountains, and plucked down the Red Hand from many a castle wall. Not for this they " preached before the State in Christ-Church," and censured the backsliding of the times, and pointed out the mortal sin of a compromise with Jezebel.

Still a good time was coming for the undertakers of the sword and cassock. Their king was caring for them. For the present, indeed, while any trace of the national confederacy remains, it is necessary to "deale liberally with the Irish lords of countreys,"* and even to tolerate their religion, "for a time not definite;" until the northern Irish "shall be more divided, and can be ruined the more easily."† Causes of offence shall arise—shall be created or pretended—and those lands will assuredly "escheat." Reformation will have its way, and the adventurers be satisfied with the bounties of their king.

Conciliation, however, was now the policy of King James. He was to rule Ireland, not with the iron rod of a conqueror whose title is the sword; but, deducing his pedigree from all the British, Saxon, Danish, and Norman kings of England and Scotland, and condescending even to count kindren with the ancient *Ard-righs* of Ireland, through his ancestors the Albanian Scots, he indicated an intention of governing the Irish with mild paternal sway, as though he loved them. A comprehensive act of oblivion and amnesty was passed and published under the great seal. All former "treasons" (as the proclamation styled a national war against usurpa-

* See Mountjoy's letter, in the Appendix—a most instructive document.
† Ibid.

tion and tyranny) were to be remitted and utterly
extinguished ; and by the same proclamation,
the very " Irishry" were informed that they were
to believe themselves for the future under the
peculiar protection of the crown ; and the king's
kindness, as his majesty's attorney-general informs us, " bred such comfort and security in
the hearts of all men, as thereupon ensued the
calmest and most universal peace that ever was
seen in Ireland."

Lord Mountjoy having thus finished his mission, and, indeed, to give him justice, having
done his errand well, repaired to England, taking
with him Hugh O'Neill and Roderick O'Donnell
to pay their homage, like good subjects, at the
foot of the throne.   Their vessel was overtaken
by a storm and nearly wrecked upon the Skerries,
but at length made the port of Beaumaris, and
the passengers proceeded on horseback to London.
Public feeling towards any distinguished stranger
is more accurately interpreted by the populace,
than amidst the stately observances of king's
courts, and judging by this criterion the name
of O'Neill was more feared than loved in England.   There were thousands of widows, tens of
thousands of orphans, whose parents and whose
husbands' bones strewed many a battle-field in
Ulster, from Clontibret to Bealach-moyre, or
whitened in heaps hard by the fatal Blackwater.
And, as the victor of Beal-an-atha-buidhe rode
on, " no respect to the Lord Deputy," says Moryson, " in whose company he rode up to London,
could contain many women in these parts from
flinging dirt at him with bitter words.   And

when he was to return, he durst not pass by those parts without directions to the sheriffs to convey him with troops of horse, from place to place, till he was safely embarked."

But at court his reception was most gracious. His pardon was confirmed, his letters patent were duly made out, his friend Roderick O'Donnell was created "Earl of Tyrconnell," first of that title; and with every mark of high confidence and honour the two new noblemen were sent home to take possession of their estates. To other chieftains, their former confederates, were also "granted" their own property with larger or smaller reservations in favour of rival claimants. As for Art O'Neill, Tirlough Lynnogh's son, (who would fain have been "The O'Neill" and had accepted English alliance for that end,) he was forced to remain "Sir Arthur," and to confine himself within narrow limits in a corner of the country. And the Rugged Niall Garbh, the Queen's O'Donnell, "had grown so insolent," says Dr. Leland, "that government was well pleased to favour his competitor." He found that his allies were his masters, and that he must yield all his high pretensions in favour of the new Earl Roderick.*

Then the Catholic religion was openly pro-

---

* Poor Nial Garbh fought zealously for his chieftaincy, "and it must be confessed," says Cox, "that he was instrumental in those good successes ; whereupon he grew so insolent as to tell the Governor Docwra to his face that the people of Tyrconnell were his subjects, and that he would punish, exact, cut, and hang them as he pleased."

fessed and its rites celebrated, not only in the
North, (where no other was yet known,) but
even in the cities of Leinster and Munster.
" Popish ecclesiastics," in Dr. Leland's phrase,
" practised with their votaries [that is, said mass
and administered sacraments] without any decent
caution or restraint ;" even monastic buildings
in some quarters arose from their ruins, and the
abbeys of Multifernam in Westmeath ; Kilcon
nell in Galway ; Rossariell in Mayo ; Quin in
Thomond ; and Buttevant, Kilcrea, and Timo-
league in Cork ; were repaired with somewhat
of their ancient splendour and occupied by religious persons as of old ; to the grievous scandal
of Dr. Ussher and all zealous Reformers.

The Earl of Tyrone returned to Dungannon :
and it is painful to follow this un-chieftained
O'Neill into his " county." Sheriffs had at last
appeared there, and made a bailiwick of it : itine-
rant judges went circuit in it ; king's commissioners travelled through it, and cleared the
passes, and surveyed and measured out the land ;
and with the customary policy of a government
which is hostile to the country it assumes to rule,
spies were planted thick around all " suspected"
persons. The haughty O'Neill soon found himself surrounded by an atmosphere of base *espion-
nage.* " Notice is taken," says Attorney-General
Davies, " of every person that is able to do either
good or hurt. It is known not only how they
live and what they do, *but it is foreseen what
they purpose or intend to do :* insomuch as Tyrone hath been heard to complain that he had so
many eyes watching over him—that he could not

drink a full carouse of sack, but the state was ad-
vertised thereof a few hours after." Yet he seems
to have had no thought of again taking up arms.
His wearied people had rest, and cultivated their
lands and practised their religion in peace; and
the grey-haired chief, though with a gloomy brow
and indignant heart, endured his detested earldom in silence, waiting for his best friend Death.

But the pre-arranged system of English government soon began to develope itself. In the
midst of this " most universal peace that ever was
seen in Ireland," the king's councillors suddenly
published in Dublin that " Act of Uniformity,"
the second of Elizabeth,* which strictly prohibited the attendance upon Catholic worship. A
proclamation was also issued on the 4th of July,
1605, whereby his Majesty, " declared to his beloved subjects of Ireland that he would not admit
any such liberty of conscience as they were made
to expect;" and commanded all Catholic clergy
by a certain day to depart the realm.† Again the
spiritual courts of the king's bishops resumed
their functions : the church-wardens were busy ;
the priests had to fly or lurk in secret places ;
and all the terrors of the penal laws were let loose

* It is sufficiently well attested (though not very material for us to remark here) that this act was obtained
in the Pale parliament surreptitiously and fraudulently.
Whether it were so or not the attempting to impose it
upon the ancient Irish, who had no part in enacting it,
and were not even *de facto* subject to that parliament a*
the time, was equally a fraud and an outrage.

† Dr. Mant admits that there was in this proclamation
an "apparent severity," p. 350.

upon the land. Such measures as these had just provoked the Gunpowder Conspiracy in England; and seem to have been intended to drive the Irish to arms, in order, as Mountjoy says, to the " absolute reducement of that country ;" but if that were the object it altogether failed ; and another expedient had to be substituted, as we shall presently see.

A very interesting account is given by Sir John Davies (in a letter to Robert Cecil Earl of Salisbury,) of a progress made by the Lord Deputy Sir Arthur Chichester, into some of the northern counties in 1607. The Lord Chancellor, the Chief Justice, Sir Oliver Lambert, Sir Garret Moore and the Attorney-General (Sir John himself) accompanied Chichester; " and albeit," he says, " we were to pass through the wastest and wildest parts of all the North, yet had we only for our guard six or seven score of foot, and fifty or three score horse, which is an argument of a good time and of a confident Deputy. For in former times, when the state enjoyed the best peace and security no Lord Deputy did ever venture himself into those parts, without an army of eight hundred or a thousand men." They encamped one night on the borders of Farney, " which," says Sir John, " *is the inheritance of the Earl of Essex ;*" then they proceeded to Monaghan, delivered the gaol, and " empanelled a jury to inquire into the state of the church in that county," which found a verdict, " that the churches for the most part are utterly waste; that the king is patron of all; and that their incumbents are Popish priests, instituted by bishops authorized from Rome." It appears, however, that the dioceses of Derry, Raphoe and Clogher had at last been provided with a king's bishop, who was resident in England, and "whose absence," says Davies, " being two years since he had been elected by his Majesty, hath been the chief cause that no course hath been hitherto taken to reduce these poor people *to Christianity*, and therefore *majus peccatum habet.*" Of another bishop, one Draper, Davies says, " there is no divine service or sermon to be heard within either of his dioceses."

From these intimations, it would appear that there was not in the year 1607 a single Protestant in all the North, except the soldiers in garrison ; so that the religious " Reformation" was still unknown there.

The second night after leaving Monaghan they arrived at Lough Erne ; and " we pitched our tents," says Sir John, " over against the island of Devenish, a place being prepared for the holding of our sessions for Fermanagh in the ruins of an abbey there." Thus they proceeded through all Mac Gwire's, O'Reilly's and Mac Mahon's countries, administering justice, and holding a kind of inquisition into both ecclesiastical and civil affairs.

In the latter department also the Deputy found that much remained to be done, before English institutions and government should predominate in the North. As an instance of the tenacity with which the people adhered to their ancient customs, Davies mentions the case of an O'Reilly, " to whom Sir George Carey had given the cus-

tody of the land (Breffni) during the king's pleasure, whereof, he continues, the poor gentleman
hath little benefit, because, not being created
O'Relie by them, they do not suffer him to cut
and exact like an Irish prince."

In concluding his narrative Davies says: "If
my Lord Deputy do finish these beginnings, *and
settle these counties,* as I assure myself he will,
this will prove the most profitable journey for the
service of God and his Majesty, and the general
good of this kingdom that hath been made in the
time of peace by any deputy these many years."

And truly it did appear full time to "settle"
the North. All apprehension of an Irish war
was at an end. The power of the Ulster chieftains was utterly broken; and hungry undertakers were waiting for their prey. English
statesmen had now fully adopted the expedient
of getting up fictitious plots, and fastening them
upon whatever party they designed to ruin: and
on this occasion we find a choice instance of that
policy.

Doctor Jones, the king's bishop of Meath, gives
the generally received account of the matter in
these words:* "Anno 1607, there was a provi-
dential discovery of another rebellion in Ireland,
the Lord Chichester being deputy: the discoverer
not being willing to appear, a letter from him,
not subscribed, was superscribed to Sir William
Usher, clerk of the council, and dropt in the
council-chamber then held in the Castle of Dublin; in which was mentioned a design for seizing

* Curry's *Review.*

the Castle and murdering the Deputy, with a general revolt and dependence on Spanish forces and this also for religion : for particulars whereof," says the bishop, " I refer to that letter dated March the 19th, 1607.

Another version of it is given thus by Anderson (Royal Genealogies): "Artful Cecil* employed one St. Lawrence to entrap the earls of Tyrone and Tyrconnell, the lord of Delvin and other Irish chiefs, into a sham plot, which had no evidence but his."†

And there is yet a third story given by Dr Carleton, bishop of Chichester—that one Montgomery, who is called Bishop of Derry, was informed that O'Neill had got into possession of certain lands belonging to his see (concerning which he was much more solicitous than for the souls of all the diocese)‡—that he instituted a suit to discover these lands—that he found one of the O'Cahans of Derry, able and willing to assist his researches, and to give evidence in his cause—that processes were issued calling upon O'Neill to appear and answer in the cause of "the Lord Bishop of Derry against Hugh Earl of Tyrone—and that O'Neill, "having entered into a new conspiracy in which O'Cahan was, began to suspect, when he was served with a process to answer the suit, that this was but a

* Robert Cecil, Earl of Salisbury, the discoverer, and some say contriver. of the gunpowder plot.

† This is the account adopted by Mac Geoghegan.

‡ This must be the same absentee bishop mentioned by Davies, who had taken no course to reduce his people to Christianity.

plot to draw him in, and that surely the treason had been revealed by O'Cahan."

It matters little in which of all these ways it fell out that O'Neill came to be charged with this conspiracy. By some means or other, by anonymous letters, or vague rumours, "artful Cecil" succeeded in fixing upon O'Neill and O'Donnell a charge of treason, to sustain which there has not been, from that day to this, a tittle of evidence. They were informed however that witnesses were to be hired against them,[*] and believing this highly probable from the whole course of English policy towards Irishmen, knowing also the rapacious views of James, and that their presence in the kingdom would only draw down heavier misfortune upon their poor clansmen, and having moreover a wholesome terror of *juries* since the fate of Mac Mahon; they came to the resolution of leaving their unhappy native country, and seeking amongst the continental powers, either arms and troops to right the wrongs of Erin, or at least a place to end their own days in peace. They waited not for the toils of Chichester to close around them; but in the autumn of that year, on the festival of the Holy Cross, they embarked in a vessel that had lately carried Cuconnaught Mac Gwire and Donagh O'Brien to Ireland, and was then lying in Lough Swilly. With O'Neill went his wife, the lady Catherina and her three sons, Hugh, whom they called the Baron Dungannon, John and Brian, Art Oge son of Cormac Mac Baron, Ferdoragh son of

* Anderson. Royal Genealogies.

Coun (who was a natural son of O'Neill,) Hugh Oge and others of his family and friends. Roderick O'Donnell was attended by his brother Cathbar, and his sister Nuala,* Hugh, the Earl's child, wanting three weeks of being a year old, Rose, daughter of O'Dogherty and wife of Cathbar, with her son Hugh, aged two years and three months, Roderick's brother's son Donnell Oge, son of Donnell, Naghtan son of Calvagh who was son of Donnell Cairbreach O'Donnell, and other friends :—surely a distinguished company ; and " it is certain, say the reverend chroniclers of Tyrconnell, that the sea has not borne, and the wind has not wafted in modern times a number of persons in one ship more eminent, illustrious or noble in point of genealogy, heroic deeds, valour, feats of arms and brave achievements than they. Would that God had but permitted them," continue the Four Masters, " to **remain in their patrimonial inheritances until the children should arive at the age of manhood!** Woe to the heart that meditated—woe to the mind that conceived—woe to the council that recommended the project of this expedition, without knowing whether they should to the end of their lives, be able to return to their ancient principalities and patrimonies." With gloomy looks and sad forebodings, the clansmen of Tyrconnell gazed upon that fatal ship, "built in th' eclipse and rigged with curses dark," as she

* This lady had been the wife of Niall Garbh, but had left him on his taking arms against her brother, Red Hubg.

dropped down Lough Swilly, and was hidden behind the cliffs of Fanad head. They never saw their chieftains more.

Here was brought about the very state of affairs that King James had long desired. "Nothing," says Dr. Leland, "could be more favourable to that passion which James indulged for reforming Ireland, by the introduction of English law and civility." So very favourable, indeed, as to leave little doubt that it was all contrived by that man of plots "Artful Cecil;" and so vague and suspicious are the accounts of "the conspiracy of the Earls," that Dr. Curry is tolerably safe in concluding "there never was any such conspiracy; and these accounts were then framed, however injudiciously, to give some colour of right to public acts of slander, oppression, and rapine."*

Instantly commissioners were despatched to the North to deal with "traitors," and take account of lands which were to escheat to the crown. The two Earls, with other chieftains, were duly attainted by process of outlawry; their lands and titles were declared forfeit; and the Plantation of Ulster commenced.

* Historical Review. The king, as if anticipating this conclusion, published a proclamation, in which (amongst other things) he says: "wee doe professe that it is both known to us and our counsell here, and to our deputie and state there, and so shall it appeare to the world, (as cleare as the sunne,) by evident proofes, that the only ground and motive of this high contempt, in these men's departure, hath been the private knowledge and inward terrour of their own guiltinesse," &c. But no attempt to give these proofs was ever made.

These operations, indeed, were interrupted the following year by the rising of Cahir O'Dogherty, chief of Inishowen.   O'Dogherty quarrelled with Sir George Pawlett, to whom Docwra had intrusted the government of Derry; and on the first of May, 1608, he took Culmore fort by stratagem, surprised Derry, put both governor and garrison to the sword, plundered the town and laid it in ashes.   Three months he kept the field against Marshal Wingfield and his army; but at length fell, either in battle, or by the hand of private vengeance (for the chroniclers differ), and the last obstacle was removed to one of the most enormous schemes of sweeping plunder that history has to record.*   In the six counties of Donegal, Tyrone, Derry, Fermanagh, Cavan, and Armagh, a tract of country, containing five hundred thousand acres, was seized upon by the King, and parcelled out in lots to undertakers.   The "domains" of the attainted lords were assumed to include all the lands inhabited by their clans; and so far were the King's new arrangements from respecting the rights of the ancient natives, that "the fundamental ground of this plantation was the

---

* The act of Parliament passed upon that occasion thus recites—"And whereas the divine justice hath lately cast out of the province of Ulster divers wicked and ungratefull traytors, who practised to interrupt those blessed courses, begun and continued by your Majestie for the generall good of this whole realm, by whose defeetion and attainders great scopes of land in those parts have been reduced to your Majestic's hands and possession," &c.

avoiding of natives, and planting only with **British**."*

Now at last the undertakers had their will of Ulster, and the King's clergy had that corner of the vineyard opened to their labours. Now all those Wingfields, and Caulfields, and Blaneys, and Chichesters had their long-expected estates. The Lord Deputy alone received for his share the entire peninsula of Inishowen—the broad erenach and termon-lands wherewith ancient piety had endowed Saint Columba's Teampol-More, formed the richest bishop's see in Ireland (perhaps too rich for a bishop who had neither flocks nor clergy); and the entire territory of Arachty was allotted, by letters patent, with much Norman law language, to certain drapers, grocers, skinners, vintners, and other guilds of tradesmen in the good city of London ; and the noble old Irish race, the clansmen who had pierced the mailed ranks of Bagnal and Norreys, and had trampled Saint George's banner on many a battle-field, worn down by famine and disease, without leaders and without hope, were driven to the desolate mountains, were hunted like wolves, and from their inaccessible heights could see those rich valleys where they and their fathers dwelt, flooded by hordes of Scotch and

* Sir Thomas Philips, in *Harris's Hibernia*. "It is true, says Sir Thomas, that after a prescribed number of freeholders and leaseholders were settled upon every town land, and rents therein set down, they might let the remainder to natives for lives, *so as they were conformable in religion, and for the favour, to double their rents*." See also for full information on the details of the plantation, Captain Pynnar's " Survey of Ulster."

English adventurers.   Surely it was a heart-
breaking sight to see ; and no man can think it
srange if deeds of stern and bloody vengeance
were sometimes done.

How it fared with the exiled chiefs and their
associates, we have no minute or very authentic
account ; and if we had, it were indeed one of
the saddest stories.   At first they sailed directly
to Normandy ; then proceeded to Flanders ; and
finally to Rome, where the Pope (Paul the Fifth)
received them with hospitality and high consideration.   But who can describe, or imagine,
with what bitterness of soul the aged Prince of
Ulster heard of the miseries of his faithful people, and the manifold oppressions and robberies
of those detested English ; with what earnest
passion he pleaded with Popes and Princes, and
besought them to think upon the wrongs of Ireland.   Ha ! if he had sped in that mission of
vengeance—if he had persuaded Paul or Philip
to give him some ten thousand Italians or Spaniards—how would it have fluttered those English in their dove-cotes, to behold his ships standing up Lough Foyle, with the Bloody Hand
displayed !   Assuredly he would have disturbed
their "letters patent," would have made very
light of their "statutes, their fines, their double
vouchers, their recoveries."   Spanish blades and
Irish pikes would have made "the fine of their
fines, the recovery of their recoveries."   But not
so was it written in the Book.   No potentate in
Europe was willing to risk such a force as was
needed ; and after wandering from court to court,
eating his own heart, for eight years, he be-

came blind, and so, with darkened eyes and soul, died at Rome some time in the year 1616.[*]

* Borlase.   Reduction of Ireland.

Borlase says that his son (probably that Henry who was recalled from Spain) was, some years after, found strangled in his bed at Brussels; "and so," he observes, "ended his race."

From the fine Elegy so beautifully translated by Mangan, it appears that O Donnell also, and his brother Cathbar, and O'Neill's three young sons, all died at Rome, and lie buried there together:—

> Two princes of the line of Conn
>   Sleep in their cells of clay, beside
>   O'Donnell Roe :
> Three royal youths, alas! are gone,
>   Who lived for Erin's weal, but died
>   For Erin's woe!
> Ah! could the men of Ireland read
>   The names these noteless burial stones
>   Display to view,
> Their wounded hearts afresh would bleed,
>   Their tears gush forth again, their groans
>   Resound anew!
>
>   *   *   *
>
> And who can marvel o'er thy grief,
>   Or who can blame thy flowing tears,
>   That knows their source ?
> O'Donnell, Dunnasava's chief,
>   Cut off amidst his vernal years,
>   Lies here a corse,
> Beside his brother Cathbar, whom
>   Tyrconnell of the Helmets mourns
>   In deep despair—
> For valour, truth, and comely bloom ;
> For all that greatens and adorns
>   A peerless pair.

APPENDIX.

A LETTER FROM LORD DEPUTY MOUNTJOY TO THE LORDS OF THE COUNCIL IN ENGLAND.

MAY IT PLEASE YOUR LORDSHIPS—Although I am unwilling to informe you often of the present estate of this kingdom, or of any particular accidents or services, because the one is subject to so much alteration, and the other lightly delivered unto all that are not present, with such uncertaintie; and that I am loath to make any project unto your lordships, either of my requests to you, or my owne resolutions here, since so many things fall suddainly out, which may alter the grounds of either; yet since I doe write now by one that can so sufficiently supply the defects of a letter, I have presumed at this time to imparte unto your lordships that I think fit to be remembered, or doe determine on; most humbly desiring your lordships, that if I err in the one, or hereafter alter the other, you will not impute it to my want of sinceritie or constancy, but to the nature of the subject whereof I must treate, or of the matter whereon I worke: And first, to present unto your lordships the outward face of the four provinces, and after to guesse (as neere as I can) at their dispositions. Mounster, by the good government and industry of the Lord President, is cleare of any force in rebellion, except some few, not able to make any forcible head; in Leinster there is not one declared rebell; in Connaught there is none but in O'Rorke's country; in Ulster none but Tyrone and Bryan Mac Art, who was never lord of any country, and now doth, with a body of loose men, and some creaghts, continue in Glancomkynes, or neere the borders thereof. Cohonocht Mac Gwyre, sometimes Lord of Fermanagh, is banished out of the country, who lives with O'Rorke ; and at this time Conor Roe Mac Gwyre is possessed of it by the queene, and holds it for her. I believe that generally the lords of the countries that are reclaimed desire a peace, though they will be wavering till their lands and estates are assured unto them from her Majestie ; and as long as they see a party in rebellion to subsist, that is of a power to ruine them, if they continue subjects or otherwise, shall be doubtful of our defence. All that are out doe seeke for mercy, excepting O'Rorke, and O'Sullivan, who is now with O'Rorke, and these are obstinate only out of their diffidence to be safe in any forgivenesse. The loose men, and such as are only captaines of Bonnoghts, as Tirrell and Brian Mac Art, will nourish the warre as long as they see any possibilitie to subsist; and, like ill humours, have recourse to any part that is unsound. The nobilitie, towns, and English-Irish are, for the most part, as weary of the warre as any, but unwilling to have it ended, generally for fear that upon a peace will ensue a severe reformation of religion ; and, in particular, many bordering gentlemen that were made poore by their own faults, or by rebels' incursions, continue their spleene to them, now they are become subjects ; and having used to helpe themselves by stealths, did never more use them, nor better prevailed in them than now, that these submittees have layed aside their owne defence, and betaken themselves to the protection and justice of the state ; and many of them have tasted so much sweete in entertainments that they rather desire a warre to continue there than a quiet harvest that might arise out of their own honest labour ; so that I doe find none more pernicious instruments of a new warre than some of these. In the meane time, Tyrone, while he shall live, will blow every sparke of discontent, or new hopes that shall lye hid in a corner of the kingdome and before he shall be utterly extinguished make many blazes, and sometimes set on fire or consume the next subjects unto him. I am persuaded that his combination is already broken, and it is apparent that his meanes to subsist in any power is overthrowne; but how long hee may live as a wood-kerne, and what new accidents may fall out while he doth live I know not. If it be imputed to my fault that, notwithstanding her Majestie's great forces, he doth still live, I beseech your lordships to remember how securely the banditoes of Italy doe live, betweene the power of the King of Spaine and the Pope. How many men of all countreyes of severall times have in such sort preserved themselves long from the great power of princes, but especially in this countrey, where there are so many difficulties to carry an armie, in most places so many unaccessible strengths for them to flye unto: and then to bee pleased to consider the great worke that first I had to breake this maine rebellion, to defend the kingdom from a dangerous invasion of a mightie forraine prince, with so strong a partie in the countrey, and now the difficultie to root out scattered troopes that had so many unaccessible dennes to lurke in, which as they are by nature of extreme strength and perill to bee attempted: so it is impossible for any people naturally and by art to make greater use of them. And though with infinite dangers wee do beat them out of one, yet is there no possibilitie for us to follow them with such agilitie as they will flye to another: and it is most sure that never traytor knew better how to keepe his owne head than this; nor any subjects have a more dreadfull awe to lay violent hands on their sacred prince, than these people have to touch the person of their O'Neales; and hee that hath as pestilent a judgment as ever any had to nourish and to spreade his owne infection, hath the ancient swelling and desire of libertie in a conquered nation to worke upon, their fear to bee rooted out, or to have their old faults punished upon all particular discontents, and generally over all the kingdom the feare of a persecution for religion, the debasing of the coyne, (which is grievous unto all sortes) and a dearth and famine which is already begun and must necessarily grow shortly to extremity: the least of which alone have been many times sufficient motives to drive the best and most quiet estates into suddaine confusion. These will keepe all spirits from settling, breed new combinations, and, I feare, even stir the townes themselves to solicit forraine aide, with promise to cast themselves into their protection : and although it bee true that if it had pleased her majestie to have longer continued her army in greater strength, I should the better have provided for what these cloudes doe threaten, and sooner and more easily either have made this countrey a rased table, wherein shee might have written her owne lawes, or have tyed the ill-disposed and rebellious hands till I had surely planted such a government as would have overgrowne and killed any weeds that should have risen under it : yet since the necessitie of the state doeth so urge a diminution of this great expense, I will not despayre to goe on with this worke, through all these difficulties, if wee bee not interrupted by forraine forces, although perchance wee may be encountered with some new irruptions, and (by often adventuring) with some disasters : and it may bee your lordships shall sometimes heare of some spoyles done upon the subjects, from the which it is impossible to preserve them in all places, with far greater forces than ever yet were kept in this kingdome : and although it hath been seldom heard that an armie hath been carried on with so continuall action, and enduring without any intermission of winter breathings, and that the difficulties at this time to keepe any forces in the place where wee must make the warre (but especially our horse) are almost beyond any hope to prevent, yet with the favour of God and her majesty's fortune I doe determine myselfe to draw into the field as soon as I have received her majesty's commandments by the commissioners, who it hath pleased her to send over ; and in the mean time I hope by mine owne presence or directions to set every partie on worke that doth adjoyne, or may bee drawn against any force that doth now remaine in rebellion. In which journey the successe must bee in the hands of God : but I will confidently promise to omit nothing that is possible by us to bee done, to give the last blow unto the rebellion. But as all paine and anguish, impatient of the present doeth use change for a remedie ; so will it be impossible for us to settle the minds of these people unto a peace, or reduce them unto order, while they feele the smart of these sensible griefes and apparent feares which I have remembered to your lordships without some hope of redresse or securitie. Therefore I will presume, (how unworthy soever I have beene,) since it concerns the province her majestic hath given me, with all humblenesse to lay before your grave judgments some few things which I thinke necessary to be considered of.

And first, whereas the alteration of the coyne and taking away of the exchange in such measure as it was first promised, hath bred a generall grievance unto men of all qualities, and so many incommodities to all sorts, that it is beyond the judgment of any that I can heare, to prevent a confusion in this estate by the continuance thereof, that (at the least) it would please your lordships to put this people in some certaine hope, that upon the end of the warre this new standard shall be abolished or eased; and that in the meane time the armie may be favourably dealt with in the exchange, since by the last proclamation your lordships sent over, they doe conceive their case will bee more hard than anie others; for if they have allowed them nothing but indefinitely as much as they shall merely gaine out of their entertainments, that will proove nothing to the greater parte. For the onlie possibilitie to make them to live upon their enterta:nment, will bee to allow them exchange for the greatest parte thereof, since now they doe not only pay excessive prizes for all things, but can hardly get anything for this money. And, although we have presumed to alter (in shew though not in effect) the Proclamation in that point, by retayning a power in ourselves to proportion their allowance for exchange; yet, was it with a minde to conform our proceedings therein according to your lordships' next directions, and therefore doe humbly desire to know your pleasures therein. For our opinions of the last project it pleased your lordships to send us, I doe humbly leave it to our generall letters: only as for myself I made overture to the councill in the other you sent directly only to myselfe; and because I found them generally to concurre, that it would prove as dangerous as the first, 1 did not thinke it fit any otherwise to declare your lordships' pleasure therein. And, whereas it pleased your lordships in your last letters to command us to deale moderately in the great matter of religion; I had, before the receipt of your lordships' letters, presumed to advise such as dealt in it for a time to hold a more restraynt hand therein; and wee were both thinking ourselves what course to take in the Revocation of what was already done, with least incouragement to them and others, since the feare that this course begun in Dublin would fall upon the rest was apprehended over all the kingdom; so that I think your lordships' direction was to greate purpose, and the other course might have overthrowne the meanes to our owne ende of reformation of religion. Not that I thinke too greate precisenesse can bee used in the reforming of ourselves, the abuses of our owne clergie, church-livings, and discipline; nor that the trueth of the gospell can with too great vehemencie, or industrie, bee set forward in all places, and by all ordinarie means most proper unto itself, that was first set foorth, and spread in meekenesse; not that I thinke any corporall prosecution or punishment can bee too severe for such as shall bee found seditious instruments of forraine or inward practices; not that I thinke it fit that any principall magistrates should bee chosen without taking the oathe of obedience, nor tolerated in absenting themselves from publique divine service; but that wee may bee advised how wee doe punish in their bodies or goods any such only for religion as doe professe to bee faithful subjects to her majestie, and against whom the contrary cannot bee proved. And since, if the Irish were utterly rooted out, there was much lesse likelihood that this countrey could bee thereby in any time planted by the English, since they are so farre from inhabiting well any part of that they have already; and that more than is likely to bee inhabited may bee easily chosen out and reserved in such places by the sea side, or upon great rivers, as may bee planted to great purpose for a future absolute reducement of this countrey, I thinke it would as much avail the speedy settling of this countrey as anything; that it would please her majestie to deale liberally with the Irish lords of countreyes, or such as are now of great reputation amongst them, in the distribution of such lands as they have formerly possessed, or the state here can make little use of her majestie; if they continue as they ought to doe, and yield the Queen as much commoditie as shee may otherwise expect, shee hath made a good purchase of such subjects for such land.— If any of them hereafter be disobedient to her lawes, or breake foorth in rebellion, shee may, when they shall bo more divided, ruine them more easily for example unto others, and (if it be thought fit) may plant English or other Irish in their countryes: for although there ever have been, and hereafter may bee small irruptions in some places, which at the first may easily be suppressed, yet the suffering them to grow to that general head and combination, did questionlesse proceede from great errour in the judgment heere, and may be easily, as I thinke, prevented hereafter. And further, it may please her Majestie to ground her resolution for the time and numbers of the next abatement of the list of her armie, somewhat upon our poor advice from hence, and to beleeve that wee will not·so far corrupt our judgments with any private respects and without necessitie, to continue her charge, seeing wee do throughly conceive how grievous it is unto her estate, and that we may not bee precisely tyed to an establishment that shall conclude the payments of the treasure since it hath ever been thought fit to be otherwise till the comming over of the Earle of Essex: and some such extraordinary occasions may fall out that it will be dangerous to attend your lordship's resolutions, and when it will bee safe to diminish the armie here, that there may be some other course thought of by some other employment, to disburden this countrey of the idle swordmen, in whom I find an inclination apt enough to bee carried elsewhere, either by some of this countrey of best reputation among them, or in companies as now they stand under English captains, who may be reinforced with the greatest part of the Irish. That it may be left to our discretion to make passages and bridges into countreyes otherwise inaccessable, and to build little pyles of stone in such garrisons as shall bee thought fittest, to bee continual bridles upon the people by the commoditie of which wee may at any time drawe the greatest parte of the armie together to make a head against any part that shall first brake out, and yet reserve the places onely with a word to put in greater forces as occasion

shall require, which I am persuaded will prove great
pledges upon this countrey, that upon any urgent cause
the Queen may safely drawe the greatest part of her
armie here out of the kingdom, to be employed for a
time elsewhere, wherein I beseech your lordships to consider what a strength so many experienced captaines and
souldiers would be to any armie of new men erected in
England against an invasion, or sent abroad in any of-
fensive war: But untill these places be built, I cannot
conceive how her Majestie (with any safetie) can make
any great diminution of her armie. Lastly, I doe
humbly desire your lordships to receive the further explanation of my meaning and confirmation of my reasons that doe induce me unto these propositions: for the
Lord President of Mounster, who as he hath been a very
worthy actor in the reducement and defence of this
kingdom, so doe I thinke him to be the best able to give
you a through account of the present estate and future
providence for the preservation thereof: Wherein it
may please your lordships to require his opinion of the
hazard this kingdom is like to runne in if it should by
any mightie power be invaded, and how hard it will bee
for us in any measure to provide for the present defence,
if any such be intended, and withall to goe on with the
suppression of these that are left in rebellion, so that
wee must either adventure the kindling of this fire that
is almost extinguished, or intending onelie that, leave
the other to exceeding peril. And thus having remembered to your lordships the most material poynts (as I
conceive) that are fitted for the present to bee considered of, I doe humbly recommend myselfe and them to
your lordships' favour. From her Majestie's Castle of
Dublin, the sixe and twentieth of February, 1602-3.

THE END.

PUBLICATIONS

OF

P. J. KENEDY,

Excelsior Catholic Publishing House,

5 BARCLAY ST., NEAR BROADWAY, NEW YORK,

Opposite the Astor House

Adventures of Michael Dwyer	$1 00
Adelmar the Templar. A Tale	40
Ballads, Poems, and Songs of William Collins	1 00
Blanche. A Tale from the French	40
Battle of Ventry Harbor	20
Bibles, from $2 50 to	15 00
Brooks and Hughes Controversy	75
Butler's Feasts and Fasts	1 25
Blind Agnese. A Tale	50
Butler's Catechism	8
" " with Mass Prayers	30
Bible History. Challoner	50
Christian Virtues. By St. Liguori	1 00
Christian's Rule of Life. By St. Liguori	30
Christmas Night's Entertainments	60
Conversion of Ratisbonne	50
Clifton Tracts. 4 vols.	3 00
Catholic Offering. By Bishop Walsh	1 50
Christian Perfection. Rodriguez. 3 vols. *Only complete edition*	4 00
Catholic Church in the United States. By J. G. Shea. Illustrated	2 00
Catholic Missions among the Indians	2 50
Chateau Lescure. A Tale	50
Conscience ; or, May Brooke. A Tale	1 00
Catholic Hymn-Book	15
Christian Brothers' 1st Book	13

Catholic Prayer-Books, 25c., 50c., up to 12 00

☞ Any of above books sent free by mail on receipt of price. Agents wanted everywhere to sell above books, to whom liberal terms will be given. Address

P. J. KENEDY, Excelsior Catholic Publishing House,
5 Barclay Street, New York.

1

Christian Brothers' 2d Book...................	**$0 25**
" " *3d* "	*63*
" " *4th* "	*88*
Catholic Primer.......................	*6*
Catholic School-Book....................	*25*
Cannon's Practical Speller...............	*25*
Carpenter's Speller......................	*25*
Dick Massey. An Irish Story..............	*1 00*
Doctrine of Miracles Explained...........	*1 00*
Doctrinal Catechism.....................	*50*
Douay "	*25*
Diploma of Children of Mary............	*20*
Erin go Bragh. (Sentimental Songster.)........	*25*
El Nuevo Testamento. (Spanish.)............	*1 50*
Elevation of the Soul to God...............	*75*
Epistles and Gospels. (Goffine.).............	*2 00*
Eucharistica ; or, Holy Eucharist............	*1 00*
End of Controversy. (Milner.).............	*75*
El Nuevo Catecismo. (Spanish.)............	*15*
El Catecismo de la Doctrina Christiana. (Spanish Catechism)........................	*15*
El Catecismo Ripalda. (Spanish)............	*12*
Furniss' Tracts for Spiritual Reading.......	*1 00*
Faugh a Ballagh Comic Songster............	*25*
Fifty Reasons...........................	*25*
Following of Christ......................	*50*
Fashion. A Tale. 35 Illustrations.............	*50*
Faith and Fancy. Poems. Savage.............	*75*
Glories of Mary. (St. Liguori.)...............	*1 25*
Golden Book of Confraternities.............	*50*
Grounds of Catholic Doctrine..............	*25*
Grace's Outlines of History................	*50*
Holy Eucharist.........................	*1 00*
Hours before the Altar. Red edges...........	*50*
History of Ireland. Moore. 2 vols.............	*5 00*
" " O'Mahoney's Keating.......	*4 00*
Hay on Miracles	*1 00*
Hamiltons. A Tale.......................	*50*
History of Modern Europe. Shea.............	*1 25*
Hours with the Sacred Heart..............	*50*
Irish National Songster..................	*1 00*
Imitation of Christ......................	*40*

Catholic Prayer-Books, 25c., 50c., *up to* 12 00

☞ Any of above books sent free by mail on receipt of price. Agents wanted everywhere to sell above books, to whom liberal terms will be given. Address

P. J. KENEDY, Excelsior Catholic Publishing House,
5 Barclay Street, New York.

Irish Fireside Stories, Tales, and Legends.
(Magnificent new book just out.) About 400 pages
large 12mo, containing about 40 humorous and pa-
thetic sketches.   12 fine full-page Illustrations.
Sold only by subscription. Only.................. $1 00
Keeper of the Lazaretto. A Tale.............. 40
Kirwan Unmasked. By Archbishop Hughes..... 12
King's Daughters. An Allegory................. 75
Life and Legends of St. Patrick........ 1 00
Life of St. Mary of Egypt... 60
"   "   *Winefride*.............. 60
"   "   *Louis*........ 40
"   "   *Alphonsus M. Liguori*............ 75
"   "   *Ignatius Loyola.* 2 vols............ 3 00
Life of Blessed Virgin.............. 75
Life of Madame de la Peltrie.............. 50
Lily of Israel. 22 Engravings.............. 75
Life Stories of Dying Penitents.............. 75
Love of Mary 50
Love of Christ............. 50
Life of Pope Pius IX.............. 1 00
Lenten Manual.............. 50
Lizzie Maitland. A Tale.............. 75
Little Frank. A Tale 50
Little Catholic Hymn-Book.............. 10
Lyra Catholica (large Hymn-Book).............. 75
Mission and Duties of Young Women........ 60
Maltese Cross. A Tale.............. 40
Manual of Children of Mary.............. 50
Mater Admirabilis.............. 1 50
Mysteries of the Incarnation. (St. Liguori.).... 75
Month of November.............. 40
Month of Sacred Heart of Jesus............. 50
"   "   *Mary*.............. 50
Manual of Controversy.............. 75
Michael Dwyer. An Irish Story of 1798............ 1 00
Milner's End of Controversy.............. 75
May Brooke ; or, Conscience. A Tale...... 1 00
New Testament.............. 50
Oramaika. An Indian Story.............. 75
Old Andrew the Weaver.............. 50
Preparation for Death. St. Liguori............ 75

Catholic Prayer-Books, 25c., 50c., up to 12 00
☞ Any of above books sent free by mail on receipt of price. Agents
wanted everywhere to sell above books, to whom liberal terms will be given.
Address

P. J. KENEDY, Excelsior Catholic Publishing House,
5 Barclay Street, New York.

Prayer. By St. Liguori.........................	$0 50
Papist Misrepresented..........................	25
Poor Man's Catechism.........................	75
Rosary Book. 15 Illustrations.................	10
Rome: Its Churches, Charities, and Schools. By Rev. Wm. H. Neligan, LL.D....................	1 00
Rodriguez's Christian Perfection. 3 vols. Only complete edition.........................	4 00
Rule of Life. St. Liguori.....................	40
Sure Way: or, Father and Son..............	25
Scapular Book...............................	10
Spirit of St. Liguori........................	75
Stations of the Cross. 14 Illustrations...........	10
Spiritual Maxims. (St. Vincent de Paul)..........	40
Saintly Characters. By Rev. Wm. H. Neligan, LL.D.	1 00
Seraphic Staff.............................	25
" *Manual,* 75 cts. to.................	3 00
Sermons of Father Burke, plain.............	2 00
" " " gilt edges...........	3 00
Schmid's Exquisite Tales. 6 vols.............	3 00
Shipwreck. A Tale..........................	50
Savage's Poems............................	2 00
Sybil: A Drama. By John Savage.............	75
Treatise on Sixteen Names of Ireland. By Rev. J. O'Leary, D.D.	50
Two Cottages. By Lady Fullerton.............	50
Think Well On't. Large type.................	40
Thornberry Abbey. A Tale...................	50
Three Eleanors. A Tale.....................	75
Trip to France. Rev. J. Donelan.............	1 00
Three Kings of Cologne.....................	30
Universal Reader...........................	50
Vision of Old Andrew the Weaver.............	50
Visits to the Blessed Sacrament.............	40
Willy Reilly. Paper cover....................	50
Way of the Cross. 14 Illustrations.............	5
Western Missions and Missionaries...........	2 00
Walker's Dictionary.........................	75
Young Captives. A Tale.....................	50
Youth's Director...........................	50
Young Crusaders. A Tale....................	50

Catholic Prayer-Books, 25c., 50c., up to 12 00

☞ Any of above books sent free by mail on receipt of price. Agents wanted everywhere to sell above books, to whom liberal terms will be given. Address

P. J. KENEDY, Excelsior Catholic Publishing House, *5 Barclay Street, New York.*

www.ingramcontent.com/pod-product-compliance
Lightning Source LLC
Chambersburg PA
CBHW020051030726
47498CB00006B/1735